The Widow

Carolyn Slaughter

THE WIDOW

HEINEMANN : LONDON

William Heinemann Ltd
Michelin House, 81 Fulham Road, London SW3 6RB
LONDON MELBOURNE AUCKLAND

First published in 1989
Copyright © Carolyn Slaughter 1989

British Library Cataloguing in Publication Data

Slaughter, Carolyn
The widow.
I. Title
823'.914 [F]

ISBN 0 434 71084 9

Printed and bound in Great Britain by
Mackays of Chatham

For my husband

One

AMERICA

Chapter One

Bella, it was said, was unfortunate in her husbands. Neither had survived a fifth anniversary. And there were those who, regarding her from the outside, drew attention to the indiscriminate way that tragedy visited lives that otherwise seemed filled with success and beauty.

When Joseph first met Bella, these two deaths were the only facts that he knew about her. And if no sense of calamity attached itself to her because of them, he presumed it was because it had all happened some time ago. He had no inkling, at that chance meeting in a sunny room in Connecticut, that here was a woman who could shatter entirely the cool surface of his life. Neither had he any intuition – though intuition was what he prized above all else in himself – that he was gazing into the face of a singularly dangerous woman. All he saw was an aura of radiance: the radiance of a woman at a point of perfection, poised between youth and maturity.

It happened in one of those dormitory towns some forty miles, as the train flies, from New York. Those places full of small, chic shops selling trinkets to women who had not just everything, but a good dozen of everything. People living in the shallows and reflecting a certain malaise because of it: a looming dissatisfaction with abundance, which made them a little unstable. They were a breed – he'd come to this conclusion several years before – of large appetite and small capacity.

It was a Sunday, an unavoidable brunch. Joseph's connection to the hostess was through her husband, a neurologist he'd known well in England. He arrived at their house and was immediately surrounded by the glossy smiles of trim American matrons whose bodies spoke eloquently of aerobics and whose voices, encountering friend or stranger, vibrated with that high trilling 'How are you?' greeting – so puzzling, in its intensity, to an Englishman. He knew that he would be talked at, long and earnestly – not so much because of any appeal

3

of his own, but more to do with a morbid curiosity about his profession.

And there, across the room, was Bella. She was sitting on a plump, peach-coloured sofa, surrounded by a gaggle of children. They were clearly all hers: two small, the gaps between their ages minimal, and two rather older ones, perhaps seven and ten. The oldest child was surveying her with a smile half-wistful, half-amused. A lonely boy, Joseph recognised it at once: that private face, that anxiety revealing itself in his way of watching, waiting, and then suddenly vanishing.

She was in full bloom; a woman, Joseph presumed, who had started to have her children in her mid-twenties. Now they attached themselves to her person like barnacles around a dark mussel-shell. Her long, white hands were in their curls, or restraining their grasping fingers, or smoothing a dress, or a temper that had become ruffled. Once he saw her snap her straight teeth at a small, butting cheek as it nuzzled close to her own. He heard her laughter – and what clues in that low, dark laughter – followed by the child's chuckle as she ran off. When they became too noisy, she would shoo them away to a young woman who waited at the door, wearing the blue frock, white collar and cuffs of the English nanny.

He did not approach the madonna, feeling it was pleasanter to watch from afar. But, he had to admit, there was something about her maternity that he liked. It was so far removed from the self-conscious parenting he had met so often. The offspring snapping at her heels were bright and eager, free of whining or snivelling and so alert that they charmed him. He noticed that, once dispatched to nanny, they would depart, with reluctance, but also with a clear comprehension of the nature of social intercourse and their own place within it. They had been well trained.

Joseph turned to talk to someone and, when he looked back, the children had gone. Without them, Bella seemed to change. There was something so striking about this that he found it a trifle alarming. Her fecundity had quite left her. As she walked from the sofa to a sideboard to take a glass of wine, she was suddenly a tall, businesslike woman wearing a grey linen dress, dipping her head in conversation with an orthopaedic surgeon. Her hair seemed to be bothering her or perhaps she was hot, because she coiled

4

it quickly into a knot at her neck, using the hair itself to keep it in place.

Joseph moved close enough to ascertain that the conversation was about medicine. Now she struck him as supremely confident: informed, intelligent, rather intense. Her face, speaking, seemed to realign its contours and became somewhat severe. He was put out by her transformation. Watching her with her children, he had been lulled into a fantasy of home life, of domestic harmony which, since he had never known it, he was reluctant to relinquish. Perhaps he was also irritated that she was familiar with his professional world; he had presumed that she did not work. Now he did not know quite where to place her in the medical world: nurse or doctor, do-good volunteer or, simply, a patient?

Then she looked at Joseph for the first time, tossing him a look from her side of the room – or not so much a look as a little lash of the eyes. Now, although not all that handsome, he was, he felt, not repellent, and certainly not deserving of such a glance. During the course of the brunch, he came to see that this look of hers was general, not particular – it was the way she regarded men.

There was, however, someone who was spared her disdain. He was a tall, lean man in his early thirties, with hair cut short and boyish; clothes tailored and expensive. Something about him made Joseph feel that he was soft intellectually, that too much of his business life was spent being agreeable; that he traded on charm. Bella had just been introduced to this man by the hostess, Margy – for a purpose, it seemed. As they spoke, rather formally – or rather, she did – Joseph could see her face very clearly. It was obviously a business conversation; curiosity made Joseph creep within earshot, while holding a conversation of his own with a woman intent on telling him her dreams.

The man talking to Bella, Joseph now decided, must be an investment banker. He found it interesting to watch the two of them, because Bella dealt with him so cleanly; the frisson between a man and a woman which would be present in virtually any initial exchange, was wholly absent. She kept her body apart, she had an odd way of seeming to keep it entirely to herself; her containment was quite marked. Joseph liked that. And he liked the way she maintained her directness right to the exchanging of cards. But then she did a curious

5

thing. As soon as his card was tucked inside her pocket, she dropped her businesslike manner. She smiled at him – a most remarkable smile, one that took him right to the centre of her being. It was the smile of a lover. Nothing else could be so intimate. Joseph was so startled that he began to wonder if the procedure beforehand had been a sham. Could he have misinterpreted it? Joseph looked at her again and saw how she moved forward and softly placed her hand on the man's arm. Then she walked away, a lovely, undulating walk, her face as blank as water. Joseph looked at the man for the first time, expecting collusion. But he was staring after her with incredulous eyes.

One of her children was now borne in by the nanny. He was a solemn-faced child with tears on his cheeks. Bella scooped him up into her arms and began to rock him, pressing the small body tightly into her own. She was being observed, and she knew it, by the man she had so unsettled. His face was drawn with longing for a moment, then he drank from his glass quickly.

She sat down. The child rested against her, curled his cheek into the hollow of her neck and, in a moment, was asleep. She sat very still, her face inclined towards the child's, her eyes closed. And when the man whose arm she had just touched so lavishly came and stood looking down at her, his face exposing its own tenderness and expectation, she turned a gaze upon him as formal and distant as a butler's. So chilling was it that he lost his composure and left the room.

Later, as Joseph was walking along the corridor towards the front door, he saw Bella coming slowly down the stairs, trailing her hand down the banister. When she rounded the corner and entered the corridor they began to walk towards one another. Then she looked up and saw him.

A strange sensation came over Joseph; he felt a shock in his spine; it was as if the spinal cord had been exposed and a steel drill touched the nerves. Then it was gone and he was aware only of the atmosphere in the corridor. It was stealthy and sexual. As they watched one another, he was reminded of the instinctual behaviour of animals coming upon a rival in an open space, waiting for the moment to pounce or kill.

When she said, finally, 'Hallo,' in a low voice, he felt she had the territorial advantage and he walked on quickly, opening the front door. There he stopped and turned to look back at her. She was standing very still, regarding him. The sunlight now filling the corridor rippled across her face, making her features sway, in the way a road seems to lose its fixity in the glare. Then she turned and was gone.

Chapter Two

Whenever she came to America for a short visit, Bella would stay with Margy. It was an arrangement that had existed for many years, like their friendship. But perhaps to call it a friendship would be to stretch it a little further than its natural limits. It was the kind of relationship that women often have, supportive mostly, but not in a close way.

Bella was the perfect guest, specifying the hour that she would arrive and, most importantly, the hour that she would be leaving. She always brought some wonderful gift: an exotic carving or an unusual piece of china. This time it was a deep, porcelain bowl with flowers painted on the base and sides, so it seemed to be brimming with fresh blooms. She never would say where she got her presents. If asked, she'd smile that delicate smile and shrug her shoulders; sometimes, she'd simply say 'I don't remember.' It wasn't that she was absent-minded. She couldn't afford to be. Her life was divided into neat sections – but she never needed to write anything down, not even a shopping list. Margy said Bella had a mind like a fly-paper. That's why her forgetfulness was odd. If you asked her when she'd started as an intern, she'd give you the exact date and year, but if you asked her where she'd bought one of her kids' sweaters, she'd have no recall of it. Perhaps she chose what she would remember and discarded the rest. It was a feat requiring a particular kind of mind, one that chose its own perimeters.

This time when Bella came to stay, to see about a job offer in New York, she was different. To be more specific, she was on edge. Margy had noticed it immediately. It was not like Bella at all. Margy and Otto had known Bella as the most composed of women. Often Margy would say, 'Bella, how d'you live this way? How d'you cram so much in, work fourteen hours and still get to go to the hairdresser? It makes me sick!' Bella would laugh, making it all seem effortless. She never complained.

Now for the first time Margy saw signs of strain. Watching Bella over the years, she had come to the conclusion that Bella worked harder than Otto's physicians, and they didn't have four little kids to worry about. A doctor without a wife couldn't function, Otto maintained. He had Margy to manage his domestic life and to provide a haven he could creep back to after the punishing hours spent at the hospital. Like his wife, he found it hard to understand Bella's achievements, but it wasn't something that Bella had ever been prepared to discuss.

'Have you noticed how twitchy she is, Otto?' Margy asked after the brunch. He shrugged in an infuriating way and went on reading the paper.

'Listen to me, Otto, damn it, I'm speaking to you. D'you think she's worried about the job?'

'No. They've offered it to her outright, so what's she got to be worried about? All the surgeons in that place have been clawing each other to death trying to land it.'

'Hm. Well, something's up and I intend to find out what it is.'

'I'm sure you will,' he said drily.

Next morning, since Bella didn't have to be anywhere until nine-thirty, she and Margy sat down to coffee and Margy came straight out with it.

'What's the problem, Bella? What's up?'

Bella didn't answer; she kept looking out of the window at the blossoms that now looked rather bedraggled on the trees – it had been a wet spring.

'I've got to get out of England,' Bella said, twisting her fingers just once, but hard, making the knuckles go white.

'Has something happened – at the hospital?'

Margy was intimidated by the rarefied atmosphere of Bella's work: by Harley Street, the London hospitals and the medical jargon that Bella and Otto spouted. But most of all she was intimidated by the work itself – surgery, of the heart. To Margy it seemed that Bella performed miracles in her daily life, particularly during the period when she had operated on the tiny, fragile hearts of new-born babies.

Bella shook her head.

'No, it's not the hospital.' She was quiet a long time, then she said slowly, 'Since Jack died, it's not been the same, I've not been the same.'

9

Margy was startled. Jack had been dead for over two years; he had died before Bella's last child was born. Margy had regarded it as a really terrible relationship. Jack had been a brilliant pianist, but he was a drunk, and not just a drunk, he was manic-depressive as well. He had done lousy things. Jack had adored Bella, but the marriage had not straightened him out. As far as Margy was concerned, nothing could: the man was a loser, and worse, he'd tried to pull Bella down with him. The only good thing he gave her were those two little kids and she wondered sometimes how he'd managed that.

'Well,' Margy said, tucking her thick hair behind her ear, 'if you want to get out of England, what's the problem? Just take the job and come over.' She was taking note of the number of muffins that Bella was eating and remembered that she never ate a thing at work, even if she was on duty for twelve hours at a stretch. She'd learned this when Bella had lived with them for a few months while she was at the Stanford. Bella had lived in America before that as well, while she was a resident at Boston, working with Isaac Roth. He had been her mentor. Now he was dead and she'd been offered his job in New York.

'I don't know,' Bella was saying. Then she pulled herself up. 'Oh yes, I do want the job in New York, how could I not? It's just that . . .'

She reached for the butter again and Margy had to say, 'How d'you eat so much butter and still be a heart surgeon, for God's sake?'

'I like it.'

Margy was encouraged to take some more butter herself and apologised for interrupting.

'Yes,' Bella repeated quietly, 'I do want that job. I've worked all my life for it.'

And there it was again, Margy thought: that quiet authority and that hard look in the eyes, almost ruthless. Something so certain, as if Bella couldn't possibly question or doubt herself. It was a feeling that Margy had never felt once in her entire life. But then – how strange this was – the certainty left Bella. She even looked a little nervous as she said, 'Sometimes I wonder, could I . . . should I . . . take it?'

Margy tried to hide her astonishment. 'How can you think of giving up a chance like that?'

10

The long, elegant curve of Bella's eyebrow lifted as a flicker of amusement ruffled her cheek. Then she turned in her chair and said, 'I was better when Jack was alive.' She sounded rather forlorn. Margy began to wonder if she'd ever really known Bella at all, as a human being, not just Dr Wonderful. It was fascinating. She began to watch Bella closely, seeing her in a way she'd never seen her before. And, of course, she liked her better. For here was a woman who had never seemed to need a husband, who'd never seemed to need anyone at all, going on about a man she'd spent years scraping off the sidewalk, hauling out of grotty bars at all hours of the morning and visiting at clinics while he tried to dry out. Finally, she'd had to bury him after a horrifying death. Margy was astounded that Bella felt anything at all.

'Addicts', Bella began, 'are hard . . .' She let the rest of the sentence go.

'Well, I guess I wouldn't know,' Margy said, feeling that her life was a paltry thing. 'Otto and I have been married over twenty-one years. He makes money, he works like a dog, he likes sport better than he likes me, and we get on pretty well. It's a partnership, a bit businesslike because of the demands of his patients, night and day – but we have our moments.'

At least he's still alive, Margy was thinking. Bella's husbands, apart from both being dead, had both been weird. She hadn't known the first one but she'd heard the stories. There had always been stories about Bella because she kept her life so close. Both her husbands had been eccentrics – or misfits – or worse. Once Margy had suggested to Bella that Jack was a lunatic, after he'd humiliated her quite dreadfully at some dinner, roaring at the guests that Bella was trying to kill him. Bella had been quite angry with Margy; she'd said madness didn't exist. Margy had observed that for someone who didn't believe it existed, she sure knew a lot about it.

'I have always rather envied your marriage,' Bella remarked quietly, turning her cup.

'You mean that?'

'Of course. You are such companions, you and Otto.'

'Well, I appreciate your thinking that, Bella, I really do.' It took a moment for Margy to regain her composure. 'Anyway, it certainly never occurred to me that you might miss Jack. You haven't mentioned him in years.'

'Jack', Bella said, in an odd little voice, 'took something with him when he died. Something of mine.' Then she got up briskly, picked up the honey jar and screwed its lid on tight – looking, Margy saw with alarm, not like Bella at all. She couldn't work out what it was: anger? grief? These were emotions that Bella never showed: she was too private for that. But then she saw that no, it wasn't either of those. Bella looked sad, she also looked guilty.

'I didn't think you'd loved Jack so much,' Margy said, clearing the table to avoid looking at Bella.

'Love!' Bella laughed. 'Americans talk about love as if it were a commodity at the supermarket. Besides,' she added sharply, 'it doesn't exist, not reciprocal love, not between men and women. Men love imaginary women and women love their children.'

Margy felt vanquished. Bella had a way of speaking that made you believe what she said. When she spoke about anything, it was with a confidence that came naturally to her. Margy wondered if she was envious of Bella. Otto admitted that *he* was, and he said it with the weight of a solid career behind him. Not, of course, that it matched Bella's. From the time that she was ten years old she was recognised as exceptional. She did not go to school with normal children. From her MD onwards, she had clearly been destined for great things. Bella had not fought her way through men's barricades; she had just stepped over men. In her own way, without bitchiness or aggression: just by being better. And in medicine, if you were a woman, to storm those barricades you had to be not just better, but a great deal better. First-rate. As Bella had always been.

Her words had unsettled Margy. It was an odd thing, but Margy had always felt that being a woman meant nothing to Bella. Being a mother meant a great deal, being a woman did not. It was hard to explain. It was partly because Bella wouldn't tolerate any question of gender. A journalist had once interviewed Bella in Margy's house, for *Time*. She had asked how it felt to be a woman heart surgeon.

'Would you ask that of a male heart surgeon?' Bella asked quietly.

'Well, no . . .'

'Well, don't ask it of me.'

'But in your case,' the woman mumbled, 'it's so unusual, you know, to be a woman and –'

'It's irrelevant,' Bella said, 'it has nothing to do with anything. If this interview is to continue, ask me about my work.'

'You know, Bella,' Margy now said, 'I don't know how you've done it. I know what it takes, through Otto: the study, the terrible hours, the inhuman competition. I don't know how you've managed even one side of your life, let alone the personal side.'

Bella looked at Margy as if she didn't know what she was talking about. Then, quite abruptly, her voice and manner changed. She looked away and said quietly, 'It was different before. At the beginning, I was never tired. I could work for ever. When everyone else fell back, I went on.'

'You make yourself sound like a machine,' Margy said.

Bella looked at Margy. 'Yes, it was like that. My body didn't count. You see, all those years – I just used it. I hardly even needed to eat. I didn't feel the emotions that held other people back.'

'But you were married,' Margy protested, 'at the beginning, and then, later, you married Jack. You must have felt those things.'

Bella's lips were set. 'No,' she said.

'Well, you do now. You were just saying, talking that way, about Jack, I mean.'

'No,' she repeated, her voice becoming low and hard. 'I did not.'

And that was that. She picked up her briefcase, a big leather bag that had once belonged to Isaac Roth, and got up to go to her meeting. Her face was quite composed; it had none of the uncertainty or distress of earlier. She didn't say goodbye to her children; she merely walked to the front door. Margy watched her with a feeling she often had about Bella: baffled, even a bit disturbed.

But at the door, Bella suddenly turned and walked up the stairs. Margy imagined that she was going to say goodbye to the children, after all, but when she came down, she was wearing a different outfit. Her pink dress, a lovely silk creation, had been replaced by a pale grey suit and her hair was pulled back into a tight knot.

This time, when Bella reached the front door, she turned and looked at Margy. Then, with a touch of scorn and also a touch of mischief in her face, she said, 'It was all nonsense, you know, what I said – about Jack.'

13

Chapter Three

Bella got out of the taxi and walked briskly down the street. It was hot and everyone was impatient, sweaty and in a hurry. She did not sweat, had no recollection of ever having sweated and, consequently, her clothing was as immaculate as when she'd first put it on. She looked up at the hospital building and smiled, as if, within the grand scale of its masonry, yet another challenge waited to be overcome. At the desk, she asked for Philip Modlinger and was immediately taken to the top floor.

His office was predictably furnished: Chippendale furniture, Indian rugs, a Hockney on a wall by the window, silk curtains, a sense of opulence. Philip Modlinger was a man in late middle-age, handsome, well groomed and, she felt, perhaps a little distant in the way he rose to greet her. He observed how very cool she looked, almost serene, and compared it to the ravaged demeanour of the cardio-vascular surgeons who worked on his team.

'I'm grateful you could come over so promptly,' he said, without any introductory pleasantry. 'As you can imagine, we want to get this settled. The suspense about where the job goes isn't good for morale.'

Bella's eyes narrowed; she was surprised that there was any question about its direction. As far as she was concerned, the job was hers: offered to her and accepted by her two weeks ago.

The chief surgeon smiled for the first time and said, 'As in London, there's a pecking order in these top appointments. I have an embarrassing situation where two senior surgeons are certain, I'm told, that the post will be theirs.'

'Oh,' she said quietly. 'Is there any reason why it's been left in question?'

His smile was rather strained. 'We hadn't heard from you,' he said carefully. 'I couldn't get you on the phone. Obviously, I didn't want to make an announcement before getting your acceptance.'

14

Bella broke in quickly, 'Didn't you get my letter?'

He shook his head.

'I sent it by express mail over ten days ago.' She was confused and embarrassed.

'I didn't get it.'

'Oh, heavens, this is ridiculous!' Her hand swept across the glossy slope of her hair and rested at the back of her neck. It was a wonderfully graceful movement and, for some reason, it lightened the atmosphere between them.

'Well?' he said, raising an eyebrow. 'Do you want it or not?'

'Of course.' She smiled. She was silent for a moment and then said, 'Though whether I could ever match Isaac's skill, I very much doubt.'

'Well,' Modlinger said quickly, 'he certainly had no doubts.' There was something just a little spiky in his tone. When he saw that she had picked this up, he continued, 'As you know, he wanted you to get this job. He asked me to agree to it before his operation, in spite of my hesitations – not about you, of course, just about the way of doing it, going over the heads of my own people.'

'I'm quite happy to make an application along with the rest,' she cut in quickly, but with confidence, lifting her shoulders with an easy movement. 'There's no need to abide by his wishes.' She gave a small laugh. 'I've never benefited from the old-boy network.'

He smiled. 'You've never needed to. No, it's all been agreed, was passed by the board before our offer was made. And in any case' – his lips stiffened – 'he was my friend; I respected his judgement in all things, so I certainly wouldn't doubt it in this.'

'You must miss him,' she said softly, making a direct connection with Modlinger. It upset his balance a little. She did not cover his emotion with conversation but waited until he seemed righted.

'I am sorry to have messed you around, I'll have to check and see what went wrong with my acceptance letter.' She looked perplexed for a moment and then added, 'There's no question about my wanting the job; I'm honoured by the offer. Thank you for making it.'

The grace with which she conducted herself was appealing to him, reassuring too, in a world that he'd begun to feel was becoming increasingly mordacious.

15

He looked up as his secretary walked in and placed a tray of coffee on his desk.

'Will you have some?'

'Thank you. I'm sorry you couldn't get hold of me,' she said. 'I had to be out of London – a conference in Aberdeen – which is why I didn't get your calls. I'm so sorry, I can imagine how sensitive the area has been.'

'No problem.' He had not expected her to be so likable. Clearly, this honour, and the others in her sparkling career, had not affected her in the normal way. She seemed quite without arrogance. It was restful: he was constantly having to cater to someone's ego in the hospital hierarchy – usually a surgeon's.

'Isaac', he said, putting down his cup, 'spoke about you a great deal. He felt you were unique.' He noticed how Bella's attention seemed taken up by the rather harsh cry of a bird in the tree outside, so much so that she didn't seem to have heard him.

'It's an odd cry, isn't it?' he said. 'Kind of like a baby's.' He continued to look out of the window. 'I like it up here, being at the top of the hospital. You get away from the sounds and smells. I hate them.' He realised then that the conversation had drifted away from its focus and that neither of them was thinking about work at all.

She was looking at the palm of her hand and her face, tilted downward, looked frail, the eyes too dark and large. 'Isaac', she said gently, 'was quite remarkable. I owe him . . .' She stopped and placed her hands together in her lap. 'I've never met anyone so technically brilliant, and yet he was the kindest man, took hours with patients.' She smiled. 'I always thought he didn't really like surgery at all; he was always looking for alternatives. And how rare that is.' She leaned her head over her coffee cup.

'So you miss him, too?' he said quietly.

She looked at him and said with touching directness: 'He was the most important person in my life.'

'I suppose', he said, 'you, too, didn't know how ill he was – until the end?'

'Yes,' she said, 'I did. He told me he had cancer a year ago, but said it was under control.'

Modlinger was hurt; he now wanted to move on.

'There are a few things, Bella,' he said, 'that we should discuss.' He rubbed a hand across his eyes, more in a gesture of clearing his vision that out of weariness. 'First, I have to be sure that you'll be quite happy with the arrangements here. That's to say, that you'll work full-time with us. And receive a salary. I know that an impressive title and an easier schedule doesn't make up for the lack of a full private practice – not to mention some of the freedom and wealth that goes with it.'

'I've considered that,' Bella said. 'There's no problem as long as we can agree a schedule that allows me enough cases. I'm used to a strenuous schedule. And I like that.'

Modlinger raised an eyebrow. 'Yes, I'd heard that. Would you want to continue at such a level? You'd find it exhausting with all the other commitments.'

'It's what I do best,' she said simply. 'I definitely want to participate in the teaching programme, but I don't want it to interfere too much with my operating time.'

'Well, all right – if you've got the stamina. I'm certainly happy to let you do things your own way, there won't be any restrictions. You come with a great reputation and there are people here who can't wait to see you perform.

'The other thing,' he said with some hesitation, leaning forward, 'is extremely confidential, but I want to mention it to you right from the start.' He was surprised at himself; he hadn't expected to confide in her. He wondered if it was because she was a woman, though she used no womanly wiles, no sexual manipulation; there was just something straight and approachable about her. He felt he could trust her and he knew that he would find it very hard to do so were she male.

'Go on,' she said.

'It's just that I'm thinking of retiring soon.' He threw it out and it seemed to rise high in the air and then come whizzing down to earth.

If she was startled, she did not show it. He was struck again by the steadiness of her manner.

'I know it's pretty weird.' He smiled, feeling comfortable, not just with the idea of retiring, but with her, too. 'The fact is, I've been locked into this game since I was twenty. And I've come to the conclusion,' he said quietly, 'that I've had no life. My wife tries to reassure me that I've saved lives, but that's no substitute for a proper life. My life has been – well, it's not been mine. It's belonged to the hospital. Everything else has been neglected, and that includes me, too.'

17

Because of his preoccupation, he did not notice her distress. Staring at the desk, he went on, 'There isn't any point in feeling guilty. I made the decision. I've loved the work.' He looked up swiftly. 'It's just that, well, I'm fifty-two and I don't have to go on with it. So I've decided to quit.'

Her agitation was receding; she could hear his words plainly again. The raucous song of the bird beyond the high window had ceased.

'When?' she asked.

'It depends on you. You're the next one down now. I wanted to know how you'd feel about it. Don't want to chuck you in the deep end.'

His implication was clear and she felt a rising sense of power. So complete was it, that the feeling of agitation, of being torn, that she'd experienced a moment before, seemed not to have happened.

'You may change your mind,' she said.

'I will not,' he said, carefully.

'You are brave, then.' In her voice, so low and melodic, there was a little envy.

'It doesn't take much courage to do what you want to.'

'Power is hard to relinquish . . . ' – she turned her cup in her hands – 'and, not to operate again, I don't know, I don't think I could give that up.'

He shrugged. 'You'll have to, one day.'

It was as if this came as a shock to her. She stared at him, she looked down at her hands and she would not believe that her skills would ever diminish, her powers ever fail.

He said, with a touch of amusement, almost without condescension, 'I was thirty-eight once, too. I know what it is to be thirty-eight and fifty-two. I wish I'd known then what I'd feel today.'

'You're saying it's not worth it.'

He shrugged. 'I know nothing exhilarates like surgery, nothing gives such prominence and glamour in medicine. But no, it's not worth it. The toll is too great, the complicity with all that's sickening in the world, too total. I was not really dedicated, I was just greedy.'

Now it was back, the agitation, and for a moment she felt quite dizzy. Her mouth went dry and blood pounded in her temples. It was as if the bird's cry had moved to the centre of her brain.

'Are you all right?' he asked quickly, rising up from his chair.

His distress banished her own. Within a few seconds, she was able to laugh lightly, 'Of course. It was simply what you were saying; it reminded me of Isaac.' She laughed again. 'He used to caution me.' She had covered herself, but he was left with a nagging doubt: was she stable?

She now took control of the interview and directed the conversation towards professional matters. Talking to her now, with such ease, well, there was no question about it: the woman was superb. No one was better qualified for the job and, surely, no one could bring to it more vitality and life. He had never heard anyone speak about their work as she did. It was as if he saw open-heart surgery from the outside, as if she sliced through to the heart, held it in her hands and said: look at this, now let me show you what can be done to heal it. How the woman would teach! Who could not be inspired by such wonder! She was one of those rare people who made of every word, or thought, an excellence. There was no cynicism in her, no boredom, nothing jaded or predictable. She had the rapt belief in her art – for to listen to her you felt it was an art, not a science – of an ancient faith healer, but one who knew every shred of modern technology.

He knew now that he had done the right thing – or rather, that old Isaac, clearly besotted by this virago ('I taught her, but in the first weeks I knew she would soon overtake me'), had sent him precisely what he needed. Now he could safely make his own exit, preserving at the same time the high reputation of the hospital. It amused him also: those prima donnas of the operating rooms had better watch out – she was a real piece of work. He would send out a memo, cataloguing her triumphs, leaving the best bit till last – that she was a woman.

Chapter Four

She was smiling as she walked down Fifth Avenue. Her hips moved in a way that was efficient and yet voluptuous; it caught the attention of the men on the street but it enabled her to navigate the currents of humanity faster than her fellow travellers. Thinking about her conversation with Modlinger, her smile widened. He is grateful to me, she thought with amusement, for being sufficiently different to make comparisons between us impossible. And he's tired; she smiled now with the superiority of one who had not even begun to pace herself. He's tired of the bureaucracy and the politics; he's sick to death of those surgeons scrapping over his desk, of a wife grown bitter on neglect and loneliness. He's tired of his life and he thinks he can remake it. He'll be gone in a year or, possibly, I can get him out sooner. His hands shook – oh, barely, imperceptibly, but they shook. Something else is wrong too. It gives me a year, eighteen months at most, to work the system. If I can maintain his support, I'm halfway there.

For the first time, then, she looked outside her brain and the street caught her eye. Three hobos were playing jazz on a street corner, their bodies perfectly in tune with the strong, spring heat. Her eyes were drawn up the sheer perpendicular slopes of the buildings. They were awkwardly beautiful, angular, seeming to have been randomly placed. She thought of the stately formality of Europe, its harmony and grace. Here, she felt, squinting at the steep cliffs of glass and concrete, it had all been speedily constructed and would be demolished just as fast. A view would not outlast a decade. What did it do to people, she wondered, such acceleration of change, such frequent and total violence to a landscape? What will it do to me? She shuddered and walked on.

Abruptly, she came to a halt, so much so that the man behind her cursed. She didn't hear or see him. Her mind had fixed. There was only one imperative now: to get to the

20

station at once and catch a train home. She ran into the street and began looking around frantically for a taxi. Other people were of the same mind. When finally an empty cab appeared, Bella rushed up to it, outdistancing the competition, putting her hand possessively on the door handle. Inside, she leaned back, closed her eyes, her brows and lips flexed with concentration – trying to remember, but unable to.

When she got back to Margy's house, she rushed straight to her room, where she began digging around in an attaché case. She could not find what she was looking for, took a deep breath, and began again, sifting more slowly through the deep pile of papers. Still she could not find it. Kneeling on the floor, she searched her briefcase, which was where she kept her letters. Then she stopped, exasperated, her hands resting on her thighs. She returned to the attaché case and emptied it onto the floor, going through each piece of paper methodically. It had to be here; she never lost anything, she never forgot anything. There was always a record; in this instance, a yellow carbon copy of her letter of acceptance to Philip Modlinger.

She did find something, but it was not what she was looking for. She held it a long time. In her hands was her hand-written version of the letter to Modlinger, and, neatly stapled to the back, was the top copy that her secretary had typed. Across this typescript, in a rude scrawl, large and ill-formed, even childish in its roundness, someone had written in a red pen: *Not to be sent. Destroy.*

Her first reaction was shock, followed quickly by anger. Something made her turn the piece of paper over. Written very small, down at the bottom of the sheet, were these words: *This is one thing you're not going to have.*

Her face took on a strange pallor, her anger evaporated and in its place a weariness took hold. She found herself putting the papers back, placing the one she had been looking for where she had found it, tucked inside a side pocket she hardly ever used. And then, not knowing quite why she did it, she drew it out again. With the prescience of one who covered herself at all times, she tore up both copies and flushed them down the lavatory. She was calm again; she could not understand why, but it was so, and it remained.

21

Chapter Five

When Bella awoke the next morning, very early, as she always did, the sun was slicing through the slats of the blinds. Getting out of bed, she opened the blinds and sat in a chair where the sun could completely cover her. She had woken from a dream feeling very cold. She knew this chill; it was as persistent as a premonition.

Light was flowing across the cream walls of the room; it rippled across the pale curtains and in and out of the windows. The light had the same opalescence in the room as it had out in the garden among the tall trees. It filled her with nostalgia. This was not the cool, flat light of England; it was the crystal light of the Mediterranean, the tropics, or the Sargasso Sea. It made her happy; it even took some of the chill away.

The light brought back memories of France where, as a young woman, having just finished her examinations, she had gone to a small village in Provence. Her doctor had ordered her to rest, because her studies, on this single occasion in her life, had brought her to breaking-point. He had asked Bella's mother not to accompany her to France, feeling that there was something seriously wrong with the girl and her mother. He'd asked to see Bella alone several times after that, and had questioned her about her mother: the nature of their life together, the pressure Bella had been subjected to in terms of her studies. He was startled to find that the girl seemed to have no memory of certain things; she was not refusing to remember, she simply did not remember – and said so. Bella's mother brought these visits to a halt. Bella was dispatched to France. It was the first time in her life that she'd ever been completely alone.

She lived above a small patisserie, in a long room with narrow windows and sloping floors. The walls and ceiling were painted the colour of country butter; and every morning, when the sun shone across her bed, she felt she was swimming. The room now came back to her with total recall, engaging all her

22

senses. The little shop below with the green shutters, the smell at dawn of the yeast rising, the warmth of the ovens coming up through the loose floorboards. She would lie in idleness, waiting for the smell of the crusty baguettes to reach her, the soft sweet odour of the rolls, the vanilla mingling with the apricots as they soaked in brandy, their scents released slowly as they nestled in hot beds of choux pastry. Later, she would go down and work with Madame, learning to cook for the first time, feeling the easy, strong pleasure of baking, using her hands and her mouth and letting her brain go cold.

It was a far cry from her own home, that world of scholarship and discipline, of striving for an excellence that outshone all others. It had always been her mother's insistence that dragged her more than her father's, but by now it was more lethal, it had become her own. She was unable to separate herself, so inextricably was she bound, and now, away from her mother's orbit, she felt the first thrilling flares of hate and rage. She fed on them even as she glutted herself on the pastries in the bakery downstairs.

Madame had a nephew, a wild, laughing boy who came to work with his aunt on Saturdays. He was Bella's first lover; he was also the first boy she had had any close contact with. Thinking of him now, after several years of chosen celibacy, she could feel his hands and how they had affected her. His haste and her wonder – not at the sensations of her body, but at the miraculous realisation that this was the beginning of her creative life. The destiny that she had chosen – medicine, surgery; the cutting back of pathology to bring forth health – this was a paltry thing in comparison. Her body would create life, would grow from seed her own children. She would watch them as they grew, knowing that they would still be laughing when her own breath was gone.

Looking at her lover as he lay back on the fat, goose-feather bolsters, she had seen his proud arrogance and felt sorry for him. His apparatus, of which he was so proud, for all its aggressiveness was yet so inadequate. It could only ignite, while her body was the centre of the world. Out of this knowledge came a little disdain, which had never quite left her. She had understood then what he could not: that his arrogance was merely a defence against her creative gift. She knew also, as her mother had sought to prove by her life, that

23

power belonged to women and that was what all the rumpus was about. But, getting up and leaving her lover in her nest, she vowed that she would not repeat her mother's life – that life where everything and everyone was sacrificed to the great work. She, Bella, would live a complete life. She would have as many children as she could as well as a career of great brilliance. She did not consider a father for these children; after all, she had lived most of her childhood without one.

Bella walked to the cot where her youngest child lay sleeping. She saw the lilac veins over the closed eyelids, the clenched fists and parted mouth. She had achieved all she had ever wanted. Yet looking at the small boy she was filled with the sadness of loving him. She couldn't place it, beyond a feeling that he was not really hers and never would be; that this desire to capture and hold fast, which was the measure of her maternity, could not be achieved – was even a violence that she must avoid. She shook off the sadness; she was able to do so efficiently because her sadness was oblique, seen only in glimpses, like the view from a speeding train.

The sunlight had shifted in the room, so that now it lit up only one corner, leaving the rest in shadow. It occurred to Bella that it would be at least two hours before the children woke. She had work to do. It had always seemed sinful to waste time. She knew this was part of her mother's legacy, but it didn't bother her: she had used it for her own ends. As she walked obediently to the table that served as a desk, all the warmth that had risen from her memories left her. The chill was back and it seemed that her body grew flat and lifeless. Yet as soon as she picked up the folder and began to read, it was as if this disfigurement left her. Her pulse quickened as her eyes sped along the text of a paper reporting the remarkable success of a new artificial-heart centre. She read on, scribbling her thoughts down next to the text, wondering whether this was an area she should become involved with again. She'd done research on a similar project some years ago, in London, but technically this was far more advanced.

She had become so engrossed that she was startled to feel a hand on her arm, a hand hesitant but heavy, letting down its weight. She looked up at a sleepy face with mussed hair and smiled at the boy in his stiff, new pyjamas. 'Will.' Her arm reached around his waist and drew

24

him closer to her. 'Couldn't you sleep? It's not even seven o'clock.'

'Daisy snores like a pig.'

'She can't help it. It'll be better when she has her adenoids removed.'

'The sooner the better.' Then he pulled at the edge of her nightdress and asked, 'When are we going home?'

'Don't you like it here?' She turned down his collar.

'It's okay, but I want to go home now.'

She laughed. 'We've only been here four days.'

'Five.'

'I was glad to have you with me, Will.'

He smiled, an odd, wistful smile that revealed his uncertainty about her.

'Get a chair, Will. Let's have a talk, while we're alone, without the little ones. I need your advice.'

He went for the chair, lightening his step as she cautioned, 'Don't wake the baby.'

'He's too old to be a baby.' He put his chair down beside hers.

She took his hand. 'Will, how would you feel about moving to America?' He didn't know how to reply. She continued, 'You know the job I told you about? The one I came over to see about? Well, I'd like to take it and of course that would mean coming to live here.'

'With Margy?'

'No,' she laughed, 'we'll get our own house, a big one, with lots of garden so you can have a tree-house. What d'you think?'

He felt her excitement and didn't want to disappoint her.

'I'd have to move to a new school.'

'Yes, but the schools here are nice, they're much more friendly and easy-going than your prep-school.'

'I'm not very easy-going myself,' he said with a frown.

She hugged him. 'No, but perhaps you should be, a little more, anyway.'

'They probably wouldn't like me – the other boys, I mean.'

'Why ever not?'

'Because I'm English.'

'Oh, the Americans love English people,' – she laughed – 'though the English rather loathe Americans.'

'Do they?'

25

She nodded and wondered how long it would take for the cultured tone to fade from his voice. It had always been a pure voice, carrying no trace of any other land. Her own had a twang that was decidedly European, with faint echoes of Vienna and Germany.

'Will,' she said warmly, 'you mustn't worry. You'll find new friends, as you did when you moved to Sussex House.'

He looked at her directly. 'It's decided, isn't it? We are coming.'

She looked at him just as directly. 'Yes, it is decided.'

He turned his face away and, in the gesture and in the expression on his face, all the loneliness of a fatherless boy was manifest.

She pulled him back to her. 'Will,' she said, 'I won't lie to you, any more than I ever promise anything I know I can't make come true. It will be hard at first. For both of us, very different to get used to. The little ones won't mind, but we will, because we like things to stay the same.'

He was comforted because she had found words to describe how he felt. He was happy because he liked this moment of exclusiveness, liked the close contact with his mother, the way her hand rested on his arm.

'Whenever I get used to one of your hospitals,' he said bleakly, 'you move to another one.'

She was startled. 'But Will, I've been at the same hospital for nearly four years.'

'Oh,' he said, but it meant nothing to him, who was aware only of her absence.

'Will,' she said, 'would you like to see this hospital? I could take you to New York and show you, it's a wonderful place, with machines you'd just love.' Immediately she made the offer, she felt uneasy; she kept the two sides of her life very separate.

But Will's face lit up. 'Oh yes, I would. I've never been to one, except that time . . .' His voice trailed away in confusion. It was a memory concerned with his father's illness and he did not want to remember it. He looked at her with a smile of such tenderness and pleasure that she winced. 'I'd like to see where you go all the time.'

Her shame was a new thing, and it was so painful to her that she averted her face. But Will, with his keen sense of mercy, leant across and kissed her.

'Don't worry, Mummy,' he said, 'I don't mind that you work so much, honestly. You make people better. You give them new hearts.'

She didn't duck it. 'But I leave you alone.'

'I'm used to it,' he said gallantly, 'and besides, I have a lot to do these days. It was worse when I was little.'

'Was it?' she whispered.

'Oh yes,' he said, because now her emotions were too deep for his detection. 'I used to wait for you, sitting on the wall outside, when we lived in Flood Street. I used to wait and wait and then, when you still didn't come, I'd go inside again.'

She couldn't take it.

'Will there be anyone else you'll miss, coming to live here, apart from your friends?'

He thought a moment. 'No, not really. Will Alison still be our nanny?'

'I hope so.' She brightened. 'Couldn't do without Alison, she's one of us. We'll make her come.'

She was grateful that, at least, she didn't have to uproot him from a father.

He knew where her thoughts had led her and said, 'It would be more difficult, wouldn't it, if Daddy was alive.'

'Yes.'

'Why did he die?' he asked, with a tone to his voice that she found accusatory. She had a sense of the boy's will, of the robust nature of it – as if she could reach out and take it.

'It was a risk he took – doing what he did. He could have died at any time. He knew that.'

'Because he was an explorer?' There was pride in Will's voice, and envy, too.

'Yes.' She had always referred to his father as an explorer because Will liked to think of him that way: he was fascinated by jungles, deserts and wild places. William had, in fact, been a professor of tropical diseases. He had been ill many times; his body had been exposed to more rare and mysterious diseases than it could bear. She remembered these illnesses now with horror – she who so hated illness that she could only deal with it by cutting it away with clean, sharp strokes.

Will was dreaming of those little tree-frogs who flew with the grace of gliders from branch to branch in the rain forests. She

27

knew how he yearned for those places that he called ones that no one knows the way to, and saw in it his father's compulsion to escape the world.

She said, suddenly, not knowing why she did, 'I'll take you to some of the places he went to, Will.'

He was unused to such spontaneity in her. 'Will you?' he asked eagerly. Then, 'But how could you? You wouldn't have time.' He was not reproachful, merely puzzled.

'Will,' she said, taking both his hands, 'I really do want to change our life.' When she'd said it, she knew it was true. The time had come, it could not be put off much longer. 'I want to be with you all much more. It's hard, working the way I do, but I want to make it better and I will.'

His face flushed. 'I know how hard you try,' he said softly. He would forgive her every neglect if she would just stay the way she was now, the way she'd been when he was little: tender, protective – there.

There was a cry from the cot in the corner, followed by a chuckle.

'Oh, Will dear,' she said, 'the baby's woken. Will you get him for me?'

He rose with reluctance from the cushion of intimacy. He resented the baby for being another, seemingly more deserving, candidate for his mother's time and affection.

'Smelly little beast,' he said, dumping the sodden bundle in Bella's lap.

'Wash your hands,' she teased, 'or you might catch something.'

She picked up her smallest child (her last child, as she thought of him) and held him close. The smell of slumber and spit mingled, filling her with love. She stood, taking the weight of him upon her hip, wiping the crusts of sleep from his eyes as she went, talking softly. The older boy swatted his jealousy aside with an impatience reminiscent of his mother's. But she caught it where it landed, turned and put out her hand to him, drawing him to her other side.

'What shall we have for breakfast, Will? Shall we be English and have porridge, or American and make pancakes?'

The choice was hard, but patriotism prevailed.

When she had changed the baby, she walked down the stairs towards the kitchen, one son perched upon her hip and her arm

28

resting on Will's shoulder. Her hand, as she smoothed his hair, was the same hand that took the knife and cut into the muscles and flesh of a living chest and through to the beating heart, cut with precision and concentration; strong hands, steady, unflinching. The same hands, which now touched her sons tenderly, also pulled together the wounded clefts of a body and held them so, for someone to stitch the seam.

Chapter Six

Three days after the brunch, Joseph telephoned Bella. Margy had given him the excuse he had needed. They'd bumped into one another in the parking lot outside Otto's hospital and Joseph had asked after Bella with what seemed to Margy no more than polite interest. Margy, fond of boasting about her friends' achievements, was only too willing to give Joseph the information he was after. So now he knew not only precisely what Bella did, but why she was in America. He was impressed.

He had known that she was a widow, but Margy repeated this news with a sad sympathy not entirely lacking in satisfaction – as if, in extolling Bella's brilliance, she needed also to have some aspect to pity.

'She needs support right now,' Margy declared. 'I mean, she's taking on a big life-change and the first thing she needs is a home.' She launched into a description of the assistance she intended to provide, but Joseph cut her short. It had occurred to him that he knew of a house that might suit Bella perfectly; he felt he knew the kind of house she would like. In fact, since he had first seen her, he had thought about her so much that he felt he knew _her_.

He had decided that it wasn't really a sexual attraction, even though that moment in the hallway had been pretty charged. Bella wasn't his type. He preferred less formidable women, though he couldn't abide stupid ones. Also, he felt that achievement on a level as vaunted as Bella's was normally detrimental to character. Bella sounded too smart for her own good and certainly for his.

Besides, he didn't need sex or love. He put sex first because he had always questioned the existence of love. He did not feel he had ever seen a mighty love or a great devotion; one was hard pressed to find a couple who even granted one another the courtesies of friendship once they were caught in the grid-lock of mutual need. To put it more simply, he had come to believe that the world was made up of man's violence to woman and woman's to man. This point of view had not been formed entirely by working within the penal system.

Joseph was not after sex, he was quite sure of that. For sex there was Susie. They had been lovers for almost two years. It had begun as a commuter love affair: she'd travel miles to see Joseph and he'd catch a plane or train to meet her. Heady at first, the lustre had disappeared from the arrangement once the American Express bills came in and, nowadays, their blood was cooler.

Susie was usually available, although her job was taking her on location more often these days. Joseph felt certain she would not find this view of her offensive. They had an arrangement that suited them both. And besides, Susie tended to think of herself in male terms, while regarding men as the opposition.

Joseph was exasperated by women, feeling that there was considerable confusion in the female mind, now that the main lashing-out was over. They were still too eloquent on the subject of what they did not want and remarkably dumb about what they did want. Of course, they wanted what men had, so why this reluctance about reaching out and grabbing it?

His fascination with Bella – because he knew he was fascinated – had to do with a long and intense interest in people who are not what they seem; people whose art of deception and duplicity is so highly developed that, unlike the rest of humanity, they do not need to use their faces as masks. You could always expose the face behind a mask, but if the entire person was a mask it was far more difficult. Joseph had met a number of such types: a few were psychopaths, one a murderer, one a gypsy and one a tramp who called himself a world traveller. These people, when you look in their eyes, do not reveal the truth because the truth is not with them. All that can be seen is mystery and void. They are eccentrics who possess a secret, sometimes unknown even to themselves, which makes their personalities skittish and inexplicable.

Bella, he felt, fell into this category, and yet he could not say how or why. When he thought of her, he remembered the baby curled up on her lap and a face almost beatific in its tenderness. But immediately the impression was eclipsed by her inscrutable face looking up at the banker.

31

Joseph was confused by his reactions to the woman, for many reasons. Why was it that when he thought of her, he thought always of her body? He felt he had outgrown the need for bodies. He had glutted himself on nubile flesh in the years after his marriage had failed, he'd reached sufficiency with sex and was bored by sensation.

This question of body: Susie's was twenty-seven years old, Bella's closer to thirty-five. But, Joseph's preference had moved towards the latter. Susie's body, like Susie herself, had no give and take. It was a hard, lean body. And it was a lecherous body, demanding but ungenerous, unacquainted with the true nature of its desires. Susie had an I'm-gonna-grab-as-much-as-you-fuckers-do philosophy in all her dealings, yet, as far as Joseph was concerned, she had no decency or honour in her. He found that he went off her when he was not with her; he could forget her entirely in a fortnight. Besides, he was beginning to see that, without the ignition of real feeling, his powers were flagging: this was not an area to expect mercy from Susie.

He knew now that there was something sweeter, more lenient, about a body that had done longer service. He could forgive his own more easily if it was lying beside another with some sag and spill. He was in two minds as to whether this was maturity or decline, but no longer cared too much.

Professionally, Joseph had chosen to eschew the body and concentrate on the mind. As a medical student, he'd considered surgery, but the draw to psychiatry had been far stronger. There was a great divide in the medical world between the body- and the mind-factions. Physicians and surgeons, he always found, would stick to the facts with great tenacity because it was their refuge from feeling. With the mind, there were few facts; there was the slippery world of emotion, thought and speculation, coupled with a vast amount of guesswork. A body chap couldn't bear the lack of categorisation: it made him pedantic. Pedantry was not something Joseph wanted to foster in himself.

And Bella, he thought (reaching for the phone), had chosen bodies in the deepest way possible: she went straight to the vital organ and took her knife to it. Surely such work must reveal something about the desires of the woman?

Chapter Seven

'Bella?'

'Yes.'

'This is Joseph Sunderland. We met at Margy's house on Sunday.'

She gave a murmur that revealed neither recollection nor the absence of it.

'I believe you are looking for a house and, as it happens, I know some people with one to sell.'

She hesitated. 'Can you tell me something about it?' He noticed, for the first time, that her voice was beautiful – low and quiet.

'It's near Tarrytown. Do you know that area?'

'No.'

'It's pretty close to the city, you could get in easily enough. It's a decent house, old, sort of a farmhouse with plenty of outbuildings, most of which are falling to pieces, but there's lots of room: five or six bedrooms and a big garden. It needs attention, but I'd say it's pretty sound.'

'And your friends? How soon would they be prepared to sell?'

'Immediately. They've just got divorced and the cash from the property has to be divided. It isn't on the market yet, but will be in a few days. That's why I thought it might be a good idea to get in first. Would you like to see it? I'm going that way tomorrow and could take you.'

'Would the morning suit?' she asked immediately. 'I have an appointment in New York in the afternoon.'

'That would be fine. I'll pick you up about ten?'

'That sounds perfect. Thank you.'

The phone went dead and he looked at it reproachfully, as if it were in some way to blame for her brevity. Then he grinned; there was a feeling of exhilaration in him: the first connection was made, they were off.

The next morning, he was at Margy's house at precisely nine-thirty. He'd got away earlier than expected and liked the idea of confounding her by being early. He suspected that her habits were as regular as a German train. Margy was not at home, but the cleaning lady directed him to the kitchen.

Bella wore a bright red apron and her hands were covered in flour. Three children were cutting shapes from a flat round of pastry. Bella didn't even notice his entrance until the boy nudged her.

'Oh,' she said, looking up, in no way confounded. 'You're early.' She introduced him to her children with polite graceful formality and they responded accordingly.

'Don't rush,' he said, sitting down on a small sofa to be out of the way.

'Can you wait till these go in the oven?' she asked, in a manner that could not be faulted. 'Otherwise the children will be disappointed.'

'Of course.' He watched as she placed the star-shaped biscuits on a tray. Disappointed, he thought, they certainly were. She was smiling at them, but they had now begun to stare at him with irritation. The boy tossed him a look of disdain so like his mother's that Joseph wondered why he was putting himself to any trouble on her behalf. He noted Will as a potential trouble-maker in his dealings with Bella.

Bella ignored him. She handed each of the children little cups of coloured dots and cherries and they began to decorate the rather grimy pastry. He was watching her hands – ringless, domestic – as they smoothed out the dough. Little plump fingers darted in and around her own; it was a tender scene. And her hands – how strange, he thought, one would imagine she might be a fine pianist. The fingers were long and sensitive; and yet they were most serviceable hands, the nails cropped and wide.

They had forgotten Joseph and he rather liked that. It allowed him to observe her ménage. Watching Will, Joseph could see that the boy felt close to his mother, although he was undemonstrative. It was possible that he didn't quite trust her: he kept checking on her face in a way that was uncertain. The bigger girl, Daisy, was very interesting: quick and inquisitive, she kept well away from her mother. The younger one, Mary, worked quietly, her attention directed at what she did. The baby

34

sat on the table and squashed the snippets of pastry between his clenched fists. He was rather close to the edge but there was no question of his falling: Bella's eyes had a restless vigilance that encompassed them all.

What was it, Joseph wondered, that was amiss here; what little disturbance in the atmosphere was he picking up? It was that sense of things not being what they seemed, and yet what could be more normal? The small girl, Mary, was complaining that her cherries were being pilfered; Bella had only to look once at the culprit for them to be returned.

Will announced flatly, 'I suppose you'll be gone till late?' Joseph watched his face carefully, but there was no censure in it.

'No,' she said, 'I won't, and this is my last meeting before we go home. We have two whole days together.' Her face lit up as she said it. The faces of her children rose to look at her; the little tension that began as she took off her apron and prepared to leave was stilled. She put the tray of biscuits in the oven and scooped the crumbs off the baby. She picked him up and nuzzled his cheek. 'Will, can you check on these biscuits in about ten minutes? When they're pale brown they're done and you can take them out.'

'I know,' he said, watching her plonk the baby down on the sink and wash her hands. The two little girls ran to the door; they were allies, clearly, and their solidarity excluded their brother.

'You won't forget what I told you, Daisy?' The child's face went suddenly stiff and awkward. She shook her head. Mary's curls jangled as she dragged her big sister off down the corridor.

'And you, Will,' Bella said softly, 'what will you do?'

'Watch the biscuits,' he replied in a dull tone.

So thoroughly did she understand him that she did not need to make any acknowledgement of his mood. Joseph admired, again, this steadiness in her. The boy might not like it, but at least he knew where he stood. Joseph doubted whether he could be so even-handed himself.

'I do have some work to do,' Will said.

'I see.' Hers was a small, sweet smile. 'Well, I'll be back later.' She kissed him on the cheek and turned to Joseph. 'I'll only be a second.'

She was gone. Joseph watched as Will's alienation returned and waited to see how he would deal with it: all the trails left

35

by the children led directly back to the mother. The boy pulled round; it was clear that he was familiar with disappointment.

Bella was back, as she had said, in a second.

'Sorry to keep you waiting,' she said.

'That's okay – not often that I see a bit of family life.' In spite of himself, he heard the sarcasm in his own voice. She looked quickly at him to see if he mocked her but he stared her out. The small child was still with her. He noticed how practised her hip was in the accommodation of a child's body and how protectively her hand went to Will's stiff back. Her reluctance to leave them was palpable, yet she would not bend; she made her exit quick.

'I'll just take Harry to Alison and I'll meet you at the front.'

The door closed after her.

Joseph had the unflattering certainty that he counted nothing at all for Bella. He saw her as committed in two directions which she would not allow to conflict. He sensed that nothing and no one had intruded upon that symmetry. Bella was physician and mother but probably never woman, never wife and never beholden to any man. It was a strong and eerie sense in her: it made her seem incomplete and rather vulnerable. All humans, to Joseph, had their *doppelgänger* in the animal or insect world. In her black eyes he saw the killer instinct: that ruthless expenditure of what she did not need or could not use. She was a widow spider and, from the body-count behind her, rather a proficient one.

As he stood in the hallway, digesting his analysis, he shuddered, just once, and then there rushed through him a great sense of possibility and excitement. He was determined to have her, or to break her. He would make her move towards him; he would wait, a still victim, and then trap her within the skeins of her own web. He sensed the strength of those skeins, built as they were of discipline, solitude and single-mindedness. It was territory he knew well himself.

He had a vision of her as a Joan of Arc figure, one who hung up her armour at night and waited, disarmed, in the moonlight, for someone to breathe life into her dark soul. Well, he might just give it a whirl. The sheer audacity of it made him laugh.

'What are you laughing about?' she said, from behind him.

He turned, very slowly, to give himself time. 'I was thinking of you as Joan of Arc,' he said.

'I'm related to her, on my father's side,' she said coolly, 'and I don't like fire.

Chapter Eight

In the car, he noticed that now she looked a little different. Her hair, which had come loose in the kitchen, was severely put in its place at the nape of her neck. Her dress was almost austere in its lines, unsoftened by any adornment. She wore little make-up and no scent. Where that rather delicious smell of vanilla and baking had gone he had no idea – she'd not had time to shower. But gone it was and nothing replaced it, not even a body smell. She had been wearing glasses in the kitchen and now did not.

She used none of the pleasantries of conversation that he found trying in Americans. Bella sat beside him and said nothing. He followed suit. In the silence, he detected all sorts of interesting clues: it was as if a vibration came off her; a low, dangerous murmur.

His only success was to get her to begin the conversation.

'You're a criminologist, aren't you?'

How pleasant to be able to correct her; he didn't feel he'd often get the chance.

'No, I'm a psychiatrist, but I work with criminals. I'm with the Home Office in London.'

'So, what brought you to America?'

Damn it, he thought, she sounded a bit bored, as if she expected him not to be up to this enquiry – as if she were well used to the inferiority of other people's minds. He was particularly annoyed because he was accustomed to an eager, ghoulish interest in his work.

'I'm involved in a seminar on American state prisons,' he said. 'Our purpose is to introduce reforms.' The set statement bored him.

But then his attention quickened: he had picked up hostility in her. She said, 'To refuse parole seems to be about as heartless as you can get.'

'Prisons get a lot more heartless than that,' he said with an acuity equal to her own; 'many states have penal systems and jails that would rival Turkey for barbarity.'

She was quiet, then she said in a low voice, 'And you?' She looked directly at him. It was hard not to flinch from her gaze; he turned his eyes back to the road.

'Is it possible', she asked softly, 'that you have come here to peer into the lives of appallingly damaged human beings only to parade their grievances in front of a bunch of professional voyeurs?

'Steady,' he warned, 'there's no need to presume the worst of me quite so quickly.' Then he laughed with pleasure. The woman had a point of view! There was passion in that well-trained voice: the unimpeded passion of a vigorous intellect.

'I'm not drawn to zoos,' he said, watching her with amusement. What a joy it was to talk to someone you knew instinctively was an equal, someone who could accompany you down the arduous roads of politics, philosophy and morality and not be lagging behind with a stone in her shoe. Perhaps, with Bella, argument could even be kept on the clean tracks of reason.

He couldn't wait to do combat with her. The sparring began then and there, in the car, seemingly stripped of eroticism, but anticipating it all the same. Her intuition was as sharp and fresh as a slap in the face and she used her intelligence with precision. Such an intelligence, he knew, often burned out quickly, exhausting itself in conversation. Hers did not. This was the way he had felt once playing chess with a master: his own powers were startled into focus. If he tossed out a question, she would pursue it; if he gave her an advantage, she would use it. If either went after the other in some deceit or platitude, it was attended to. For the first time in a long time, he knew that he was dealing with a marksman whose aim and return were up to his own.

She wanted to know precisely what he did for a living. This was not cocktail talk: each definition was investigated, each step of his career put under scrutiny. She found a loose bit of stitching in a rather well-constructed curriculum and went for it.

'Why didn't you take up that post in Glasgow? It could have taken you deeper into research. Why did you go for the safe London job?'

39

'There were reasons at the time.' He knew that not taking the opportunity to work with the best criminologist in the country had been a great blunder – one he had always regretted.

'These reasons: did you perhaps put them down to a wife who impeded your progress with her concerns?'

'That's perceptive of you. Venetia certainly had a phobia about Scotland.'

She ignored the interruption. 'Or, was it more truthfully a failure of nerve – your own?'

He winced. 'Well, Sherlock, I suppose I have to say that you're right and also that I'm not particularly enjoying this cross-examination, but, for now, you may proceed. Yes, I botched it: my career would have been more glamorous and exciting had I gone for it. We all have our moments of mediocrity.'

'Indeed we do!' She laughed, making him feel her moments were few and far between.

As for the exact nature of his work, he gave up on simplifications. She was very well informed on the criminal mentality and she knew far more about psychology than a brief course in medical training would have taught her. Having encouraged him to express his reasons for coming to America, she then proceeded to dissect those reasons. She did this with neither arrogance nor superiority, but simply to test him against her own standards. Clearly, she was one who put herself and her life under a microscope and she was doing the same to him. She kept after him.

'I'm not used to being the one under scrutiny,' he said, 'so let's move over to you.'

'If you like.'

When he investigated her career and motives, he was surprised to see that she seemed to have scant interest in telling him the statistics of her triumphs: where most people became expansive, she became reticent.

'The price of your dedication to your work', he said, 'must be paid elsewhere, by others?'

'Isn't that true of anyone?'

'Only if one has dependants. Which is why, of course, it's much more difficult for a woman.'

'No,' she said quickly, 'the difficulty doesn't lie in the fact that I'm a woman: it's because a man can leave the house every day and not feel guilty about it and I can-not.'

'So you think a man doesn't feel guilty about walking out of a house full of kids to take up his selfish labours?'

'No, I do not.'

'Why? Because he can do as he pleases?'

'No. Because he doesn't feel guilty. He's chosen someone to relieve him of that feeling.'

'I see. And what if the woman is a lazy slob and a lousy mother, or simply a neurotic soul who cannot keep the wheels of life turning? Does he feel guilty then?'

She laughed, quickly and lightly. 'I doubt that he would feel guilty. I think he'd probably believe that he'd made a poor choice.'

'Perhaps. I'll give you that one! But I do have to take you to task about your laughter.'

'My laughter?'

'It's in very poor health: it comes from your head when its proper location is in the belly.'

'It seems that you'd like to lower it.'

'Definitely.'

She would not be drawn; she began to look impatient. 'When will we get there?'

'Soon enough.'

She moved the conversation back to criminals: she had asked him before why he'd chosen to live with the riff-raff of society. Now she said – and there was something pretty odd, he thought, in the way she said it – 'The worst criminals are walking around free like you and me. Isn't it just the stupid who get caught?

'Yes, of course, they're official scapegoats, punished on our behalf.'

But he was puzzled: he could see that this wasn't what she meant; it wasn't a glib interpretation that each of us, in our own way, was of a criminal mentality, for the occasional fixing of taxes or a swiped towel from a hotel. She was talking personally. When he failed to follow her into her private domain, she aban-doned him and went on alone. She was silent a long time and her abstraction was so intense that he could not break into it.

He saw, signposted at the side of the road, a nursery, and remembered that he wanted to buy some flowers for the

41

wife of a colleague he was visiting that afternoon. He turned to Bella and was about to ask her if she'd mind if they stopped for a minute, when he saw that something was very much amiss. She was huddled in her seat. Her shoulders were drawn round to protect her, her legs pulled tightly together: it was as if she was no longer a tall woman.

He stopped the car outside the nursery and turned to her. He said carefully, 'Are you all right?'

'Perfectly.' She smiled, she was herself again.

'It's just that a moment ago you seemed upset – extremely so.'

She shrugged. 'It was nothing, I just felt cold.'

He looked outside at the sun and balmy blue skies. 'Cold?' he persisted.

'Yes,' she said, firmly; 'it has nothing to do with the weather.' Then, altering her tone a fraction, but only a fraction, so that he should understand she would proceed no further in this direction. 'There are times when I feel cold. It's an internal process, nothing to be concerned about. Let's get your flowers.' She opened the door of the car and stepped out, an imposing woman, wearing an elegant linen dress.

Chapter Nine

Inside the nursery, he lost her. 'I know nothing about flowers,' she said and left him to his own devices. When he had bought a bunch of lilac, he looked for her and saw that she had disappeared. The nursery was large, with a central aisle leading down into a jungle of tall vegetation. He walked in this direction until, finally, he found her. She was sitting on a stone bench; in front of her was a large pool in which scarlet fish swam. She was watching them and he could see that the abstraction was back; this time it was even more marked. Her face was drawn and sad and her body had closed in on itself as before. He did not go any nearer, but watched her from the seclusion of a dark corner.

A wide fan went on in the ceiling and began to whir; she looked up at it, startled, and then resumed her brooding position. He wondered if she could possibly be cold, as she had claimed. Her body suggested she was, though the air was close and damp. The fan had caused some small, copper chimes to play their sharp, sad melody and, as soon as she heard it, great agitation registered in her face. Her head flew this way and that, trying to locate the sound. He was astonished: Bella was afraid, that was the only word for it. She got up in a childish, awkward way and began to run towards the exit.

For a moment Joseph was too astounded to do anything but watch her retreat. He was not quite sure how to proceed. The woman seemed really quite loopy; he had better be careful, he had no wish to get entangled. But he had to do something. With reluctance, and some annoyance, he followed her out of the nursery and into the bright sunshine. There he saw her, her arms folded, looking out at a line of rose bushes with their roots encased in green sacking.

'Bella?' She looked up slowly and, to his further dismay, it was as if she did not recognise him – something she was quick to conceal. 'Bella – are you all right?'

43

She nodded her head, sadly, it seemed to him. He had no alternative: his curiosity now took on a detached concern; he took her arm and led her over to a bench under some pine trees. 'Let's sit here for a moment. Or would you rather sit in the sun, are you cold?' He had taken her reality as the frame-work of a discussion and it shocked him to see how quickly he had reverted to his professional self. They sat thus, in silence; she whispered a few words and then just sat, her head down.

Then she looked at her watch, as if she had remembered some appointment, and he said, 'It's all right, we have enough time, we don't have to be at the house till one o'clock.'

Instantly, she relaxed. She looked across the road to the sprawl of urban dwellings and said, 'How can they build such ugly places? Look at them, flat roofs, flat sides, no towers, no spires, no domes.' He wondered for a moment if she was confused; it was as if she was in Europe. 'How can they bear such ugliness?' she asked.

He laughed. 'None of it will be here in a couple of years. See that Sunset Motel? It will be demolished very soon, you can tell just by looking at it.' He added drily, 'Americans live with daily wreckage. To them, change is progress.'

He felt he had given her enough time to recover and now asked, 'Did you live in Germany?'

'No, I visited it a few times,' she said quickly. 'My mother was German. Why do you ask?'

'Because you spoke German a few moments ago.' He watched her face lose colour.

'I don't speak German.'

'I see,' he said quietly.

'Perhaps we ought to be on our way?'

'Perhaps we should.' He looked at her smooth face with admiration. How had she managed this transformation? What flick of the brain had returned her to normality? He wanted to pursue it, but hesitated. After all, this was not at all what he had envisaged. Deep down in some envious recess of his mind, he knew he was a little relieved to find something wrong with her. Better to keep clear of the woman. But then, without warning, out came a question.

'How often do these things happen to you?' he asked.

She looked at him then from an aloof place; he was surprised, he'd not expected such command of herself. 'The

44

last time,' she said, 'was six years ago, when my mother died.'

Her candour shamed him.

'And what, may I ask, brought on this one?' Was it possible, he wondered, looking at her face, that she, too, was disappointed in him, as he was with her.

'You may not ask,' she said, 'because your interest is unkind.'

'There are many things you want to know about me,' she said quietly, 'because you are looking for an explanation.'

'For what?' he asked.

'For my success.'

He was startled by the validity of this insight.

'You're the kind of man', she went on, 'who needs a reason to justify his opinion. And your opinion is that it is not possible for me to be a successful surgeon and the mother of four children without there being something wrong somewhere. You would like to inflate a small incident into something that will tidy me up for you. Perhaps' – she smiled – 'you are even one of those men who can only deal with a woman as a mother, or a wife? And when asked to extend your vision, to encompass both these things and a rigorous profession, you can't do it and refuse to deal with me.'

'I'm ready to admit some of that,' he said, 'but don't let's fool ourselves that it explains everything.'

'I'm not in the habit of fooling myself about anything,' she said. In the quality of the quietness, he wondered if her explanation of her behaviour was merely a mask.

She gave a low laugh. 'Really, it's quite simple. There's nothing more profound about my situation than there would be about yours. But you find that hard to accept.'

He was forced to be impressed but he certainly wasn't forced to be silent another second. He was being pinned to the wall by a woman who, just a short while ago, had behaved like a jabbering psychotic simply because of a few chimes.

'I'm sorry to be indelicate,' he said coolly, 'but bizarre behaviour, followed so swiftly by great control, interests me. I would like to know what that was all about – in the greenhouse?'

Her eyes on him were cold.

'I will tell you just this,' she said, as if speaking to a child; 'there was a slight trauma in my childhood. Sometimes, it resurfaces against my will. I have no memory of it now.'

45

There was no way for him to proceed. He was irritated: he had no interest in, nor compassion for, the Bella of the greenhouse. He wanted her only as Bella the sharp-shooter. He wanted to quarrel with her, to be lifted to intellectual flights with her. He wanted no truck with some messy, psychological tangle. Sensing this, she turned on him with some aggression of her own.

'Now,' she said, 'since you won't be content until I've explained my career to you, let me say I reached this place through concentrated selfishness – like anyone else.'

'That kind of selfishness is not easy,' he said, narrowing his eyes. 'How did you manage it?'

She looked at him as if she held his words up to the light.

'You are asking how I did it, being of my sex?'

'If you like.'

'You're wondering how I pulled it all off without benefit of a wife?'

'No,' he scoffed, 'many women have "wives". In fact there's a movement right now to turn men into wives, complete with guilt, resentment, fury and neurosis.'

'How is it doing?' she asked. And then, with a short, cool laugh, she said, 'How little it takes for you to show your hand. You have no respect for women, do you? That's why I'm an irritant to you. Until just now, when you saw an Achilles heel and thought to stick your knife into it.'

There was a silence.

'No, I don't respect women much,' he admitted, 'though I would like to.'

'Perhaps you have just been unfortunate,' she said, adding, 'You should know that I'm not interested in the women's question, if this is a subject you wanted us to lock horns on.'

'Okay, Bella, let's drop all that tedious stuff and get to what I want to discuss: you. You're quite correct, I do want to know what magnetised your career. We'll stick to that for the time being.'

'The truth at last.' She gave a little sniff. 'There's not much to say,' Bella said, folding her legs to one side. 'The graph of anyone's career, man or woman, is of their own making. I've never been interested in taking sides. I have never recognised that I had a problem, so my sex never was a problem. I have probably had to work harder, but I would have done so anyway.

I was brought up to be very industrious, very ambitious.' She laughed. 'That is the German I haven't forgotten.'

He lifted an eyebrow. Well! That was very cool indeed.

So, he thought; she had made her way not by being as good as a man, nor by being better; she had done it by being herself. She had never been in opposition; she had never asked for privileges. Being so much herself, she seemed to have forgotten that she was a woman. He felt that this gave her a certain grandeur. Her mind was truly individual and it used all its faculties cleanly. Consequently, her career would be free from any sense of injustice or grievance. It took genius to keep such integrity in the patriarchal pool she had chosen to swim in. This might be the key to her: she felt herself without limitations; she wielded the scalpel in her own way, knowing that if she used it as a man, it would turn upon her.

'I am happy enough to discuss women with you,' she said equably, 'as long as my own life is kept clear of their complications.'

'But how can your life be clear of their complications when you have four children?'

'Children are not impediments to success.'

'Not to a man.' He wanted to be just as scrupulous about his gender as she was about hers.

'Nor to me.'

'And husbands, I believe you acquired a couple of those, too?'

'To have children, one must have fathers,' she said.

He found it a strange comment.

'You see men as studs?' As soon as he'd said it, he deplored the cliché and hoped that she wouldn't be part of it.

'Isn't that how they see themselves?' Ah, he sighed, she too had slipped. What a pity.

'How do you see them?' he demanded.

'I did marry to have children,' she said, with the simplicity he found so appealing.

'Well, that at least is what women have always done,' he said shortly. Perhaps, after all, she was not as novel as he'd believed.

'I suppose,' she said, 'we must both resist the temptation to generalise: I speak only for myself.'

'You're right. However, I will ask you this: since it's always being pointed out how very difficult it is to be a

47

mother and a professional – why don't these things make conflicts for you?'

She breathed out; she looked away. 'Oh, but they do,' she said bleakly, startling him again by the shift in her mood. It was extraordinary: a moment ago she'd seemed invincible. Now, a little girl had crept nervously from behind a curtain. He changed his own voice and spoke briskly.

'Okay, then, indulge me for a while. Allow me to discuss women generally with you for a change. I'll give you a theory I have and you can tell me what you think.' He saw that she was quite composed again.

'I've noticed', he said carefully, 'an unpleasant change in womankind in the last couple of years. There is a phenomenon and, as it happens, this woman whose house you are to see, is a perfect example of it. I call it the Salome Syndrome.' He laughed, looking ahead, not at her. 'Now before you go for the jugular, which I know you're bound to do, hear me out.'

She drew up her knees in a graceful movement. 'All right,' she said, 'you have my full attention.'

Chapter Ten

They had left the nursery and were in the car. As he drove, it was the first time she had bothered to look closely at him. He was tall and strongly built, though a bit bony. It was nothing if not an English face: a rawness of complexion, because the skin was too fair; sharp, shrewd eyes, mouth too full, a rather angular jawline. It was a face full of character and good humour. He'd got away with too much, she decided; people had admired him too freely. He'd had his acolytes because of the persuasiveness of his personality; what he needed was the challenge of more demanding intellects. To his credit, he knew this. In the same way, she felt, he knew that his life lacked depth and quality. He was impatient, on the brink – wanting something remarkable to happen to him, but doubtful that it would. He was woman-wary, world-weary, too old for a man of, say, thirty-five.

She noticed that he often spoke metaphorically and found this refreshing; it wasn't part of the coinage of her world. He was using the woman whose house they were to visit as a test-case for his theory.

'Linda's husband,' he began, speaking forcibly, 'is a politician. Certainly, he has most of the scabby traits of the breed and she's had to suffer those. But he's not been a bad husband or father. Now,' – he looked quickly at her to make sure she was listening – 'as he began to reach a crucial stage in his career, Linda demanded they leave Washington and move to the country. Hence this house we are going to see. Linda then developed anxiety attacks and depression, which had the effect, naturally, of hurrying him along. Not fast enough though. She then baled out as wife and mother (roles she had never played with much enthusiasm) thereby forcing him to pick up the slack. This left him further removed from his work and the chance of political glory which, I admit, the poor jerk was virtually slavering to have –'

'And her purpose?' Bella interrupted, 'ultimately?'

49

He looked at her and frowned with amusement. 'You don't have much patience with a story, do you? Well, we're doing this my way, for a change. The purpose is, of course, the sacrifice of the man's career.'

'This happened?'

'Yup. And I have seen it more than once. It's definitely connected with men's withdrawal from women and their present reluctance towards marriage.'

'I trust we are not speaking personally here?' she said archly.

'Certainly not, smarty-pants, we agreed to keep off all that. As I was saying, it goes like this: the man, reluctantly, responds to the woman's manipulation. He changes his life somewhat; he adjusts his work, a bit, to accommodate his wife's needs; he ceases to react to her furies with belligerence. In other words, he capitulates. She despises him still. When the disease has fully taken over the marriage, he throws in his job. The sacrifice is done. The syndrome has reached its conclusion.'

'Well,' she said, 'this seems to me to be the old story of woman's wickedness.'

'Of course. But it's the new twist that interests me. It's far more successful than the oldest manipulation: sex, which we always imagined had the greatest power. This is totally effective because it kills a man where he lives: his work, his creative life, the only challenge to her maternity.'

'What disturbs you, then, is the success of this syndrome. For the first time, you feel, men are sufficiently adrift to be destroyed.'

'Yup,' he said grimly, 'the worm has turned and frightened off the plough.'

She laughed softly, and he thought, how wonderful to be discussing this without seeing fury and hatred in your opponent's eyes. This was discussion so pure that the subject stood out in sharp outline, blurred neither by his rancour nor her defensiveness.

'What's your problem with this, Joseph?' she asked. He liked the fact that she used his name like an intimacy she had been hoarding. How unlike the American way, he thought. They will grab your name at the first opportunity and use it until all the personality has been choked out of it. This 'Joseph', so quietly uttered, was almost an endearment.

'Do I have a problem?'

50

'Well, you're not discussing this as if you don't really mind which way the argument goes. Something is muddying the water and' – she looked directly at him now – 'I'd say it was rage.' It was as if she shone a light directly into his face.

He smiled. 'What should I be angry about?' He felt the excitement of an animal who knows his pursuer is gaining ground.

'Does a Linda hover in your life?'

'No.'

She looked weary. 'Life for both sexes is difficult enough. Why must we pit ourselves against each other?'

'Because we hate each other,' he said, quite without passion.

She looked up. 'Yes, we do.' For a moment he could have sworn that she spoke of their relationship.

She was uncomfortable with the way he regarded her. 'This husband of Linda's, is he being destroyed personally in the process?'

'Of course. His career can't be salvaged and now they're getting a divorce.'

'And perhaps,' Bella asked, 'he will be made to look after the children? And she will take up a career?'

He beamed with pleasure. 'Exactly. He keeps the children and she goes out into the world he has vacated.'

'That is certainly very uncomfortable.'

'It's no wonder that men don't marry.'

'The world may run out of children.'

'Not with you around.'

'Do you have children?'

'I do not.'

'But you'd like to?'

'Yes.'

She was quiet a moment, then, 'It must be hard – and of course I'm speaking generally – to feel that as a man your career is no longer inviolate; that there is no wom- an willing to protect you from disturbance; no devoted, exemplary person hinged to your success and pleasure, the rearing of your children and the picking up of your socks.'

He laughed loudly. 'Yes, it's quite sickening.'

'And instead, there's an enemy in your house, hell bent on your dislocation.'

51

'If you're suggesting', he said tartly, 'that I personally need those supports, you would be wrong.'

'I see. Well, why are you so unsettled by your syndrome? It must mean that you would like to marry and are disappointed.'

He snorted. 'Would I like to marry?'

'Yes, and for most of the reasons we've just discussed. I too would miss such support and selflessness if it's what I was brought up to expect.'

'You put too much emphasis on me,' he said. 'I'm an observer. You're saying my illusions about women are being shattered, but I have none.'

'You are a great liar,' she laughed.

'And here we are,' he said, turning down a long, straight road, and feeling something like relief. 'It's right at the end of this road, a bit out in the woods. You'd like that, wouldn't you?' He looked at her sharply. 'Some splendid isolation?'

She shrugged.

And suddenly he was quite furious with her – with her smug assurance that he was threatened by these women and their sick need to have the head on the platter before they could go out and make a success of their lives. For some, this head was their single success in life. What he objected to most was the tarnished old sword they struck with: illness, dependency, weakness. Fight a man and there was an end to it. Fight a woman and the hostilities never let up.

He snarled to himself and got out of the car, slamming the door behind him, leaving her to fend for herself. He strode ahead of her up to the house, knowing that he'd come off rather badly in their first round, but determined to get even.

Chapter Eleven

Bella stepped out of the car and looked up at the house. All her thoughts were concentrated on how suitable it would be for her and her children. It was a handsome house, well worn and elderly, a little shabby, but with the stern qualities of an old tweed coat. The stone was grey, the shutters bold green – reminiscent of the French countryside. The garden was neglected, but flowers still pitted their wills against the weeds. If this house was left another winter, she thought, it would go beyond repair. It could even be lost to the elements. Close up, it was in a very bad state: the paint was cracked, the wood warped. The roof would have to be re-tiled; the window frames would probably fall out if you opened them. A place with potential, she thought grimly. She walked round the side of the house and looked briefly at the secondary life of barns, garages and sheds that meandered around the side and back. Not much comfort there. But an enticing peek into a walled garden, with apple- and pear-trees breaking into blossom and rhubarb plunging up through the warming earth – this was comforting after the highways they had driven along.

Joseph was knocking loudly on the front door. He is no stranger to irritation, Bella thought with amusement; he likes his own way, but will not be seductive to get it. Admirable. She regarded him now with far more tolerance than she had in the car. He's all right, she thought, nothing wrong with that mind; it's just rather cranky and needs oiling. She watched him push open the front door.

Bella waited on the doorstep. Finally, a curly-haired woman arrived and looked at Joseph in an unwelcoming manner. He took Bella's arm somewhat rudely and led her inside. She frowned at him, not liking this hasty ushering-in of her person. He kept his hand planted firmly at the base of her spine.

'It's a lovely old house,' Bella said, moving smartly away from Joseph and looking up at a graceful, curved stairway.

'Doesn't look as if a duster's been applied to it since I was last here,' Joseph said breezily, stepping over a child's bike.

Linda glared but said nothing. She turned to Bella. 'We haven't put up a sign yet,' she said, stuffing her hands into her pockets. 'Ted wanted one and I didn't.'

Looking at her, Bella saw how discontent and spite had sullied an attractive face.

'Is Ted here?' Joseph asked, expecting him to walk out clutching a dish-cloth.

'No. I'm doing the sale,' Linda said. Her voice, Bella noticed, was always on the verge of anger. 'The boys are with him this week.'

'Oh?' Joseph looked surprised. 'I thought he was going to a conference in Boston.'

'It's his turn,' Linda said. 'This week it's his turn.' Then she turned to Bella and said rudely, 'Of course, you wouldn't have these problems.'

'What problems?' Bella asked vaguely, moving into a long drawing-room, wonderfully light and spacious, with a sprawl of dismembered toys on the floor and two dog's bones on the sofa.

'The turns problem.'

Bella was mystified. 'The turns problem?'

'You know – whose turn it is. With children. You don't have kids, I don't suppose, being a surgeon. That's what you are, isn't it? A brain surgeon?' The question was so aggressively put that Bella stared at her for a moment, speechless. She said shortly, 'Heart. I'm a heart surgeon.'

'She has four children, as a matter of fact,' Joseph said, smiling broadly.

As Linda strode out of the room, Bella grinned at Joseph and shook her head slowly. It was a great look, he thought, acknowledging a complicity, a shared point of view. He winked at her; she seemed to respond; her cheeks grew rosy.

Bella was now studying the pine floors. 'The wood is wonderful,' she said, bending, running her hand along the grain. He watched the long curve of her waist, the roundness of her hip as she balanced on her haunches.

Entering the room, Linda said, 'The last people did the floors. It's an easy house to keep clean, if that's relevant. The floors never show the dirt.'

'It's always relevant,' Bella said, observing that the house was filthy. She had moved to a window where a magnolia tree threw a pink glow across the walls and where the crystal light washed over the floors, turning them golden. Her walk now seemed altered. It had slowed, as had all her movements. Standing with her back to him, her arms rose in a most sensual way as she released the clasp of the tortoise-shell grip that held her heavy hair in position. It fell down, settling around her neck. She turned very slowly, and looked at the room in a way that was almost trance-like, so dulled were her features and languid was her body. He could see in her face how she loved the domestic life and, finding this quality in her, he forgave her.

She walked through the rooms, inspecting the kitchen carefully, like a woman who would spend her days there. She wandered in and out of the sunny bedrooms, choosing one for each of her children. Linda had left to answer the telephone. They were alone, he and she, in one of the boys' bedrooms. There was a rat's nest of dirty clothes in one corner and the remains of a half-eaten pizza on the window sill.

'You'd think she'd have cleaned it up a bit,' Bella whispered. 'She did know we were coming, didn't she?'

'Not her turn,' Joseph whispered, picking up a heel of bread smeared with peanut-butter and studying it with interest. 'I ask you,' he said with an endearing smile, 'is this a woman who would cook a meal for her family?'

'I suspect', Bella said, 'that they are left to forage for themselves.' He was pleased to find her so amiable.

She went on into the main bedroom and gave it a brief inspection. Then turned and walked into Joseph, who was standing too close. She backed away and raised her head to study the ceiling, which had some bad cracks running across it. He had the strongest desire to place his hand across her throat.

'A house', she said, 'needs so much maintenance – as much . . .' she hesitated, 'as a marriage.'

He felt a quick pity for her. Her marriages – perhaps they'd been happy? It was an odd thought, one he'd not had before. He'd felt that she'd be an impossible woman to live with; that she was capable of a high class of violence. But now he wondered.

He watched her walk down the stairs and out of the front door. He waited at the top of the stairs, not wanting to follow her into the garden. Linda walked to the foot of the stairs and looked up at him.

'So,' she said, 'will she take it?'

'Doubt it,' Joseph said. 'Looks like a tip.'

She let out her breath and without it she seemed defeated, almost pathetic. 'I wish you wouldn't always pick on me,' she said miserably. 'Why can't you leave me alone?'

'I think', he said quietly, 'you like to be picked on. You're always looking for a grievance.'

'Don't start on that,' she said, her arms flying up as if to ward him off. 'I don't have to listen to you, there are enough people in this world to make me feel good about myself, I don't need you to –'

'Linda,' he said with exasperation, 'can your mind never rise above cliché? Can we have a straight conversation?'

'Yes,' she sulked.

'Do you want to sell this house? Or are you just trying to create a long-drawn-out confrontation with it?'

She hesitated. 'Yes, I want to sell it. I need my half of the money.'

'All right. Then you will need to clean it up, it's that simple.'

'It's not my responsibility', she said angrily, 'to do the cleaning.'

'No, it isn't,' he said patiently, 'but you can either use that point of view to keep the place on the market indefinitely, or you can get someone in to clean it. And', he added drily, 'split the bill with Ted.'

She was quiet for a moment and then she added, 'That's the first time you've actually said anything constructive.' He got up and walked down the stairs. She looked at him and tilted her head to one side. 'You've changed,' she said.

Bella could be heard coming quickly down the corridor; he realised that he was anxious to see her again. She walked into the room, looked across at Linda and said, 'I'll take it.'

'Just like that?' Linda said, shaken.

'Would you like it wrapped?' Joseph asked. Bella ignored him. She stood in front of Linda and said, 'I'll get a survey done immediately, if that's all right. I'll give you the asking price, on condition that it's a deal. I haven't got time to wait. I have to get my affairs in order very quickly and I hope you can do the same.'

Joseph moved towards her. 'Hey, steady on a bit, Bella. I think the price is a bit steep – it needs a lot of work.' He looked at both women. 'Look, you're not going through an agent, so why not cut that percentage?'

'Just like a man to try and take over,' Linda snapped. 'This is none of your business, Joe . . .' She hesitated, looking at Bella. 'Or is it?' Bella ignored the implication. She said, 'I need this house in a month's time, empty and clean. If you can do that, you can have the asking price. I'll speak to my lawyer this afternoon; can you get me the name of yours while I take another look at the basement?'

Joseph sat down, impressed by her speed and efficiency yet puzzled as well. In this sharp, economical exchange she had shifted her ground again. The gentle, domestic animal moving through the rooms of her new lair had become a swift executor of a deal even Linda wouldn't be stupid enough to bungle. But he was well pleased with the outcome. He could see Bella living here, he could even imagine what she would do to the place. She would restore it to its former elegance and create a home and shelter here. He wanted to be around to see her do it.

They walked together down the drive towards his car.

'So now you have a house – congratulations.'

'Thank you.'

'I hope it doesn't turn out to be more that you can handle.'

'No. It looks worse than it is: the former owners did quite a lot of constructional improvements. The roof will have to be redone,' she mused, 'but there's no damp and it's sound.'

'Good,' he said. 'And what did you make of Salome?'

'I saw what you meant.'

'Well, what did you make of her?'

She considered it. 'She's not my type, I can't get on with women like that. She's greedy but she's lazy and indulgent.'

'You don't pity her?'

'No,' she was emphatic, 'her weakness is aggressive: she uses it as a weapon.'

'I wonder what she thought of you,' he said with a nasty grin.

'She did not like me,' Bella said.

'Why not?'

'Because she felt I wasn't on her side. She's only at ease with certain women – those with a sex-bias, a consciousness of sides.' Stepping into the car, she laughed softly. 'Even though

I'm sure I could make a better sponge than she, and even though my rooms are arranged in a way that's called feminine, she'd still put me in your camp, the men's camp, because I succeed. And most of all, because I do not give her sympathy.'

He laughed. 'I couldn't have put it better myself, and you don't even know the woman! But why do you deny her sympathy?'

'Because she doesn't deserve it.' Click went the safety belt into its anchor. 'And because she doesn't try hard enough or think hard enough. She takes easy remedies.'

'Okay,' he said, 'enough of the subject for now. We can discuss it at another time. I don't want you to be late for your appointment.' She shook herself a little, as if the appointment might have slipped her mind. 'You are still going?' He turned to look at her and was puzzled by her expression: what on earth could be the matter? She looked anxious; she sat on the edge of her seat.

'Of course I'm going,' she said in an agitated way.

'You don't have to go,' he put out a hand instinctively and found hers; to his surprise, it was shaking a little. 'We could just as easily go to tea or', he smiled, 'to the movies.'

'Oh,' she said, in a queer voice, 'I haven't been to the . . .' She hesitated at the word, '. . . movies, for so many years.'

He looked at her. She looked down. They drove on in silence. It was some time later that she reached over and touched his arm, tenderly, it seemed to him, and said, 'Thank you for my house.'

In that moment, he was certain that he would marry her.

Chapter Twelve

Bella returned to Margy's house just after midnight. On the way up to her bedroom, she stopped to look in at the children. Will rolled quickly onto his side and looked sleepily up at his mother.

'You weren't still awake, were you?' she asked, sitting on his bed.

'I don't know.' She could just make out his face by the moonlight that lit up one window.

'What time is it?' he asked.

'Just after twelve o'clock.'

'Did you forget?' he asked with the patience of an adult.

'Forget what?' She brushed his hair down with her hand.

He was quiet. Then he said, 'Forget that you said you'd be coming home early.'

Some vague recollection was shaken loose in her. 'Oh, I'm sorry, Will!' she said, smoothing her hand along the covers of the bed. 'Yes, of course. The thing was . . .' and here she retreated a little from his scrutiny '. . . I had to stay on to meet the other surgeons and cardiologists – and then, well, I was rather forced into going out to dinner with the boss. Will –' she grabbed his hand with excitement – 'it's going to be such a fine job, a real challenge: I can do some of the things I've . . .' Will's expression steadied, then silenced her. He had begun to wind the stuff of the counterpane around his fingers.

'Oh Will!' She took his hand and unbandaged it from the cloth. 'I *am* sorry.'

'So it's decided then?' he asked.

'Yes, if that's all right with you.'

'It's all right with me,' he said, lying down and thereby freeing his hand from hers.

'Will, you aren't angry, are you?' She leaned forward, concerned.

Slowly, he made himself say it, 'I don't know why – these days – you forget things.' His voice was flat. 'You used to say you wouldn't make promises because you never knew if you could keep them - now you promise, but you forget.'

'I didn't forget,' she said lamely. But there were many things that she couldn't quite remember these days – blanks in her mind, in her days: time lost that couldn't be made up. That business in the nursery that morning, it was frightening that it could still happen, after all these years. Things were going wrong. She was exhausted by it, and by the child, who pulled on her so much, drawing off her strength. It was as if Will had become her custodian. Look how he watched her, his face brimming with pain and mistrust. Well, she had forsworn guilt: it was indulgent and wasteful. But she felt it. She saw in his face the neglect of her own childhood.

She got up from the bed. 'Were the others all right?' she asked. The tone in her voice moved him to compassion.

'Oh yes, they were fine. We went to McDonald's, with Alison. It was all right.' He was protecting her, as was customary. She stooped to kiss and tuck him in. 'Sleep tight, Will.' He saw her face quiver with an old suffering and he could not bear it. His arms came out of the covers and around her neck, pulling her face against his cheek. Tears came to her eyes – of confusion and fear – an old fear. They shared it for a moment. She kissed him again and left. He lay in the dark a long time, but tonight, even plotting his course down the Nile could not comfort him.

Bella, too, lay in the dark and could not sleep. She was troubled by Joseph: by his insistence and by his anger. She knew that he disliked women, as she disliked men. He was attracted to her because she seemed to live outside the scope of his dislike. At the end of the journey back from the house he'd pressed her for information about herself. She'd felt her hostility mount. She would not be pushed. He was trying to place her in a position where he could handle her. She had spent too long getting rid of the obstacles in her life. It had taken blood. She would not be joined – for to be joined meant to be weakened. She had told him so. He had disagreed, trying to convince her of the greater strength of a united life. But she knew, too well, what that meant. Sacrifice. Hers. No, he must look elsewhere.

What alarmed her about Joseph was his way of behaving sometimes as if there were an intimacy between them. It was ridiculous; she hardly knew him. But it frightened her because of her memory lapses. There was something of the same problem with James Venables, the investment banker. He had also contacted her after Margy's brunch. She had met him again for purely business reasons. She'd had a plan, one that she'd discussed with Otto, about starting a new centre for heart diseases. There was considerable corporate interest in funding heart disease; James could have got the finance together. But after seeing him she'd decided to go no further with the plan. She didn't like his attitude towards her; didn't understand his familiarity. It must all be shelved. She didn't have the strength; she knew just how much pressure she could bear. She had to concentrate.

It was strange, but now the recollection of Joseph was tinged with regret. There was something warm and earthy about him that reminded her of the better days of her dead marriages. He was alive and quick in a way that she knew to be quite rare. He had laughed at her and said, 'I'm the man for you, Bella dear, no one else would take you on. And don't imagine that a corpse or two will frighten me off!' And then he had whispered with an evil smile, 'You did kill them, Bella, didn't you? Admit it.'

Two hours later, she was still not asleep. Her discipline failed her, again and again. In an attempt to pull herself round she thought she would make a record in her diary of the details of her contract with Philip Modlinger.

It was cold in the room and as she went to shut the window she saw the shadows of the trees standing like sentinels on the grass, sombre in the moonlight. She thought for a moment that she heard chimes, but it was some other sound in the distance. She switched on the desk lamp and opened the drawer to get her diary, a handsome leather book sent by a pharmaceutical company.

Inside the drawer, the diary was open. She had not left it so. For a moment she stood there, staring at it. Then, slowly, she lifted it out. The book fell to the floor and the pages crumpled. She stooped to recover it, placed it on the table and slowly smoothed out the pages, turning them to find again the entry that had alarmed her.

61

The diary had been open at the page which recorded her acceptance of the hospital post, with the commencement date written beside it. Now all this had been obliterated by a single, large 'NO' scrawled over the top of her small, regular handwriting. Underneath were these words: *You will not take my children out of England. I'm out. And I'm coming home. You cannot stop me.* The graffito – for so she thought of it – was signed. Signed by a hand that was clearly shaky and afraid, but signed all the same: *Rebecca.*

Chapter Thirteen

She sat down slowly and closed the book. Her fury was still as a frozen lake. Her face had no expression, her eyes showed no feeling; no light penetrated their centre so they appeared almost colourless.

She breathed out. So – Rebecca had come back. After years of absence she had come back, sneaky and insidious as ever, tracking her down to this moment of triumph and waiting to deface it. The shock of it: she had been *here*! In this house, this room. By the handwriting – and how well she knew it – Bella assessed that Rebecca was still weak. But, weak or not, she had got out again and into this house. How had she found the strength to assert herself after that last perdition?

'I wanted her dead,' Bella whispered in despair. But the thought of Rebecca seemed only to provoke images of life and warmth: of a little rocking laugh; of a pretty woman sitting on a lawn in sunlight, surrounded by people who loved her, who fetched her a cool glass of lemonade, a hat for her head, a bunch of pale roses. Rebecca, watching children run this way and that for things to please her. Sweet, gentle Rebecca, who knew how to love, who was loved. Rebecca, sitting at a piano playing Chopin in an empty room with the sunlight streaming in and turning to find Papa standing there, applauding her.

Bella's face twisted with pain. She would banish this intruder. But how to do it? How even to make contact with her? Things were different now. She would have to use the method they used as children. Rebecca had written in the diary and then gone. Bella would have to do the same.

She picked up the pen, but found she could not write. Some power kept her hand where it was. She tried again, and failed. No word came. She sat there, staring ahead of her. Tears began to run down her face, tears she did not wipe away or even seem to feel.

After a time, she managed to right herself. The sky was no longer dark; she switched off the light and picked up the pen. Her hand began to write, fast and efficiently, filling the page in front of her with neat, legible writing.

Rebecca, this is how I used to speak to you and you give me no choice but to do it again. You have to go away. You have been up to your old tricks, doing things behind my back, things I did not understand at the time – like the acceptance letter that you destroyed. Please don't try to fight me. It will only break you.

Try to think this through. I cannot live with you again. And you cannot live alone. That much has been proved. We had an arrangement. You've stuck by it till now, and you will have to go on doing so.

I understand that you want to come back. But it would not work. I, too, have had my banishments. Yours must continue. I can go on looking after the children. Will is like my own child now. He doesn't miss you. It may sound cruel, but it's better that he doesn't miss you. Think of the pain and confusion you'd cause if you came back. Think of the children. You've seen them, I'm sure: they're happy, aren't they?

It is better for everyone if you stay away. You cannot go home to our house in England. I am leaving there, we all are. The house will be sold. Stay away. Do not come back again.

Bella.

Two

ENGLAND

Chapter One

Standing in the middle of Bella's drawing-room in London, Rebecca began to laugh.

'I am home,' she whispered.

The house was empty, quiet as if it held its breath. She walked slowly across the room, pausing to run her hand across the slope of a davenport desk. A single pink rose stood in a narrow vase, a petal spilled without a sound. Her head tilted to one side as she listened. The children were not here. She had taken care to find out their movements and knew that they had gone with the nanny to her mother's house at the seaside. But though they were absent, still she seemed to hear the sound of their feet come crashing down the stairs, their voices high as birds' – the voices of very small children. The kind of children they no longer were. A photograph of Will as a small child met her gaze like a collision. She remembered stitching the little white gown he wore.

She walked to the windows and swung back the silk curtains to let in the sunshine. The drive was empty, as was the garden. Still, she saw them – quick, small, darting; behind the rose bushes, by the pond where the goldfish roamed among the weeds, under the trees where the children gathered conkers. Surely that was a golden crop of curls – over there, under the blue rhododendron bushes where the child's house was built? And a slim shadow, running, calling, 'Daisy, Daisy! Where are you?'

Shaken, she moved back into the room. The memories were laden with loss. She needed so much to assert her presence in this house, to force it to acknowledge her return. If she could have taken a duster to it, or a brush, it might have been accomplished; she might have scrubbed away Bella's presence. As it was, the best she could do was to search among the records on the shelves above the stereo until she found, right at the back, some Bach. She waited for the sound of the organ to fill the room:

67

it was as if water rushed over and cleansed it. She repeated, 'I am home,' and felt safer.

For many years it had been Rebecca's house. She had spent months painting the walls, polishing the floors and the bright tops of tables. Now, she felt, with an old familiar pain, Bella had made it more beautiful than she ever could. She remembered how her mother used to laugh at her and say: 'You'll never be a good *Hausfrau*.' Bella had no interest in such work, but she succeeded at it. She would touch an object and it would seem to respond; she would place a piece in a certain way and it had grace and charm. Whereas under Rebecca's hands things had a way of becoming flat and dull. Still – she brightened as she thought it – mother loved me best, I could make her laugh.

She wrung her hands nervously and glanced at the door, afraid that it would swing open and reveal Bella standing there with that awful smile of hers. 'Oh,' she breathed in dismay, 'she's taken my collection of dolls from the book case – they're all gone.' She looked for the one from Vienna, Papa's home town – the one wearing the silk dress with the gold brocade. Bella's blue china was now arranged where once the dolls had been. When they were children, Bella had threatened her with these dolls: 'Do as I say, or I'll break them into little pieces.'

The full quota of her grievance rose up: Bella had taken everything from her and now would take her children away from England. Into that world of hers where there was no time for anything but work. How could she have taken care of them? How often had she been there all the years that Rebecca had been locked out? Who had looked after them – who woke them, put them to bed, cooked for them and fed them? Who had loved them?

She began to explore the house, painful though it was. She was looking for things to remember, seeking some trace of herself. It was such a beautiful house. It had been different when she'd lived here. Then there'd been the happy disorder of family life. Bella didn't like disorder. The house was more formal now: there were expensive chairs with silk coverings, delicate carvings and china vases, lamps that would tumble at the nudge of a child's elbow. But there was no evidence of a child. She knew that her dog, Max, could not lope through this house as he used to when it was hers. Bella had had him put down when that little brat of hers, Mary, was born.

68

That was when the competition about babies began: Rebecca had two, Bella felt she must make right the deficiency. Being chief resident was not enough, she must be pregnant too.

This jealousy was difficult for Rebecca to bear; she knew how much it had always sullied her. And yet when she looked at her own life how could she avoid the jealousy? What achievement could she point to? What could she look at and say, this I've given my life to, this justifies all the years; this is the result of my dedication and discipline. What but her children? And yet she knew they were only half a life. She remembered how drastic Bella's discipline had been. Mother had taught her that: Mother pushing her to try and break her. Papa was kind to Bella. He'd pointed to the outside world and said to her: 'It's for you to do whatever you want. You're a very clever child, Bella, more clever than your mama or I will ever be. It's a certain cleverness only a few have. It's a gift or a curse. Make of it a good gift for others. That way it will make you happy.' But mother, always the scientist, had insisted: *'Lerne, lerne, lerne. Dies ist nicht gut, es ist nicht gut genug, lern'es noch einmal.'* The words, the language, had been like a lash across Bella's back.

When they were small children, Bella sometimes let Rebecca copy her work. One day, when Papa came in, Rebecca wasn't able to hide her own book under the table in time. Papa snatched it up and demanded: 'What is this stupid work, look at this – drawings and scribbles all over the page! What are you thinking of? Why are you doing this?' He had not allowed her to play her piano for a whole week, dispensing the one punishment she could not bear. Without her music, she felt trapped inside a cold, dark room and, on the outside, she seemed to hear Bella laugh. Bella was laughing with Papa because she had captured him, he was her prey.

Rebecca tried hard to banish these memories, but found she had little control over them. She wanted to remember the happy time spent in the house. But the happy was all mixed with the sad because of what she had lost. So many years an exile, so much gone for ever.

She had thought that by now she would be rooted to one spot, one piece of land, here, in this place. And that each year she would make it a little more settled, as each year she watched her children grow, marking it on the door in the kitchen. She wanted to be held fast by the same habits, the same view of the magnolia tree by the bedroom window, the same burst of crocuses on the lawn each spring. Instead, she was a nomad, going here and there, homeless. She, who had wanted to stand in a garden among flowers grown from seed, to pick beans from her own soil and fill jars with the fruit from her trees, now she was to be uprooted yet again by the whim of one who cared only for herself. She would remain an outsider, her face pressed to a window, watching her children guarded by a nanny, not knowing their mother, never hearing her name spoken. Like the dead.

The hatred was back. It focused on the way Bella lived her life: her days pinned down, each day pressed flat so that more could be laid on top, and more, and more. A life without breath. But Bella could juggle it and make it all look effortless. Rebecca could not, nor did she want to. She wanted only to sit quietly day by day and fill the bowls and watch them empty again; walk on the common with the dog and see her son riding his bicycle; make dresses for Daisy and sit with her as she practised her scales. There was no piano in this house any more. There was no life.

And here her face turned spiteful: you took it all from me with your ambition and your greed, your hatred and your jealousy. Oh yes, you were jealous of me, too. After Daisy was born, that was when you knew you had to get rid of me. And you did it through William, William whom I loved, William, who loved me. And that's why you hate Daisy, Daisy who looks like William, Daisy who is my daughter and whom you will never steal as you have stolen Will.

Her eye caught sight of a child's chair: a delicate thing made of rosewood with a small, round cushion. She thought with pleasure: she's made a cushion for the rocking-chair we had as children. But then she was uncertain. Had she made the cushion herself? She seemed to remember stitching the white appliquéd sheep and the moon sailing in a blue sky. Who had made it? Bella or herself? She wanted to take it with her. She held it protectively against her shoulder and walked with it to the door. But there she hesitated. She looked down at the cushion, rested her forehead against it a moment, then, heavily, returned it to its place on the chair.

The music had come to an end and she must go.

Chapter Two

The day after arriving back in London Bella had, with typical efficiency, handed in her resignation and, by nine o'clock, proceeded to the theatre for her first operation of the day.

It was a routine case: Peter Watson was a robust forty-five-year-old whose angiogram showed triple vessel disease. Medication was causing him side-effects and he was anxious to have the operation – more anxious, she now remembered, than he needed to be. Because she was in the habit of trusting her patients' instincts about their conditions, she went to look at the notes and X-rays again and checked with her assistant that there had been nothing irregular in the pre-operative investigations. Everything was as it should be.

The operation went well and, leaving the house staff to take the patient off bypass and close the chest, she put away all thoughts of Peter Watson. The memo announcing her departure would have been circulated by now; the news would set the consultants buzzing. What she had not expected, however, was the hostility she picked up from her colleagues. She dismissed it as anti-American feeling: there had been cracks about high fees, high-tech surgery, unscrupulous greed. She shrugged it off; already she was able to distance herself from a hospital she'd worked in for four years and whose reputation had been enhanced by her presence. Besides, there was a lot to do: her work schedule was heavy, cases having accumulated in her absence. She sat down with her secretary to work out a programme for the next month to try and avoid too much squabbling about her operating time-table – always a fraught issue. If she could leave the hospital in four weeks, she could have a week at home to organise the move and the children. It was a bad time of year to be leaving: people were on holiday, there would be emergency cases and her most experienced nurse was ill. Not to mention the fact that she'd promised Will a trip to the country to go fishing.

71

Once the schedule was done, she telephoned the estate agent and said she wanted to sell her house. Then, shippers: she chose three and arranged times for them to come and give estimates. Next, a transference of funds to her American bank account and letters to solicitors both sides of the Atlantic. The last thing would be the sale of her Mercedes. Now, as her mind quickly collated the activities of the next two hours, she decided she could get home to show the estate agent the house and be back at the hospital by seven to do her ward round.

At six o'clock the estate agent informed her that changes in property values, and her improvements, had doubled the value of the Victorian house facing Clapham Common. She was surprised, taking little interest in such fluctuations.

Much later that night she found a large For Sale sign posted outside her front door. She was affronted. And shocked: the speed was indecent and it made her feel treacherous. Sadness filled her: how soon it would be gone, and all the years of living there assigned to memory. She would miss the old Polish woman across the street, whose husband she had operated on a year ago. She walked into the drawing-room and looked about her at the marble fireplaces, the delicate cornices, the walls cluttered with dark oil paintings. The elegant furniture had belonged to her grandmother – how would it travel the seas? How would they all settle in a new country? Her background was German and Viennese, but she felt English now. The house she was buying in New York State – it could be made just as beautiful, but had she the strength?

The For Sale board stared at her through the window, with insolence, she felt. There was a message from the estate agent to say that the house details would be sent out in the morning. It was done. She had done it. In a spirit of resistance, she went down to the basement, got out her tool box and took down the sale sign. For a moment she felt dizzy and wondered whether she should go at all.

She sat down in the drawing-room, having no inclination to go to bed, although it was now two in the morning. She wandered aimlessly over to the stereo and, without noticing what was on the deck, switched it on. The house was very quiet. She walked into the kitchen and opened the door to the fridge. As she did so, she heard the first notes of Bach's Fantasia and Fugue in G Minor. Her head jerked up and turned towards the sound with disbelief. An image came: her father, clapping his hands, calling out, 'Bravo!'

She closed the door of the refrigerator and, with an even step, walked back into the drawing-room. She stood for a moment, watching the record revolving on the deck. Then she snatched it off; her hand was not steady and there was a squeal as the needle cut across the grooves. She held the record, staring at it as if to understand something. Then she snapped it in two.

Chapter Three

Rebecca came back the next day and read, with interest, the house details on the front table. Her eyebrows rose when she saw the exorbitant price that Bella was asking for the house. Not many years ago – what was it, twelve or so? – they had bought this house together, putting their childhood enmity behind them, not easily, but with determination. They had never been companions, but once or twice, as then, buying the house, they had been equals. Looking back, it seemed to Rebecca that her life, for the first time ever, had been more tangible than Bella's had been then. If that was indeed so, then it was due only to one thing: Rebecca was loved, William loved her. It made her more real than Bella could ever be.

Stepping now into the drawing-room, Rebecca at once saw the broken record. She picked it up and ran her forefinger slowly along the sharp, straight edge. Then she smiled: she had made Bella angry. What an achievement that was!

Bella's face at eight years old, when the children threw pebbles up at the window where she stood looking down at them. They called her names because she did not go to school but sat trapped in a close room with her tutors and her books. But no taunt could touch Bella; her eyes barely blinked as she regarded the leering faces below. Once, the window was broken and a stone struck Bella on the cheek, making a deep gash in the skin. She wiped the blood away and went on with her studies.

It was hard not to admire such self-discipline, Rebecca thought; Bella always showed great courage. She remembered Bella at twelve, coming into the kitchen, holding a letter and announcing that she'd won a scholarship. The way Mother looked! The jealousy on that mask-like face. Their mother, who had achieved so much in her own life, who seemed so invincible, who was both scientist and owner of a booming drugs company – actually jealous of her own child! Rebecca's face grew stiff as she remembered what had happened that day. Their mother had, with no word of explanation, taken hold of the long, heavy hank of Bella's hair and cut it off at the neck with the kitchen shears, tossing it in the rubbish bin, on top of some burnt fat. Bella looked at her mother, touched the back of her head, looked at her hair lying in the fat and walked out of the room. Their mother had screamed after her, but Bella had not so much as flinched.

'Why do I pity her?' Rebecca said out loud. 'Why should I? She's never pitied me, not once in her life.' But she could not stop the pity returning as she thought of how Bella had been locked in the small cupboard in the corridor with only a small torch to see by. She was left there, cramped in the dark, for five hours at a time; Mother would not let her out until the work was completed to her satisfaction. Even this did not break Bella, although once she had come out with her nails all ripped and bleeding.

Rebecca now forced herself to venture further into the house than she had dared to go on her last visit. Slowly she climbed the stairs and made her way down the corridor to the room in which Will had slept as a baby. She opened the door. The room was unrecognisable. There stood his old wooden crib, but everything else was changed. Another child had inherited Will's place. She closed the door quickly, her heart thumping, and walked on. But each of the rooms frightened her. Here was the bedroom that she had slept in with William; now it was Bella's room. The once pale walls were dark with rows of books and strange paintings; the white chairs had been covered in a bold blue material. She hated the colour. She hated the bed. It was her bed, she had bought it in Portobello Road, the first thing she and William had bought together. Their children had been conceived in that bed. William had been ill in that bed . . . She wrenched her mind away from those days. For this was also the house that she and William had come to when they were first married, when Bella had gone and Rebecca was strong and fearless because of it. This had been their first home together, where they had been so happy.

The only difficult times had been when William went abroad on research trips. Rebecca found the loneliness unbearable. She had never been alone in her life. Before William there had always been Bella. But with Bella completely gone and

William often away, she felt afraid again, cut off from the world. The house was like a long corridor which she paced up and down, up and down, waiting for William to return. But then, slowly, something changed in her. In her fear, she turned to the house that represented both Bella and William; through it she found she could domesticate both her fear and her loneliness.

Loving the house was an extension of loving William; it was also her first attempt at existing normally in the world. The house was hers, not her mother's, not even Bella's. She began to paint the walls, made new curtains, changed the furniture around, removed Bella's books and desk to the basement. She filled it with lovely things bought at antique markets. William brought exotic statues and carvings back from his travels in the East; she made cushions and drapes from the silks and brocades that he gave her. She turned her attention to the garden and grew scented flowers wherever there was soil: sweet peas, roses, lilies, wall-flowers and lavender. She dug and weeded: vegetables sprouted, magnolia blossomed, wisteria took over the walls. She felt that a curse had been lifted from her: her hands, brilliant only when they flew over a piano keyboard, now brought everything to life.

Her body, too, was changing, filling with her first pregnancy. She sailed like a barge down the days, not caring if her nails were broken, her hair uncut and her dresses unironed. She was domestic, happier than she had ever been. And she was free. Her mother had washed her hands of her; there was not a word from Bella. She was in full command of her life.

Their first child, William, was born. He seemed to replace the family she had lost, most particularly her father, who had died when she was a child. Will looked a little like him, or so she cared to think. She carried the child close to her all day, often strapped to her side. It was a love affair, but one tinged with fear: the fragility of his life terrified her; she was always waking in the night to see if he still breathed. She did not feel it was possible to love anyone so, not even her husband, because the love was so completely without ambivalence.

She had arrived now at Will's room and she entered it, feeling that at last she would get some real trace of him. It was a room that could only belong to Will. The walls were hung with maps and there were red lines, indicating journeys, in all the

76

most remote regions of the world. She stared with pride and amazement at this glimpse into the mind of her lost child. In a large box, he had put together all the paraphernalia of survival: compass, knife, binoculars, a solution for purifying strange water, rope, matches, first-aid kit. It was as if he had been preparing for years for a journey into a region where he would have to fend for himself. She laughed softly. Genetics were at work, for here was the son of a wanderer, William's child.

Then her hand flew down into the box and pulled out a battered old army beret. At the sight of it, she was so overcome by grief that she collapsed onto the bed, holding the beret to her face, rocking her body to and fro. Finally, she stopped her rocking, smoothed out the beret and placed it on her lap.

She and William had found this beret together in a junk shop, on a very important day, some time after their marriage. They had agreed that day that she would stop work, that the academic life (which he felt her parents had forced on her) should come to an end, to free her from the tyranny that pressed her so hard. Her mind was a fine one, but it was this very fineness that made for its fragility. William wanted to protect and help her; when he had first met her, she seemed to be living on the very rim of stability.

It was hard for Rebecca to stop working for she had never known a life without study. But, through William, her life was changing so much that she felt she could do it. And then there was Will, and not so very long afterwards, she became pregnant again.

Rebecca stood up, rubbing the tears from her face. She laid her hand gently on the pillow where Will's head must rest each night. 'I have missed his whole life,' she breathed. 'It has all gone and I was not with him as it went by. He was alone and I was alone; he was my child but I barely knew him, as I've barely known my daughter.'

Slowly, insistently, her sadness was replaced by rage as she vowed that Bella would not steal the rest of the years, would not force her back into the darkness. Suddenly it was not only monstrous but impossible that Bella had actually been able to do it: that she had frightened and threatened and blackmailed her to such a degree that her will was broken.

Such was the force of the memory that Rebecca began to shake as she remembered the day Bella had returned after her long absence. How Rebecca had been alone; William in Borneo; how cold it had been; and all day long the sensation of fading, of slipping: that her life was falling into disarray, as it had when she was a child. She had felt these things before she understood their message: Bella was coming home and that meant Rebecca could not remain.

The headaches began, the ones that William always kept a record of in his diary. They became so bad that she could not stand. Her dread of Bella (she could not be wrong, she'd had these premonitions before) took all the happiness from her domestic life. Now, when Rebecca looked about her at the bowls filled with flour and sultanas, the meat cooking in the pot, the beans sliced and resting in water, the little clothes cavorting on the line, the piano open with her Chopin and Debussy – all the things that she loved, that filled her days – now she felt them decompose under Bella's eyes.

Balancing Will on her knee, her stomach swollen with her second child, she tried to practise her scales, all the while waiting for Bella to walk in and reinstate herself on the third floor. Will had the flu and the central heating had broken down. Rebecca seemed unable to apply herself to anything, to get anything done. She just walked around, clutching the child.

And Bella came back. She took a quick look at the situation and assumed command. She picked up the small boy and brought down his temperature: she got on the phone and had the central heating mended. She found a cleaner and a nanny. She threw out all the flimsy oriental covers and ordered elegant but serviceable furnishings from Harrods. When things were back to normal, she went off on a series of interviews at the hospitals she had chosen to approach.

For a fortnight Rebecca struggled against this invasion. Once she managed to get Bella out of the house for two days, but so awful was the anticipation of her return that little pleasure could be derived from her absence.

William was still not back from Borneo and he could not be reached. Rebecca could have tried to fight Bella, but she did not. She had entered a placid, almost lifeless, state. It had been the same when they were children; there came a time when it was useless to fight Bella because she would always win.

Daisy was born, two months premature, small and frail. The birth and the anxiety about the baby's health shattered what was left of Rebecca's resistance. She gave in. She let Bella take over, and relinquished her baby to the nanny. It was if she no longer existed.

She began to have dreams about Bella capturing William when he came home. She knew how it would be and she knew she hadn't the strength to resist any of it. When William came back he would see Bella and Bella would be the one he would want. She would take him, he would be her prey.

She packed her life away and left.

Chapter Four

It was three a.m. Bella was asleep in the small office that the surgeons used when they stayed overnight at the hospital. She was woken with the news that one of her patients, Peter Watson, had just suffered a cardiac arrest. She was surprised as she'd seen him earlier in intensive care and his condition had been stable.

When Bella got to him, her most experienced nurse, Theresa, was working on him. There was no pulse. Machines surrounded his bed and that particular tension hung in the air. Her hands went cold. Brushing Theresa to one side, Bella checked the drip, snapped out a question, adjusted the electrodes across the heart, and said quickly: 'Increase it to 400 and repeat the adrenaline.' Theresa was looking at her with a strange expression, but did as she was asked.

Within a minute, Bella had cleared the area around the patient, reopened his chest and begun to massage his heart with her hands. Theresa knew it was useless; she had tried everything. Bella could not give up. She looked frantic. She began to will him to recover, fixing her mind on him as she worked the material of his body. She looked at Theresa and saw surprise in her face. The great heart surgeon has lost her cool, it seemed to say. There had been rumours about Bella lately – of appointments made and not kept, patients left waiting, calls not made. Theresa had denied any suggestion of such negligence: it was absurd and was caused by jealousy. But all the same it was odd. She too had noted inconsistencies in Bella's behaviour over the past week. Now this.

Peter Watson was dead. The people around his bed all knew it, but it was as if Bella would not allow it. The machines hummed with a flat finality; Theresa stood back and looked at Bella, then moved forward and clicked off the defibrillator. Bella stood up. Her hands shook a little.

'There was nothing you could do,' Theresa said firmly in her soft Irish accent. 'Come on, let's get some coffee. You look worn out.'

Bella's stiffness went out of her, her body seemed to sag. It was this vulnerability that enabled Theresa to cross the divide between their respective positions and say: 'If I remember correctly, this is only your second death in all the years you've been here. Certainly since I've been working with you.'

'One is too much.'

'You're not God,' Theresa said lightly, pushing the swing doors open and letting Bella go out first. 'You can't save 'em all.'

Bella was silent. She felt exhausted. There would be a coroner's court enquiry after the post-mortem. Tony, the senior consultant, had been behaving strangely lately. He'd accused her this morning of not going to the Monday meeting; she'd never once failed to attend it, and was probably the only consultant in that position. He'd implied that she was losing interest. Now it was possible that she could be considered negligent. The muscles in her stomach contracted for a moment.

Bella wasn't listening to Theresa, who was saying she couldn't account for Peter Watson's death; he was to have left the unit the next day. Abruptly Bella stopped and said, 'I must phone his wife.' She remembered the confidence of the woman, her certainty that her husband would make a complete recovery.

'Why not leave it till the morning?' Theresa suggested. 'Why wake her now? It's after four.'

For the first time Bella looked at Theresa with some interest. Accustomed to being treated with the reserve and respect that her status demanded, she was unused to hearing advice of any kind. She turned towards the lifts and said briskly, 'I'll ring her immediately. She lives in Wells and has a long way to come.'

Bella drove home, her mind blanked out by sheer effort of will. She hated cars and drove recklessly because of it. Being in a car reminded her of long journeys when, from the age of three, she'd been subjected to scientific tests with other prodigious children from all over Europe. Sitting in the back of her parents' car in the dark, she had listened to them whispering in German, her father's voice raised in protest or anger. She had learned to shut herself off from the fear and exhaustion by entering a trance. She had forgotten how to do it until it had happened spontaneously in the nursery with Joseph. She had to put it out of mind, and pressed her foot down hard on the accelerator, bringing the speed well above eighty.

Once home, she went straight to her bedroom. On her bed was a note from Alison to tell her Mary had a fever. She went to check on the child, who was tossing in her bed, her pillow wet with sweat. Bella woke her up, gave her some medicine and waited, sponging her face, until her temperature was back to normal.

In the morning, when Alison came in to get Mary out of bed, she was surprised to find Bella lying beside her.

'When did you get back?' she asked Bella, who had woken at the sound of the door opening.

'Oh, late. Mary was very hot.'

Mortified, Alison said, 'I would have stayed with her, only she seemed cool at bed-time.'

'Oh, that's all right. I'm just over-protective. She had a seizure once and stopped breathing.'

'Oh,' Alison said, dismayed, 'I never knew that.' Surely, she felt, it was something she should have been told.

'It was some years ago. She outgrew it.' Bella laid a hand on Mary's head. 'She seems fine now.' Bella remembered how afraid she'd been: the small child unconscious, lying on the grass where Bella had pulled her from the car and given her mouth-to-mouth resuscitation; the people watching; the man rushing into the house on the corner and coming out with towels drenched with cold water. How her wits failed her so that she had not thought to do this herself; she had behaved only as a terrified mother with a stricken child. In the ambulance she'd regained control.

'I can take over now,' Alison said, 'or you'll be late for work.' She knew Bella's schedule exactly; it was pinned on the kitchen wall and she learned it by heart every week. Had she shown inefficiency here, she'd not have survived a week with Bella.

Bella looked at the sleeping Mary and gently brushed her hair back from her forehead.

'I'll look after her today, Alison,' she said with a tender smile. 'After all, who should look after them if they're ill, if not their mother?' She added, 'I have so little time with any of them.'

Alison frowned, surprised, but too shy to investigate the remark. Bella had never seemed to feel any guilt about putting her work before her children: their school plays, sports days, holidays, illnesses. Of course, no real emergency had ever tested that choice. But, if Mary had outgrown the seizures, then this was not one either.

'Okay,' Alison said, 'I'll get Harry up.'

'Thank you, Alison.' Bella smiled again. 'Mary will wake up in a minute. Breakfast is too important for her to sleep much longer.'

Alison nodded, thinking: how would you know – you're out of the house at six every day. But immediately she regretted this meanness.

Bella remained at home all day, missing two operations, a consultation and two important meetings concerning the future of her patients once she'd gone. When her secretary, Irene, rang to find out where she was, Bella was quite rude to her. Irene was so taken aback by this behaviour that she told her friend, 'She's never spoken to me like that before, never. It's as if I was some stupid stranger. I've worked for her for four years, and she's never once treated me that way, never once.'

Chapter Five

Joseph returned to London a couple of weeks after Bella; he'd decided that he needed a brief holiday. Besides, he had some responsibilities towards the inmates of Wormwood Scrubs. But his main purpose was to track down Bella and sort her out.

She was not at the hospital; some surly secretary had given him that much help. Through a series of devious methods he had managed to acquire her home address and was driving there without calling first. He did not care for the telephone, and besides, it would be better to catch her unprepared. There were a number of things he wanted to ask her, not the least being what had happened to her the day she had promised to be home by tea-time, while he, like an idiot, had sat outside the hospital waiting for her.

When he arrived, he noticed that the nanny, the sandy-haired, quiet creature he'd seen at Margy's house, was observing him with a fair amount of curiosity.

'Any reason why you're staring at me?' he demanded.

'Oh, no, no.' She retreated from the stern-faced individual towering over her.

'Well?' He was insisting on an explanation and it seemed to her that she'd better comply.

'Well, it's just that she's not expecting you and she can be, that is, she doesn't like, she can be . . .'

'A pain in the arse,' he finished, and strode off round the back.

She was on her knees weeding a bed of yellow and black pansies.

'Hello,' he called. He watched her as she put down the trowel, as her dark head turned, her face lifted and she looked straight at him with barely a trace of recognition. Was the woman blind? What was the blank expression in aid of? He felt like hitting her. He walked up to her with determination. 'You're damn hard to find,' he said, his voice vibrating with annoyance. She said nothing, but she watched him closely, her hands on her thighs. She brushed the hair out of her eyes, making a smear across her forehead. Her eyebrows arched and then she gave a slight, definitely unwelcoming, smile. He stared, with surprise, at the state of her hands; they were cut and rough, the nails full of dirt.

He would not be frozen out. 'Your hospital was extremely unhelpful, as was some grumpy old bat in your office.' He was put out by the manner in which she surveyed him, and by her silence. He shifted his weight from one leg to the other and smoothed down the back of his hair. Still she watched him. He lost patience and crouched down swiftly beside her, hearing his knees cracking like glass. She pulled back.

'Hey!' he said, grabbing her chin unceremoniously, 'I'm Joseph, the one who found you your house in America. Remember me?'

Then she smiled, a closed and mysterious smile, full of a strange satisfaction.

'Oh,' she breathed, and stood, walking backwards a little. He was up, too, and then moved away from her, taking up his position on a wooden bench. He was ruffled still, but he looked at her shrewdly as she rubbed her dirty hands on her dress.

'Well,' he said quietly, 'this is quite a little transformation. Who'd have believed you could be so earthy?' He looked around him at the sunny garden with its square of lawn, its apple trees and beds of neat flowers. The roses were out, pale pink and fragrant, and the wisteria buds were full as grapes. Pansies and violets nestled in the rocks around a small fish pond.

'Nice place you have here,' he said. 'Lived here long?'

'Yes,' she said, then she asked quickly, 'What did they say?' She spoke in a voice that he thought he remembered as being deeper.

'What did who say?'

'The hospital.'

'Well, your secretary didn't seem to know when you would be coming in. She wouldn't give me your address either.' He laughed. 'I had to pull a few strings. A friend of mine in paediatrics managed to get hold of it for me.'

'I see,' she said. And then she walked over to where he was and sat on the grass, quite close to him. She leaned back, turning her face up to the sun, her legs spread out in front of her like a peasant woman. And, he observed, they were rather agricultural, long, strong legs. In the faded print dress, her tall body looked particularly fecund. Her hair was pinned on top of her head but wayward strands kept falling across her face. She looked quite different when it was not scraped back in that severe knot at the nape of her neck. Also, her hair looked shorter and this gave a neat, sweet shape to her head. Her beauty was more provocative than he remembered it.

'I've been at home,' she said, offering her first real communication. He felt that she'd decided against blocking him and wondered what had caused this shift. 'Mary was ill.'

'Mary's the oldest girl, isn't she?' he asked, remembering the bright, spirited child most clearly.

'No, you're thinking of Daisy,' she said, adding quietly, 'Mary is the little blonde one.' To his surprise there was a trace of dislike in her voice.

'Yes,' he said, 'of course,' not having the slightest recollection. 'Is she better?' he asked dutifully.

She nodded and began pulling at the grass.

He couldn't help but say it. 'Your hands,' he said disapprovingly. 'Can you operate with all those cuts? They're in pretty bad shape.' He leaned forward to take her hand, but she pulled back with a sharp intake of breath and quickly moved her hands into the folds of her dress. 'You must be a dedicated gardener,' he said coolly, still looking at the place where her hands had rushed to cover. 'My father liked gardening.' Chatter infuriated him, yet here he was doing it.

'I haven't gardened for a long time,' she said. 'Things have become neglected.'

'It looks fine.'

'No, there's so much to do,' she turned her head to look at some place in the garden that did not please her.

'How long have you been away from work?' he asked pointedly.

'Two days.'

'Isn't that difficult? When you're leaving so soon?'

She said with a small, childish snort: 'To hell with them.'

'Good for you,' he said.

'Why are you here?' she asked.

He looked directly at her. 'I came to find you.'

86

'Where did you come from?'

'From New York, of course.'

She nodded in a distant way.

'I needed a holiday and when I was here I thought I'd look you up. See if I could help.' He stopped. 'No, that's a lie. I wanted to see you. Our last meeting was a bit disturbing.' She did not pursue it. He sensed that there was no antagonism in her whereas the last time he'd seen her, outside the hospital in New York, she had been verging on hostility. Now she was rather docile.

'You know,' he began slowly, 'you don't seem as pleased to see me as you should be.'

'Should be?' she repeated, with a small smile.

'Yes, we seemed to get on so well when we last met. Remember the great arguments and discussions? We liked each other' – he smiled wryly – 'in spite of your curious decision to dine with James Venables rather than with me that night.'

She lowered her head. 'I do like you,' she said softly, 'as much as I may.'

He'd been about to say something snide, but now he looked at her with interest. As much as I *may*, she'd said, not, as much as I can. Interesting. He could not keep his eyes off those hands of hers: fingers so different from the pale surgeon's fingers with their cropped, immaculate nails. He was confused by the inconsistencies in her behaviour. She was seeking some confirmation from him – but he had no idea why.

He went and sat beside her on the grass.

'What's up, Bella?' he asked bluntly. 'What's going on?'

She did not move away from him as he'd expected, but looked up into his face, her eyes squinting a little from the sun.

'You're acting as if we barely knew one another.'

She looked worried, but tried to hide it. 'I'm just pre-occupied.'

He relented. 'Of course. You must be. You must have a lot to do, with the move so soon. Need any help? Seriously, I'll gladly give you a hand. I've nothing much to do at the weekend, except go to my house in Gloucestershire.'

'I might not go,' she said, pulling at the clover in the grass. He knew that she was referring to America.

'You're not serious?' He was a little dismayed. He had to be there for three more months.

'I don't know.' She sounded unhappy. 'I don't want to have to leave England.' She looked up at the house. 'We've been so happy here.' Joseph wondered if that happiness had anything to do with either of the dead husbands, but doubted it somehow. He couldn't believe she'd been happy with a man. It was hard to believe she could fully know the meaning of the word. For the first time, distinctly, he saw how deep the wound in her was. He was not prepared to get into that so he said, 'Well, it's a bit late to have a change of heart, isn't it? I thought you had already accepted the job?'

She did not reply. How odd, he thought, this melancholy in her. She was waif-like, as she'd been in that peculiar incident at the nursery.

'It's not the kind of opportunity that comes up more than once,' he said.

'Perhaps the opportunity to stay at home would be more worthwhile,' she said slowly.

He raised his eyebrows. 'And I thought you were the one who could dispense with such womanly conflicts?' he said, and then, immediately, wished that he hadn't. He was steeling himself for a sharp retort, but her knife remained sheathed. How very disagreeable that was, to find that her emotional discipline was tighter than his own. She could so easily have taken a shot. She'd proved how good her aim was on frequent occasions. Was it possible that she was in charge of herself here? Women were normally over-sensitive to any little remark, taking digs at each opportunity. Yet she remained silent.

'You see,' she said softly, 'my son, Will, is very against it.'

Now, he did remember Will all right, a tough customer with something not quite right in his relationship with his mother. He was picking this up again, in the over-protective way Bella spoke about him.

'Kids have to make adjustments,' he said briskly. 'It's good for them.' He wondered if she'd turn that steely little blighter into a nancy-boy. The kid needed some male company.

'Are you an expert?' she asked. And his heart took a bow: this was more like the Bella he knew; surely now they could take a quick turn on the dance-floor. But looking at her expectant face he saw that he'd misunderstood. Her question was a serious one; she awaited his answer.

88

'Um, no, I'm not, if you mean am I a parent. But I've dealt with kids professionally, not kids like Will, of course, but boys all the same. And' – his voice became tart – 'I was a boy myself, once.' He wanted to be done with this; he sounded like a waffler. 'He'll be fine,' he said.

'Maybe,' she said, looking over to the house, where he could see a small girl peeping round the door leading into the garden.

'Well . . .' He got up reluctantly. 'I suppose I'd better be off.'

The child had nipped back inside, but he could see that he'd completely lost Bella's attention. Her face was maternal and tender. She, too, rose.

He was disappointed. How often it was that you felt you'd made a connection with a woman, only to find, the next time you met, that there was nothing there.

'Mary!' she called, seeing the child come out timidly again.

'Goodbye,' he said, beginning to walk to the door.

'You won't have any tea?' But it was a politeness and, as such, he refused it.

'Goodbye,' she said, smiling, watching him leave, and then quickly going in to the child.

Joseph walked with some annoyance to his car. He sat there a moment and rolled down the window to let in some air. He'd blown it, no doubt about it. He'd intended to ask her to come to Gloucestershire with him, but the idea had seemed preposterous on this visit. As he turned the key in the ignition, he slammed his hand down on the dashboard.

Inside the house, the woman sat talking to her daughter, but her attention was elsewhere. She stopped listening to the child as her uneasiness grew. Suddenly, she rose and walked swiftly to the front door.

As he began to drive away, Joseph saw Bella come out of the house and stand a moment, framed by the pale pink roses daubed across the white walls. She rubbed one foot against her leg like a girl. So moved was he by the sight of her that he stopped the car, got out and walked swiftly back.

'I thought', she began shyly, 'I might have your telephone number, you know, in case there is something you could help me with. If you meant it, of course.'

He took out a pen and wrote his number on the wall, then bent quickly to kiss her on the cheek, but missed because she turned her head. His kiss landed on the side of her mouth.

'Make sure you ring,' he said, 'or I'll be back.' Her face warmed to the affection in his voice.

Will appeared from nowhere and stood beside his mother like a sentry.

'Hello, Will.'

No reply.

'Will?' His mother frowned and he walked off quickly.

'I'll see you soon, Bella,' said Joseph, and walked back to his car. When he turned and looked back, she stood in the doorway still, with her hand raised. He had the strangest feeling that she thought he was deserting her – that she would not see him again. He could not shake off the feeling, and it added to the air of unreality that seemed to haunt his relationship with her.

Chapter Six

Joseph sat in heavy traffic on Battersea Bridge. Something was bothering him. He just could not work Bella out and it infuriated him. His instincts about people were always right. He still could not dislodge his first impression of her from his mind. And today – well, she had looked like someone who earned her living digging potatoes. My God: those hands! He was trying to remember something. He jumped when a horn blared behind him because he had failed to take advantage of a six-inch space in the crawl to the traffic lights.

He was due at Wormwood Scrubs but just couldn't face it yet. He was too unsettled. He stopped at the Dôme for a drink. It was odd to be back in England again, pleasant. England never changed, it was dormant and self-satisfied, a country that had lived for too long off its past, In comparison, America was excessive, over the top in every way. Still, he had to admit that he'd rather enjoyed his first months on the committee. The people – prison officials, psychiatrists and psychologists, experts in human and inhuman behaviour – they were all rather good, for a change. An almost decent collection with an indecent job to do.

For Joseph to be able to view prisons and prisoners from a distance was something of a relief. That's why he hesitated now, thinking about Wormwood Scrubs. When he walked into that caged world he'd feel its terrible force again; the violence lurking just below the surface: massive, oppressive and stealthy. The old fear would come back to him. It wasn't personal fear; everyone felt it, it was part of the place, like the smell. The fear of turning your back, the way you would always make sure you could see the door when talking to someone there; the fascination and dread of getting that close to such casual and mindless murder. So much was so indiscriminate – so why not you next time? He realised with annoyance that because he'd been to see Bella he'd not worn his customary

91

dull garb. The inmates were disturbed by anything too bright or flashy – reminders of the living world out there. Now he saw his expensive shoes and well-cut khaki trousers, not to mention the bright blue shirt. He winced: he looked like a man on holiday – which, dammit, he was. Fuck 'em. Today, he thought firmly, they will have to bear with me, for a change.

He now realised that the 'mistake' of wearing these clothes was a way of removing himself from the responsibilities of his patients in the prison. He was liking the work less all the time. The prisoners made him an accomplice to their violence. He was far closer to evil, he felt, after he'd spent long stretches dealing with no one but convicts. He knew it was a complicity he must have sought. It had been his own choice to work with the criminally insane. He believed in evil. He'd seen it. He knew that he had the capacity to kill, like most people. Coming up close to killers, peering into their acts, was as close as you could get to doing it. Bella was the same, without a doubt: there was a woman in direct contact with her own capacity for evil. Or so he had believed, before today.

He thought about her marriages and her secrecy about them; he'd not been able to draw her out at all. He had always believed that each marriage had a killer and a victim. Peer into every lousy marriage (and most were lousy) and you would find this pattern: the destroyer and the one who was destroyed. Look closer and you saw that the roles were interchangeable. The victim invariably used his weakness to destroy the stronger one and the stronger one retaliated in kind. Had Bella ever played the victim? She seemed like a whole-hearted killer to him. But then he was astounded by these thoughts: this was the gentle, insecure woman of the garden; the sweet, maternal person with the broken hands. Yet he knew she was evil. He thought hard about it, but could not change his mind.

Of course, he was obliged never to admit that he believed in evil, particularly when questioned by the press in, say, some sensational case when everyone was panting to hear the grisly details. Then, he had to deny that evil was what he was dealing with. The poor wretches – official scapegoats – both intrigued and repelled the imagination, and appeased the conscience. The more people they could stick in prisons, the better everyone liked it. The ludicrous thing was that the public seemed to believe that if only the police could find them all, and the prison officials could punish them all, then that would be an end to violence. The more they were made to suffer in there the safer everyone would feel. He was part of a system of vindictive justice, which found its most violent expression in America, a country with a bloody history and a long and legal familiarity with murder: what was once confined to the 'red man' was now passed on to the black and the poor; the cowboy and soldier had been replaced by the electric chair or an injection that took fifteen minutes to kill. He was depressed suddenly. The committee was a sham, like all the rest. No one was interested in preventing crime, only in punishing it.

He was at the gate now and had to force himself to go in. The news of the day was that Billy the King had been battered to death in his cell the night before. And the inevitable shift of power was taking place. Joseph had liked Billy. He was vicious and quick, as his crimes had been, but there was intelligence and humour in him and a keen understanding of life in the only way Billy knew it: cheap and disposable, but exciting and real. Life was worth killing for, he used to say. Billy was a stranger to remorse and found the concept of guilt hard to understand. He had argued eloquently with Joseph on the subject. To Billy it was easy: you gave back what you got from life, mate.

Now he was dead and there was a thick silence surrounding his death, with intrigue running up and down the corridors. The warders were edgy, expecting retribution – and no one would speak to Joseph about what had happened. He felt that his small successes, those minute steps forward in communication, seemed to have been wiped away in his absence. He had abandoned the prisoners for two months and now was being made to pay for it. He had at least three more months of work in the States, including the report he'd agreed to write and, by the time he got back, the sea would have washed his tracks entirely off the beach.

He left the prison and drove slowly towards his flat in Paddington. He was still trying to shake off a rather spooky little conversation he'd had in the prison with Ray, a thug with the subtlety of a boa-constrictor, who would, most probably, take over from Billy the King.

'Know anything about Billy's death, Ray?' Joseph had asked.
'Nah,' he said. 'Got a fag?'

93

Joseph gave him the rest of the packet; he always took cigarettes into the prison.

'Thanks. It's like this, doc,' he said. 'Your pal, Billy, well, he started losing his grip. Pretty soon everyone knows it: the time comes for someone else to take over. Billy, 'cause he's gone soft, well, he makes it easy for that somebody, don't he?'

Instantly, Joseph understood why that conversation had spooked him and stayed with him all through his visit to the Scrubs. It was, in fact, nothing to do with either Billy or Ray – it was all to do with Bella. Now that he'd made this connection, he saw it. He'd worked Bella out.

And Bella, with her sure instincts, had known he would soon be on to her: it was why she had looked so orphaned when he had left her standing at the front door.

Chapter Seven

When Bella next went into her bedroom she noticed that something from her bureau had fallen to the floor and broken. She walked closer and saw that it was the last remaining picture of William – or it had been, because nothing remained of him now, all his features had been obliterated. She bent her knees and studied the wreckage. It was not the work of a child. This had been done deliberately, the sole of a shoe had pressed the broken glass into the photograph.

She gathered up the shards of glass and put them, one by one, into the waste-paper basket. She was remembering the other occasions when she had come upon ripped-up photographs of William. Poor Rebecca, poor, lost creature, who had never been loved by Papa, who had practised all those hours on the piano to please him and never got beyond mediocre. Poor Rebecca, who had never been loved by William, who imagined that he had begun to favour Bella; Rebecca, who had even believed that Bella had seduced William.

She went to a drawer – found that it had been gone through – and took out a box to put the torn pieces in: Will must not find this. She had only kept the picture because he insisted it stay in its old place. What was it about sons, she wondered, that made them so determined to admire their fathers? When William was ill with that mysterious disease he'd caught in Borneo, he'd refused to have the small boy anywhere near him. He had not treated Rebecca much better; in his delirium, he often forgot who she was. Of course Bella had been blamed for this behaviour, but how could it be her fault that while he lay dying he would have no one near him but her?

She sat down in the blue chair, still holding the small box with the shredded photograph. The situation with Rebecca was escalating; she had broken in for the second time and would have to be stopped. Bella lifted her hand and pressed her knuckles into her temple. Rebecca was coming and going in the dislocated way she had done on two occasions before: after Daisy's birth and during William's illness. It was when she was at her most dangerous. The note she had left in America was like the notes in the past, disordered and desperate, most definitely threatening: 'I'm back, I'm out and you cannot stop me.' She remembered the other notes Rebecca had written over their long, troubled history. Each word came up before her eyes, even the scrawl written on the kitchen wall came back to her precisely as it had been: *Get out, Bella, leave my house, leave us all alone or I'll kill someone. I'll kill the baby, I gave it life so I can take it away again. I'll kill William. I'd rather kill him than let you take him. I mean it so get out, get out NOW.*

Bella lowered her head slowly onto her knees and tried to think. After a while, she heard a timid sound at the door and she looked up with a swift jerk of her head.

'Oh, it's you, Daisy, what do you want?' Her voice was hard and quick and the child stepped back. She shook her head. 'Nothing,' she said. 'I didn't know whether it was you.'

'Who else could it be?' Bella snapped. Then she relented and her voice softened. 'I'm sorry, Daisy, I'm just tired, that's all.'

'Are you going back to the hospital?' Daisy asked, nervously.

'No.' Then Bella said, 'Daisy, what's that in your hand?'

The child moved her hand forward quickly. 'Oh, it's a doll. I found it on my bed. I thought you'd put it there.'

'Me?' Bella asked. 'Why would I? I know you don't like dolls.'

Daisy shrugged. 'Well, I don't know where it came from then.'

'Bring it to me, Daisy,' Bella said in a low, soft voice, 'let me look at it.'

It was a doll with a round porcelain face and fine, golden hair.

'Hm,' Bella said. 'Rather a nice doll.' She looked closely at the doll's clothing. 'This is interesting,' she said, 'come and look, Daisy' – for the girl stood rather apart. Bella was fingering the silky material; it was cream in colour and made a rustling sound. 'Do you see, Daisy,' Bella said very quietly, 'this dress was hand-made by someone. Look at the stitching, see how small the stitches are, and look at the gold braid around the hem, it has been very carefully worked.'

Bella leaned back a little, setting the doll aside.

'There was a doll', she said, narrowing her eyes, 'very much like this one, in our house, when I was a little girl.'

Daisy moved closer; it was not often that her mother mentioned her childhood.

'Was it your doll?'

'Oh no,' Bella said. 'No. I, too, do not like dolls.'

'Well, whose doll was it?'

'You ask too many questions, Daisy. Let's go downstairs. No,' she said quickly as Daisy reached for the doll, 'let me keep it for a while, you know, just to find out where it might have come from.'

As Daisy turned towards the door, Bella snatched up the doll and thrust it violently under her chair.

Chapter Eight

After Mary's illness, Bella went back to the hospital. She was a little surprised to find that her secretary, Irene, was rather distant: the woman seemed to derive some private satisfaction from telling Bella that she should see her boss the moment she got in.

Sam Gallagher, Bella's boss, looked up as she entered his room with an expression on his face that mystified her. When he spoke his voice was really quite angry.

'What the hell's been going on, Bella?'

She frowned. 'What do you mean?'

'I'm referring to Mr Watson,' he said with irritation. 'Peter Watson.' It was as if the clouds parted to reveal the land below. He noticed how the colour rushed to her face.

'My God,' she breathed.

'You're bloody right! The woman arrives here to find an empty bed in his room!'

Bella's hands went up to her face and he noticed the condition of them: good hands, the best hands that he had. She quickly moved them out of sight. Bella had always puzzled him: so composed, such an utterly reliable woman – until this fiasco. There had been a few incidents in the years she'd worked with him, but only, interestingly enough, in the past couple of months. Previous to that her record was impeccable. Now she sat there, silently absorbed in her own thoughts. It was a side of her he was most uncomfortable with; intensity of any kind bothered him.

'Why didn't you tell her about his death?' he now asked, more quietly, 'and why have you been away from the hospital?' It suddenly struck him that there might be a connection between the two: the death and the strange way she'd bolted from the hospital on the night that it occurred. Had there been some cock-up? Some negligence? All this she read in his face. She mustered her resources to deal with him.

'I meant to tell her,' she said calmly, 'I was going to break it to her that night – not that he'd died, but about the cardiac arrest, to give her time to get used to the possibility of his death. But I didn't.' She drew in her breath. 'And the next morning – '

'And the next two mornings,' he cut in. 'Jim had to cover for you. The whole thing was a mess, deeply upsetting for everyone.' He was glaring at her through his glasses; she was thinking that Jim was the worst possible person to break news of this kind to a relative.

'Did Jim tell her?'

'Of course. But Mrs Watson was furious. She said she'd asked you most particularly to tell her the truth, to let her know if you felt that his chances were poor.'

'His chances weren't poor.'

'Well, what happened?' This was a very different question; he was asking her to explain what had caused his death. She saw something else in his eyes, something she found more distasteful: a certain pleasure to have her on the rack, unable to acquit herself. He realised, with interest, that he'd always expected something of this kind to happen with Bella. He wondered why. Would it have vindicated some prejudice? Or was it simply because she had always seemed just a little too perfect?

'I can't tell you, yet,' she replied briskly. 'I haven't seen the pathologist's report or talked to Jim.'

'I have,' he said.

'Well?' she asked.

He was stunned by her self-control, by the utter lack of fear in her. 'Nothing there,' he said with an annoyance he pushed quickly out of the way. 'But of course you'll want to go through it more carefully. We should' – he looked coldly at her – 'do more investigations – '

She cut him short. 'I'll speak to Mrs Watson straight away. You'll have my report in a few hours and, of course, you have my apology.'

She was gone. He shrugged: she was brilliant but really damn odd. For a minute, when she first came in, cool as a cucumber, it was as if she hadn't a clue as to why he'd wanted to see her – as if her absence from the hospital had not occurred. Now he realised she had given him no explanation

99

for this or for any of it. Perhaps the strain of that time-table was telling on her? It had never been in his interest to question the amount of work she did before: she was the draw for all the most intricate heart surgery that came into the hospital. That was his next problem – and one he blamed her personally for: how to replace her?

He was left sitting there, feeling rather piqued. What had begun as his meeting with her had turned into her meeting. He would have felt better pleased had she burst into tears or thrown a tantrum. Instead, this clipped acceptance of respon-sibility, without excuse or complaint – like a soldier taking it on the chin. All in all, rather as a decent male surgeon would, or should, behave in this situation – but of course they didn't.

He snorted, yelled for his secretary and demanded coffee.

Chapter Nine

When her report was complete and her operations rescheduled, Bella drove straight down to see Mrs Watson in Wells. When she arrived there, in record time, she knocked on the door of a small and rather run-down cottage tucked into the side of a hill.

'Mrs Watson. May I come in?'

The woman at the door hesitated, her face in the two o'clock sunshine grey with fatigue. Bella moved forward a fraction. 'Mrs Watson, I came down to apologise for the unnecessary suffering you've been caused.'

There was no response.

'I'm truly sorry about the way you heard of your husband's death.'

The tired eyes regarded Bella's slowly; she looked directly into them, avoiding none of the emotion she saw there.

'It's natural that you should be angry,' Bella said.

'It's not natural that a specialist should lie to us. I asked you for the truth. I should have got it.'

They stood thus, eye to eye, shoulder to shoulder, women of similar strength pitted against one another.

'You got the truth,' Bella said simply. 'There was no reason to suppose he would not have made a complete recovery. It's impossible, sometimes, to – '

'Don't go into that stuff,' the widow said in a spasm of irritation. 'I've had the full explanation, some doctor, Levi, I think . . .'

'Yes, Jim Levi.'

'He explained the whole thing to me, as if I was a moron, he even drew me a little picture on . . .' her voice gave way, 'the back of a letter of Peter's. I don't need to hear it again.' She stopped, looked sharply at Bella, whose hands were tucked under her arms as though she was cold.

'He was careful to stress that it was not your fault – ' she gave a small sneer – 'an act of God, something like

101

that, I suppose, one of those things . . .' She ended on a high note, recalling with a devastating shaft of memory how Peter had sung the Sinatra song 'Just One Of Those Things' whenever he was feeling particularly happy. The last time he had sung it was two days after his operation, when he began to feel better. She averted her face, unable to forgive this cool consultant for allowing her husband to die.

'We . . .' Mrs Watson hesitated and began again, 'I had hoped that we could go to Scotland for a holiday, afterwards.' She looked vacantly at a straw hat which hung on a nail in the hallway, then forced her eyes away.

Bella tried again. 'Mrs Watson?' It was her voice that reached out to comfort, the other woman noticed, for she made no physical gesture. 'Mrs Watson, I can't tell you how sorry I am, and any excuse I give you will be almost insulting. I thought to ring you that night, but wanted to spare you till morning. The next day, my child was dangerously ill . . .' her voice shook a little and gave resonance to the words '. . . I couldn't think of anything else. She has seizures. On two occasions she has almost died . . .'

The woman looked at the doctor, appalled, her own anger pulled out from beneath her so effectively that she felt the whole structure collapse. She could only mumble the same useless words that had been spoken to her.

'I'm so sorry, I had no idea.' It was unbearable to her – any more suffering.

'It's just,' Bella twisted her hands with that strange, wringing gesture of hers, 'I felt you should know that. I wanted to tell you myself. I know it doesn't help or excuse my neglect of you. I had to come. I'm sorry if I've upset you more by doing so.'

'Oh no. No, no.' Martha Watson put out her hand to comfort the other; she laid it on her arm and said, 'Please, come in. Won't you have some tea?'

Bella looked down at Martha's hands, strong hands, that baked and scrubbed, cooked and cleaned, making a life for someone else, someone she loved and had now lost. She envied the woman her grief. Martha Watson, looking at Bella now as a woman, not merely a doctor, remembered with shame that she had heard that Bella was a widow, too.

Bella looked for the first time carefully at Martha's face and saw that it was a striking face, with a full mouth and

102

grey eyes beneath hair that had once been thick and blonde. She urged Bella to enter the small sitting-room crowded with photographs of children and dogs, a man fishing in a stream, the same man, Peter, on a boat.

'I'm afraid I can't stay, I have to be back at the hospital,' Bella said.

Martha was instantly ashamed: they were so busy, so pressed, all the time, such terrible hours. She had a cousin who was in medicine once, but he couldn't take it. The poor woman, how did she manage? With a child like that? The worry of it. No wonder. She'd been so kind when they'd gone in to see her, so encouraging, so sure that Peter would be fine, so unlike that first specialist, before they'd decided on a second opinion. She felt terrible to have been so angry, so lacking in understanding. After all, the hospital should cover a surgeon at a time like that, they must have known. And she'd come all the way down, two long hours in the car and people dying . . .

And there she stopped, at the word, dying, for it brought her straight up against the pain again. She humbly opened the door to let the doctor out. When Bella had gone, she realised, with horror, that she had not even asked whether the child had recovered.

Chapter Ten

Once behind the wheel of her car, Bella knew that there would be no repercussions about Peter Watson's death. She had herself to deal with, of course, but there was no point in trying to find some explanation for a death that, sad as it was, was unavoidable. She was a scrupulous surgeon. She did not arrive to operate when the patient was already lying cold on the table, as most surgeons did. She was always with her patients immediately the anaesthetist had finished and she remained there, listening to last-minute fears, until the patient lost consciousness. Young residents watching her would smile to see that she often smoothed a cheek or a forehead, rubbed an arm, held a hand. Her patients gave themselves up to her with complete trust. So, too, had Peter Watson.

Driving back to the hospital she felt quite sure that there had been nothing careless about the handling of this case, neither during surgery itself nor the post-operative nursing. She had gone over everything, checked all the data, spoken to the pathologist in great detail. She must let it go, there was nothing to be done.

She set it aside and now cleared her brain of all professional matters. She had to concentrate on Rebecca. Because of course it was Rebecca who had caused the fiasco. Bella was quite sure that before leaving the hospital she had changed her mind and asked the nurse, Theresa, to break the news to Mrs Watson. But the plan had been changed. It was a standard trick of Rebecca's. She would have got on the phone, said she was Bella and asked Theresa not to speak to Mrs Watson after all – that she would do so herself. The ramifications of this were frightening. It meant that not only was Rebecca making excursions through the house but she was turning her attention to the hospital. The purpose was the same as it had always been: to disrupt both life and work, to try to make it impossible for Bella to function.

Usually, Rebecca was intimidated by the hospital: she would have to find her way round it, to know Bella's exact place in it. Of course, she would not attempt to interfere with the work itself; she would move around the perimeter, causing small explosions. This last was quite a coup. Bella had virtually been accused of unprofessional conduct. And it was not over yet. She would have to deal with Theresa when she got back; she would have to stabilise her own situation at the hospital.

All of which she could do. She had dealt with Martha Watson; now she would take on the rest of them and deal with each in turn. But more important, she had to deal with Rebecca. Thinking of this, Bella's eyes – the same eyes that had smiled with such sympathy at Martha Watson – now seemed to level and take aim.

Rebecca was different this time. Rebecca was restored. This was not the work of a pitiful little widow, destroyed by William's absurd and unnecessary death. This was not the woman who had fallen to pieces, threatening to injure her own children, accusing Bella of plots and seductions. This was a woman executing a well-prepared plan: one who had got herself into hospitals and houses, made silk dresses for dolls and trampled photographs – under everyone's nose. Rebecca had come back for her children, the very children she had been unable to care for, had terrified and then abandoned.

It was alarming – the length of Rebecca's reach. Bella felt utterly weary. She knew now that she had lost hours, even days, when she could not remember where she'd been or what she'd been doing. She had failed to keep appointments at the hospital. She had broken a promise to Will. She realised that she had no recollection of what she had done after leaving the hospital in New York after her meeting with Philip Modlinger.

She was frightened: she was suffering from amnesia. It had happened only once before.

In the past, Rebecca had suffered from memory lapses and Bella had not. Thus, Bella could control Rebecca, who had suffered the kind of disorientation that Bella was experiencing now. Bella had lost a vital advantage. She could not manage if the lapses continued. Her life was far too complicated to survive such a deficiency.

Trying to find some comfort, Bella went back to a time when there had not been a relentless war between the two of them. At that time, if Rebecca had caused havoc with Mrs Watson she would later have regretted it and tried to right the situation. Clearly, this sense of pity was no longer there. Rebecca had become ruthless.

Bella knew that she had driven Rebecca to this: that she was responsible for the deformation of a sweet nature. She wondered now: did I go too far? Push her too much? Take too much from her? Did my life and success so far overreach hers that she decided she must break me or be locked out for ever? But Bella knew also that she could not afford to be compassionate: her pity would be used against her, as in the old days she had used Rebecca's.

She had arrived back at the hospital. But she couldn't seem to get out of the car. She sat there, with the hot sun beating down, trying to make herself go in. She opened the car door, then closed it. Suddenly and quite desperately she wanted to go home, to see her children, to get away from the strain inside her and the strain she would have to endure in that tall building over there.

Then the schedule on her desk flashed before her eyes, and the backlog of work came home to her. She opened the door again.

But she wanted to see Mary and she wanted to hold Harry in her arms. She thought of her house being invaded by Rebecca. She turned the key in the ignition and began to reverse the car: she must go home, she would go home.

Martha Watson's face came back to her; the face of her boss came back to her. She slammed her hand down on the dashboard. She switched off the ignition, finally, and got out.

As she walked towards the glass doors, her world began to regain its balance. The doorman smiled at her and complained of the heat. The familiar smell of the corridors, the ringing of the phones, intercom messages for the doctors, the bustle, the happy greeting of a patient who was going home – all this was an infusion to her. She smiled; she was home, after all.

She took the lift to the top floor. When the doors opened, she saw Theresa.

'Oh, I'm glad you're back,' Theresa said. 'I worried about you, what with the telephone calls. Everything okay now?'

'Perfectly, thank you.'

'I just wondered,' Theresa said, puzzled.

106

Briskly, Bella walked on.

'I hope your little girl is better.'

Bella stopped. She turned round. 'My daughter?' she said. 'Who told you my daughter was ill?'

Theresa gave her soft laugh. 'Why, you did, yourself. Don't you remember?'

Chapter Eleven

Will's head was bent over an Agatha Christie book. He was reading fast, with a concentration sufficiently developed to block out his sisters' interruptions and the yelling of Harry, who'd been left to his own devices as Alison plied the Hoover. His mother's hand, placed on the crown of his head, roused him. He looked up at her.

'Oh,' he said, 'you came back last night.'

Bella adjusted the long, cotton robe she wore. 'Did I say I wouldn't?' She cleared a place on the sofa so that she could sit beside him.

'No.' He squinted at her through sunlight that poured through the kitchen windows. It seemed to him that the sun made the large room rock a little, as if they were out at sea. He loved the kitchen, it was the best room in the house, after his own. It was the place he liked to find his mother in. She didn't seem in a hurry to leave; he thought he might be able to persuade her to make him a treacle tart.

'It was nice to have you here last week,' he said. 'We went to some good places. I liked the Natural History Museum best.'

'Hm?' she said, vaguely, scratching with her finger at some chocolate merging with the sofa fabric. Mary came over and flung herself across Bella's knees, settling there.

'Not much wrong with you, is there?' Bella said with a tug at Mary's curls.

'Oh, I'm not completely better.' Mary gave a mournful but plucky smile.

'Of course you are!' Will snorted. 'No one eats that much toad-in-the-hole if they're ill.'

Mary pouted and turned her face into her mother's shoulder.

'Aren't you going to work today?' Will asked hopefully.

'Yes, I am, a bit later.'

'Oh.'

'I think I've been off too long,' she said, with an odd edge to her voice, 'gadding about with you lot.'

'Wednesday was great,' Will said, remembering the trip to Richmond Park, which she did not.

'I'm glad you liked it,' she said, dislodging Mary, who went off to torment Daisy. Harry was trailing after Alison like a puppy. He began to cry and she picked him up, perching him on her hip as she moved backwards and forwards, vacuuming the carpet in the hall.

Looking at Harry, Will said, 'I remember you carrying me like that, when you were doing things in the house.' Bella was startled; she looked at him.

'You were a bit different then,' he said.

'No one remembers that far back, Will,' she said briskly.

'I do.' His gaze was steady and impossible to avoid, it was full of accusation.

She picked up his book and looked at it.

'You're not going to phone that man, are you?' Will demanded.

Bella looked at him with interest.

'What man?'

'You know, the one who was here the other day.'

She thought for a moment, was about to ask him a question, then shrugged. 'I don't suppose so.'

Guilty, he now felt safe enough to admit, 'That's good, because I rubbed off the telephone number.'

'You did what?' She smiled encouragingly, feeling a chill at the back of her neck.

'I scrubbed the numbers off the wall,' he said, a little defiantly now.

'Oh. That was rather out of line, wasn't it?'

'Yes,' he admitted. Then added sullenly, 'I just don't like him.'

'But it might have caused me some trouble,' she said, still smiling. 'Anyway, why don't you like him?'

'He works with murderers.'

'Who told you that?' she snapped.

'You did.'

She breathed out softly. 'Of course. Well, that's no reason to dislike someone, because of their work. You could say

109

that I work with diseased people – someone might not like me for that.'

'It's different.'

'Why is it different?'

'It's not violent.'

'Death is often violent, Will,' she said gently.

'Well, it's just spooky then.'

'Don't be refractory.'

'What does that mean?'

'Stubborn.'

He laughed and picked up his book.

'You've been reading too many mysteries,' she said lightly.

He was silent for a moment and then he said, 'When I read mysteries, I often like the murderers, but that man makes me not like them.'

'How interesting,' she said, standing, cocking her head sideways at him. 'Perhaps you are just looking for a reason not to like him?'

'No,' he said,'I just don't like him.'

'Remember how you hated Jack?' she said, then, seeing that his face fell, she added, 'It's all right, don't worry about it.'

She took Mary by the hand and said conspiratorially, 'Let's see if we can find where that telephone number was written, shall we?' She turned to Will. 'You must give us a clue, because there are too many walls to look on.'

'I know where he wrote it,' Daisy now flung in, pushing herself forward.

'You do not,' Will said.

'I do!' She looked at Bella, who looked back enquiringly. Daisy was excited: here was a chance to gain her mother's approval, something she could seldom do.

'Just outside the front door, under the bell,' Daisy said triumphantly.

Will said, 'That's just like you, Daisy, always sneaking about, spying on people.'

'Spying is not a very pleasant trait,' Bella said coldly.

'I have to spy,' Daisy said, 'or no one tells me any-thing.'

'Oh, come on, Daisy,' Will said, and walked off.

Bella went to the front door and opened it, searching for a second to find the numbers. Will had not done a good job; there was the faintest outline of a row of numbers. Bella memorised them quickly and shut the door.

Back in the kitchen she went to rescue Harry, who was now literally under Alison's feet. 'I'll take him. Stop working, Alison, you've done a lovely job.' She flipped him across her shoulder. 'I'll make some tea,' she said, moving to put the kettle on. Then she turned to Will. 'I can't remember exactly, Will, the day he came, can you?' she asked slowly.

'Who?' Will closed his book.

'The man,' she said lightly, 'the murderer man.' She laughed. 'I can't remember the day.'

'Nor can I,' he said. But his essential decency made him relent. 'It was the same day you sent the people away – the ones who came to see the house – Tuesday.'

She was dismayed by this information.

Will looked at her. 'You'll have to make up your mind, Mummy,' he said placidly. 'After all, we can't go on packing and unpacking like this.' Alison, too, was looking at her now. 'I don't want to keep getting my things in piles and then putting them away again, it's a bore.' He put his book down. 'You don't want to go to America, do you?' He said it earnestly, hoping it was true.

'Yes, I do,' Bella said firmly. She turned to the children and said, 'Now, listen, some time today' – she looked across at Alison – 'Alison can help you a little bit, you have to sort out your toys into two piles: those you want to take and those you can throw out.'

'We've done that already,' Will said, giving her a look both curious and unsettling.

'They did it last Saturday,' Alison put in.

'Of course, I know that,' Bella snapped, 'but I need you to do it again.'

'Okay, okay,' said Will.

'And this time, be ruthless. *Things* don't matter. We can't take great loads of junky toys with us.'

Will, who kept his possessions meticulously, took exception to this remark, but he said nothing. His mother was pressed, he knew the signs: she made these odd comments, forgot things, didn't do what she said she would. It didn't happen often. And besides, maybe she was referring to Daisy's junk. Daisy only liked things when they'd been gutted. She took things apart, unwired and dismantled them, then put them together again in a way she liked better. She had even begun on the household appliances; their innards lay strewn around the house.

'Well, I must be off,' Bella said, her expression preoccupied in a way that was familiar to them all. Harry had fallen asleep, his cheek curled into her neck. She kissed him and very efficiently made a nest for him on the sofa, using one hand.

'When will you come back?' Instantly, Will's face had lost its confidence. He and Mary, Daisy more so, wore the anxious faces of orphans.

'When I can,' she said. And though the words in themselves were not much comfort, still they were part of a familiar ritual of departure, and as such, less changeable than the woman who said them.

'Come back soon,' Will urged, sorry that he had been hard on her.

'Soon – soon,' chanted Mary, casting her eyes in the direction of the surrogate, who was making the reassuring sounds of household activities: the fridge opening and closing, the washing machine running, the clatter of dishes. Mary walked over to Alison and asked her for a drink. Will reached for his book and held it, his eyes trained on his mother as she left the room.

'Mummy?' he called.

The door reopened and she looked at him with – was it a touch of irritation?

'Nothing,' he said. 'Don't get tired.'

'I won't.'

Bella called out to say that she would be home the next day, so Alison knew she could have her day off.

Will waited for the sound of his mother's car turning in the driveway, but it was long in coming. He saw the sunshine pour across the stone tiles and settle on the glass vase filled with the first pink roses and the last of the lilac. She had been so happy the other day, working in the garden. It was something she never did, though he seemed to remember when he was very small, her growing vegetables and placing them in his hands. Now the roses that she'd cut from the white fence were fading, the petals falling one by one, the lilac turning grey. It was summer, but it filled him with melancholy. When they went to America, he would not be able to do all the things that he

112

normally did in the summer: the fishing trip with Russell, the visit to Cornwall to stay with his paternal grandparents, with whom he went sailing once a year. In their cottage, he could look at the pictures of his father as a boy and a young man and that last one, with his mother and father smiling at one another in the deck of a boat, her hair blowing behind her in the wind, his hand on her shoulder. He loved this picture so much that he wanted to steal it. Each day he was down there he took the album out quietly and stared at it. Once he had tried to trace it with some very thin paper, but it hadn't worked. He would not have time to go down this year, because in a few weeks – unless she really did change her mind – all this would be gone. This house would belong to other people, his room be turned over to strangers. He was particularly sad because for a short while he'd felt that perhaps they would not go, after all. But they would. Now he knew it. She had made up her mind. Stoically he sat there, trying to prepare himself for this blow, listening at the same time for the sound of her car.

But he waited a long time because Bella was not in her car. She was on the telephone, ringing the numbers that he'd rubbed off the wall.

Chapter Twelve

Will heard his mother's key in the lock and saw her go quickly up the stairs. She was in a very altered mood and went straight to her bedroom, where she stayed for a long while. Finally, she called Will and Daisy and sat them down beside her on the bed, one on each side.

She said, firmly, 'We are going to go away from here, to America. I've thought about it and there's nothing to be done. We will have to do our best to be happy there.' There was something about her that was defeated, yet she seemed filled with a fierce determination. Now Will knew it was done and that it must be faced. Daisy hardened a heart that had already grown flinty on the eruptions it had endured.

Mummy is being so sweet, Will thought, even to Daisy who she usually rather ignores. He fled from this observation into the pleasure he saw in his sister's face as their mother spoke. He was a bit puzzled; his mother seemed quite unconcerned about the hospital, even though she'd sat him down so carefully the day before to explain how busy she'd be finishing everything before they went away.

'A person has to finish well,' she'd said.

'But if you're not going back?' He was thinking how in his exercise books his work deteriorated and was a mess by the end.

'Particularly if you're not going back. How you finish is how you'll be remembered. It's more important even than starting well. You can't make one mistake . . .' and here she'd been silent for a moment, and pale, '. . . everything must be done as near perfectly as can be, every single thing you do – or it must be done again and again.'

When he asked her now why she wasn't at work, she brushed the question aside. He was grateful. She was putting them first; she was taking the trouble to explain to them why they must leave behind them everything they were used to.

114

She was taking them on a journey around their house, as if she too needed to begin the process of leave-taking.

From one room to the next they went in a little procession. She showed them the old wicker cradle they'd slept in as babies. It was down from the attic, ready for shipping.

'Every time', she said, 'a new baby came, I would make new linings for the inside of the cradle. I used to think I already knew the person who was coming, so when you were born, Will, I put in pale green silk, which has always been your favourite colour, and scarlet for Daisy.'

She laughed, her attention drawn to an old Italian globe, painted with rich dark colours for the land and cobalt for the sea. 'Will used to turn that round and round and I used to show him where his father had gone, though he was too small to understand.'

As they walked on, looking at all the things that had been in their house as long as he could remember, Will remembered his grandmother taking him to church. 'These are the stations of the cross,' she'd said, as they'd walked from picture to picture. So it seemed to him now, walking with his mother, from one room to another, saying goodbye.

'Why are we keeping all these things?' Daisy asked.

'It is our only immunity,' she said.

The children looked blank.

'It is the way we remember who we are,' she said, 'when everything around us changes. These things, belonging to us, to our family over the centuries, they remind us who we are, they keep us safe.'

'I know who I am.' Daisy said quietly. 'Don't you?'

Her mother looked startled. 'One day, Daisy, these things will belong to you and to Will and you will be glad to have them.'

'Not to Mary and Harry?' Daisy asked quickly.

Her mother walked on, saying nothing.

But it was spoilt for her now, for with the names of the other children, it was as if another presence haunted these rooms, other memories hovered in the evening air waiting only for her departure to take up a different, darker elegy.

115

'Daisy!' Bella said sharply. 'That was not very nice. It's unpleasant not to want the other children to have these things too.'

Daisy moved closer to Will, who said, 'Mummy, please.' His voice pleaded, but it also had an imperative quality.

'Come on,' she said, 'you're tired, it's time for bed.'

The children both knew that the journey had ended and they did not cavil.

Much later, when the house was sleeping, a lonely figure could be seen climbing the last flight of stairs to the top of the house, where Bella had her study. Rebecca had left this till last. She was afraid to be here at all, creeping about in the dark, but she had to do it, once, before everything was taken away. Now she opened the door; moonlight lay on all the surfaces. It was a barren place, a place of books and files. The only personal things – and it was a great shock to see them here – were some bottles of sand that William had collected in far-flung deserts and the big, beautiful stones he'd hauled back from the East. Behind these most intimate symbols of William's life, Bella had actually placed a photograph of Jack playing at a concert at the Royal Albert Hall. Rebecca remembered Jack's short but brilliant career; all her life she'd wished for just one day when she could play as he could: one day of excellence. 'A nice hobby,' her mother had said, 'but you do not have the ability to be first-rate, so please return to your studies.'

It was strange: she had simply to re-enter any of these rooms, even this most private one, and her life returned to her. Each room had its own integrity. Some were more faithful than others: the kitchen, and the bedroom where she and William had slept together, they stayed true – these places of the deepest living. The drawing-room had gone over to Bella, as had the dining-room and the conservatory, where Rebecca's sprawling, undisciplined plants had been replaced by an extravagant display of orchids, in blue pots, their black, inflexible stems breaking into blooms as lush as clotted cream. She thought quickly: the garden will always be mine. Then she knew that this was nonsense since Bella had the power to do away with it all. Their days were numbered here. She had to accept it, she must go wherever Bella went because she could not suffer another separation from her children.

116

And so she began to trail about, knowing that when the next spring came other eyes would see the honeysuckle break free of its dead tangle, the powdery roses embrace the white fence, the wisteria make its tight bunches of purple buds – and she wondered if the house would remember her. Would the sun look through the windows at the places they had lain together? Would it seek out the children and find them gone? When their colours had vanished from the walls and their breath from the corridors, would anything remain to prove that they once lived there?

She could not bear it. Perhaps nothing of her had gone on in her absence either? Everything she had tried to do to keep Bella away from the hospital had been a ridiculous attempt, she saw it now, to buy a little more time for herself. But why should she stoop to steal a little time here, the odd day there, to be with her children, when that other person took all the time she needed to devote herself to what fulfilled her most in life? These things must change. She saw for the first time that the enemy lay within, in the way she accommodated Bella and denied herself. She would do it no more.

Chapter Thirteen

'A man is just a beast, after all,' Joseph said out loud, looking around him at the chaos of his London quarters. Not that they were slovenly, far from it. But what man would stoop to make his bed, or buy milk for his breakfast, or activate the washing machine, until the last lonely sock looked up at him from the drawer? These were simple things, they had no importance. He could do them if he must but they had no importance. If the wheel of life turned, it was only because a woman's hand worked it; remove that hand or find it engaged elsewhere, and the wheel stopped. Was this a matter for remorse or celebration? If the hand that turned that wheel was stiff with rage in the doing of it, then that hand must let go. But of course, and he smiled ruefully, there was damn little satisfaction in this state of affairs for anyone – man, woman or child. There was an impasse between men and women and he wondered whether it would ever be cleared.

Then the phone rang. He was reluctant to answer it because there were three unanswered messages from Susie on it, and one from the prison. He wished to avoid both. He was on holiday, after all. When the six rings stopped he could hear Susie's voice barking petulantly at him, demanding his attention. He snapped the machine off, then, remembering something, he rewound the tape.

The day before, Bella had called him. It was why he was feeling rather chipper this morning. Some instinct, following his realisation about Bella on his way back from the prison, had made him tape their conversation. Now he played it back.

Bella, with a low, laughing voice; Bella sounding far removed from the remote and shaky individual whom he had seen and talked to in the garden a few days before. He noticed that his own voice had put on a cloak, to hide his pleasure and curiosity that she'd called.

118

'How are you getting on?' Joseph asked.

'Oh fine, things are improving slowly.'

'Worked off your feet at the hospital?'

'Oh, I'm managing.'

'Hands cleared up, have they?'

'What?'

'Nothing.'

'No, what are you talking about?' So authoritative was the voice that he obeyed.

'Your hands, after all that gardening, you'd really cut them up quite badly.'

A pause.

'I was merely', he said carefully, 'enquiring as to their health.'

'Oh, I see.'

There was a significant pause.

'Well then, did you come up with anything I could do for you?'

'No.'

'That's a shame. I'd like to help.'

'Thank you, but everything's organised.'

'You can do it all yourself, eh? Don't need any help from anyone?'

'Something like that.'

'So it's all done then?'

'Not quite, but the house is almost empty.'

'That must be rather depressing.'

'No, not really.'

At this point he had realised that she wanted to get off the phone. She'd learned what she'd called to find out. He heard himself rally as he said, 'Why did you call, Bella?'

'Oh, just, you know, to thank you.'

He hesitated. 'For all my back-breaking work in the garden, you mean?'

A pause, then, slowly, 'It was kind of you.'

'No trouble at all.' He wanted desperately to point out her blunder, but restrained himself. Instead, he had seen a way of manipulating her difficulties and, at the same time, finding out for certain if she had any recollection of their meeting in the garden.

119

'Well, I hope you haven't forgotten your promise to me.'
Now, as he listened, he saw the ugliness of his behaviour
towards her. What could she do but bluff, or lie?

Her voice, with just a tremor of uncertainty, 'What promise
are you referring to?'

He heard the cockiness of his voice as he said, 'To come
to my house in the country?'

She was playing for time now and asked casually, 'Where is it?'

'Gloucestershire.'

'Oh yes, of course.'

'You remember our conversation, then?'

'Of course.'

His voice now rose with pleasure. 'You're not a walker,
by any chance?'

She laughed and said, with cool, wry humour, 'Not a
serious one; I don't have boots.'

He felt she was strong enough now for him to go after her
without equivocation. 'So you'll come then? This weekend? As
you agreed?'

She was thrown. '*This* weekend?'

'Yup.'

'Oh,' she breathed, 'I'm not sure *that* much gardening could
have been done.'

He laughed, enjoying her. But her voice had changed. 'I'm
awfully sorry, I'm afraid I can't possibly, you see, I'm behind
with things, I have operations scheduled this weekend . . .'

'Can't be done,' he said blithely. 'You promised me and you
do owe me.' He enjoyed the fact that she could not know what,
if anything, she'd promised. 'Bella, you do remember our time
in New York, don't you?'

'Driving to New York, you mean?'

'Yes. And you'll remember how we enjoyed one another's
company. All I am asking for is one day, Saturday, to get to
know you a little better.'

Surely, he thought, she'd refuse outright. He didn't understand her hesitation. Some part of her wanted to come.

'Go on, do come, it'll do you good.'

'Well, it's difficult, I've been rather recalcitrant at the
hospital lately.'

'Oh really? That's not like you.'

'No. But it's why I have a heavy case-load now.'

'Be a devil. Cancel them, do them next week. You work too hard.'

'What are your motives?' she asked sharply. 'It's not me you're thinking about, is it?'

A pause.

'No, you're right. But think of all the rows we can have, isn't that a good reason to come – a chance to straighten each other out?'

She laughed. 'All right, on those conditions, I'll come.'

This was said in so level a way that he was disarmed.

'I'll collect you early on Saturday morning. Clean your duelling pistols.'

'Would I allow them to get rusty?'

'Not a chance. I'll see you just after dawn. Goodbye.'

He now felt sorry that he'd put her on tape like that. She was right: he was a lot more threatened by her than he'd imagined. Trying to force her out into the open had made him do the same to himself. He began to wonder seriously about his motives.

The phone rang again. It was Susie, complaining bitterly now. He told her that he would not be seeing her again, that their arrangement must come to an end. He waited for the full squalor of her personality to emerge. Instead she said quietly, 'I think it was a little more than an arrangement, don't you, Joe?'

'You're quite right, it was and I apologise for minimising it.'

'But all the same' – her voice was sober – 'whatever it was, you want it over with, am I right?'

'I'm afraid so.'

'Hm.' She was quiet for a full minute and then she said: 'What is it, d'you think, that makes me feel you might be in love?'

'Me? In love?'

'Yes.'

'What ever makes you think that?'

'Well, for one thing you always told me not to throw you over until you'd found someone else.'

He laughed. 'How true. And, well yes, I have, as a matter of fact.'

'Have what?'

'Fallen in love.'

My God! He couldn't believe it. He'd actually voiced it.

Chapter Fourteen

Unfortunately, Bella was unable to keep her arrangement with Joseph. On Thursday afternoon, while playing on the common, Will and Daisy disappeared.

Alison had waited until dark before sounding the alarm, because the common was a place where the children played every day by themselves. But supper came and went, and she went out to look for them – in vain. Bella drove home from the hospital and informed the police. She was advised to contact every person she could think of who might know their whereabouts. When this proved fruitless, she answered questions at the police station until she was white with tension: _of course_ she had thought of everything, looked everywhere. She drove up and down the familiar streets until the phone's magnetic pull drew her home again – only to be disappointed. She settled down to a vigil by the phone. Alison sat huddled in the only chair still unboxed, speechless with misery. Finally, she dared to ask, 'Do you think they might have run off because they don't want to go to America?'

'Of course not.'

Bella couldn't bear to be in the same room as her and paced the kitchen until three in the morning. Walking around the rest of the house was upsetting: the walls were marked with dirty squares where pictures had hung, the bookshelves were empty, the floors bare. Without her things the place had lost all beauty and serenity. But she couldn't sleep so the pacing went on. Finally she went to the top of the house, where she noticed that all William's possessions had vanished. She hadn't packed them because she was going to throw them away. Will never entered this room so it was not he who had saved his father's things. She did not have the strength to be affected, and pushed it behind her.

The next morning she was haggard and incapable of making a decision. She thought to go to the hospital; surely work would distract her? What was the point in hanging around at home, wasting vital time? She could be back in half an hour, the police would call the second . . . But then, how could she possibly concentrate? How operate with her nerves like this? She had a repeat bypass to do, it would be tricky. But it would be still more tricky if she cancelled again . . . And if they came home and she wasn't here, what then?

As she sat trying to juggle these options, yet coming to no conclusion, Alison watched her with amazement. Here was a woman who made decisions with the speed of a dealer on the stock exchange, a woman incapable of hesitation, one who knew precisely where her duties lay and went to them. Now Alison watched her as she dressed for work, got into her car and started for the hospital only to end up roaming the streets around her house, returning home hours later, having failed to get there. Then she made several rushed calls to her secretary and got her to swap round theatre time so that the bypass could be done as she'd promised. Bella set off again and reached her destination. She performed one operation and cancelled the second. She had a furious row with a neurosurgeon who infuriated her by saying: 'Take a grip of yourself, doctor,' in the most pious of tones, so that she could happily have taken the scalpel to his throat. Her rage disturbed her. She was out of control and did not know how to right herself.

But at least at the hospital she could achieve something. At home she had simply to wait and it drove her to distraction. The police had begun their search of the area, but would not specify how thorough it could be. 'Early days', the sergeant kept repeating. Another officer suggested that the children were 'probably having a whale of a time, hiding in a friend's attic'. He would not understand that Will wasn't capable of such stupidity. Alison kept hearing Bella mention Will's name, never Daisy's – it was as if she had forgotten the girl entirely. This disturbed Alison, as did the fact that Bella had taken to carrying Harry around all the time she was at home.

By the end of Friday there was still no sign anywhere. Now Bella's mind was venturing, in spite of her resistance, into dark areas. She could not rid herself of that story in the papers about the child-molester who was attacking children on their way to school. He had still not been caught. And there was a photograph of a lost child's face that had hung so long in the Post Office that it had faded to transparency. Didn't these things always end with a mutilated body dumped a few miles from the child's home? In her terror, she began to search the tip where broken furniture was abandoned, the long grass under the deserted stand of trees, the junk-yard behind the closed garage. Finally, she became obsessed by the pond in the middle of the common, but did not have the courage to ask the police to drag it.

That night she spent up on the third floor packing all her medical books with a hopeless urgency: where was the point? How could she plan to go anywhere now? And yet the shippers were arriving on Monday. If she did not do it now, when could it be done? Besides, it kept her busy, it stopped her from imagining. And if she waited? But if she continued, believing they would be going in ten days, then, surely, she tempted the gods to prevent her?

The books were packed. Light streamed through the small windows onto the dusty floor. A woman sat there, motionless, so possessed by her thoughts that she did not feel the hours pass, nor even the edge of fatigue. Her eyes were wide and staring and they seemed to see from a very high point. At dawn – a beautiful blue dawn with the sun making the leaves sparkle on the trees – she walked out of the house with the slow tread of a sleepwalker and made her way to the common.

Chapter Fifteen

There is an island in the middle of a large pond on the common where fishermen wait and ducks fly. It is overgrown with trees and ivy, honeysuckle and reed. The soft, muddy edges of the island are treacherous, making it virtually impossible to stand there without sinking up to the knees. There is also something forbidding about the place; it does not tempt children to explore it. It simply lies there with its moat of thick brown water, and now and then a duck will rise out of its dark centre, or the geese will land on their way to a more agreeable habitat. It has danger signs posted, but no boats sail the pond, as it is neither large nor appealing enough.

As the sun rose, a woman walked across the emerald turf of the West Common. She walked straight ahead, crossed the main road and continued with slow, regular steps. As she neared the pond, she stopped and seemed confused. The place was deserted: no fisherman sat on the cement path, no dog ran after a stick; so quiet was the pond that it seemed as though all the wild birds had deserted it.

For a long time she stood there, her eyes trained onto the circle of land in the centre of the pond. She could not walk on. The sun rose higher and released a little heat. It would be a warm day. She wondered what day it was, she seemed to have lost track. She walked to the edge of the water and looked across at the island, her expression fixed. She could not leave the spot and sat on a bench, waiting. She put her hands over her eyes and bent her body down over her knees until her face rested on them. She seemed to hear the sound of chimes in the wind, far away.

Slowly, her face lifted and its expression changed: the eyes dulled by fatigue and strain grew bright. She rose quickly from the bench – so quickly that she stumbled. She began to run. Then she stopped, hesitated, looking behind her at the pond for a moment. It seemed as if she was going to call out but could not do so. Whatever it was that she tried to do, she could not. She gave up and ran very fast, looking like a frantic girl, across the road, the West Common and on, not stopping until she reached her door.

Chapter Sixteen

She was horrified to find, parked outside her house in his car – Joseph.

He rolled down the window and said, 'I do hope you haven't forgotten. We said just before seven.'

Reluctantly she had walked closer, so now he could see how breathless she was and how flushed and hectic her face. He said, with his particular mixture of humour and irony, 'D'you always run so fast? That was rather violent for jogging.' Then he stopped because now he had really seen her. He got quickly out of the car and went to her; she backed away.

'Hey.' He took her arm. 'What's the matter? What's happened?' He put an arm protectively around her and felt her slump. He led her into the house.

In the kitchen, Alison was staring at a cup of tea. She moved quickly towards Bella, startled by her expression.

'Did you,' she began, frightened, 'did you find anything?'

Joseph looked from the woman to the girl in confusion. 'Will someone please tell me what's going on here?' He looked sharply at Alison; of the two she seemed rather more in control of herself.

'The children,' Alison said dully, 'or at least Will and Daisy, have been – I mean, they've disappeared.'

'Since when?' Now he looked at Bella.

'Thursday,' she said, in an odd dreamy voice, moving over to the window.

Joseph realised that he was going to have to deal with Alison. He put out his hand. 'We've not been introduced, but I'm Joseph Sunderland and you must be Alison.'

'Yes.'

'Could you be a dear and make Bella a cup of tea?'

Alison nodded. She was balancing on a thin line, trying not to cry. 'Do you want some?'

'Please.' He smiled at her encouragingly.

'Bella,' he said, as if he spoke to a child, 'please come into the other room and tell me exactly what's happened and then we can see what to do.' His voice calmed her for a moment and then she brushed him aside. She pulled herself up and spoke in a voice that he noticed was both rational and overwrought at the same time.

'We must get a boat,' she announced.

Her demeanour was so odd that he began to reconsider: was he in fact dealing with an hysteric? He had dismissed this prognosis in favour of another, before. When she made for the door, he grabbed her arm none too gently. 'Hey – where are you going?'

She stopped and, in an instant, her manner became passive. 'I need to get the boat,' she said quietly.

'What boat? And why?' Now he stood facing her, holding both her arms; but she was unlikely to resist him.

Alison came into the room with two cups of tea. She said quietly, 'There's a boat in the cellar. Bella said she didn't want it packed with the other things down there.' Alison's blue eyes, wide in her round face, were reluctant to leave Joseph's. They regarded one another for a moment. 'It's a rubber boat,' she said.

'Would you mind getting it?' he asked.

Alison shook her head. She opened the door to the cellar and he could hear her feet as she went down the stairs. Still Bella said nothing.

'Now Bella,' he said gently, 'why do you need the boat?'

'To fetch them,' she said, her voice so low and sweet that he was startled. He noticed the loveliness of her face: her long, almond-shaped eyes were dark and troubled, her skin was very pale. She reminded him of someone and then he knew why: she had the same madonna beauty that he'd first seen in Margy's house and had not seen again until this moment.

The phone rang. She ignored it. He wasn't able to so he picked it up, listened for a moment and then handed her the receiver. 'It's the police.'

'Don't tell them anything,' she hissed with a sneaky look on her face. She took the phone reluctantly. 'No, no word. Nothing. No, I can't think of anything else. Of course. Thank you.' She replaced the receiver and stared ahead of her as if she had no idea what to do next.

128

'Bella,' he said patiently, 'you need the boat to fetch whom?'

She turned wide eyes on him. 'The children, of course.'

Aware that he'd begun to speak to her rather as if she were a lunatic, he now asked, matter of factly, 'You know where the children are?'

'Yes, of course I do.'

'I see.' He was calm. 'Well, why didn't you tell the police?'

She smiled gently at him, as if he were simple minded. 'I can't tell them anything yet,' she said. 'I must fetch them first.'

Alison appeared at the door with an inflatable boat. 'I couldn't find the oars,' she said.

'They're in the corner, under the stairs,' Bella said. Then added, with a frantic note, 'Get them, get them quickly.'

Alison caught a sympathetic look from Joseph and nodded. 'Okay.' In a minute she was back and gave Bella the oars.

'All right,' Bella said in her normal voice, turning to Joseph. 'Will you come with me?'

'Of course.'

'We can drive some of the way.'

They walked outside and he put the boat, the oars, and the woman in the car.

'I'll show you,' she said.

'Now,' he said, once safely behind the wheel and driving, 'perhaps you can explain all this to me?'

She said, 'I'm sorry it's all such a mess. I hope I'm not holding you up?'

His head jerked in her direction. Then he was surprised that he could still be surprised by her. Clearly, she had forgotten the weekend plan. She ran her hand through her hair, which was falling out of the pins that held it in place at the back of her head. She shook it loose.

'Just tell me what's going on,' he said wearily. It was all a bit much at eight in the morning.

'It's hard to explain,' she said, looking down. 'I don't think you'd understand.'

'Try me.'

'Can you turn right here, then right again at the end?'

He did so.

'May I explain later?' she pleaded.

'By all means.'

'Because we're here.'

They made their way to the pond; the place was deserted. The boat took a long time to inflate and he struggled with it. It was not the time to ask questions; her concentration had become utterly focused and, though she had asked him to come, he felt superfluous.

'I'll have to get them one at a time,' she said, putting the boat on the water. He looked across to the island.

'I presume they're on that island?' he said, containing his need to blast her with questions.

She nodded and started to get into the boat.

'Can't I go? I'm not sure you should do it . . .'

She shook her head vehemently and got in, finding her balance quickly. He held the boat so that she could not leave. 'You *think* this is a place they might have gone to – or, do you know they're here?'

She looked at him. 'I know . . .' she began, '. . . what I mean is, it's a place Will went to once when he was unhappy, ages ago, so I just thought he might have gone there again, with Daisy.'

'You took a long time to think of it.'

'I . . .' she hesitated, then looked him straight in the eye, 'I haven't been myself,' she said quietly. Then she moved back in the boat. 'Now, please, let me go.' He was obliged to let go of the boat because she pulled so hard with the oars. She turned her face up at him; it was sad, even innocent – the face of a girl who could not fairly be pushed beyond her limit.

He stood, watching the boat move swiftly through the water. She handled the oars well. He wondered if he'd made a mistake. He felt concerned, even responsible. She was unstable: why on earth had he let her go? She was nearly out of sight, rounding the bend of the island; he walked quickly round the pond to follow her progress.

He saw her get out of the boat, holding on to a log to steady herself. Evidently she'd known exactly where to land. He wished yet again that he hadn't let her go, but knew that he couldn't have gone with her – or without her, for that matter. He watched anxiously as he saw her stumble. Her legs were covered in mud. Soon he couldn't see her at all; she had disappeared into the trees and he thought, inexplicably, I wonder if I'll ever see her again?

She made him feel that there was no fixity in her, no reality at all. She was, at that moment, like someone from a place that existed only in memory; someone who didn't inhabit the world as he knew it. She was impossibly evasive and strange and yet, seeing her gone, he felt quite forsaken.

Chapter Seventeen

Sitting on the grass with his knees pulled up, Joseph tried to work out what was going on: was the story about the children a fantasy? An elaborate ruse? He remembered with relief that the police had called; they must have believed her. Surely the children couldn't possibly have been left alone, all night, in that dark tangle of trees? *Had* she known they were there? That was ridiculous, too. And then it came to him coldly: of course, she knew they were there all right. Because she had put them there. Then it made complete sense to him: it was bizarre, but quite logical.

He waited for quite a long time. Two fishermen had taken up positions on the other side of the pond, close to the road where his car was parked. A tall woman walked a labrador. His eyes returned repeatedly to the boat, to the island. It was as if he expected both, at any moment, to disappear. Nothing happened: he grew hot and moved over to the shade. Half an hour passed, then an hour. He reached the point where he felt angry enough to leave, but suspected this might be the design behind her delay. He waited more out of stubbornness than devotion. He would wait all day, all night, if necessary. He was going to see this thing through to the end.

Perhaps she suspected as much, because some minutes later she could be seen entering the boat, helping Daisy in, balancing the boat and then setting off. Will stood back in the trees; he made an outline both still and forbidding as he watched them row away. Then he lifted his arm and held his hand up for a moment; seeing it, Joseph felt an excruciating moment of empathy with the boy's loneliness.

As they moved closer, very slowly, Joseph got up and walked across to the water's edge. The boat drew up and he helped Daisy out. Her face was stiff and unhappy but indomitable as well. Bella, with a quick, 'Daisy, wait here,' went back to her rowing. She had glanced at Joseph briefly, that was all. Now, she seemed to send Daisy a quick, silent warning and he saw that there was complicity between them.

He felt sorry for the child who stared after the boat.

'Hello, Daisy,' he said. 'I'm Joseph, a friend of your mother's. Are you all right?'

She surveyed him with what he'd once thought was her mother's frankness, then nodded in reply to his question and turned, very slowly, to look back across the water, where the boat made its journey to the island once more. Her back was eloquent with her refusal to converse with him, her gestures so deliberate that he wondered if they were voluntary.

People now strolled across the common; a few took up sunbathing positions, though it was hardly warm enough. An old man fed the ducks. He turned to Joseph and said, 'People aren't supposed to go there, you know,' jerking his head at the island. 'It's prohibited.'

'Really?' Joseph said, disliking the fellow.

'Accident on there once,' the man said in a monotone.

'What kind of accident?'

'Don't know.'

Joseph looked away, but the old man said petulantly, 'She's not supposed to go there.'

Joseph ignored him. Soon, he walked off, muttering, and began to repeat his message to the next person he encountered.

'Daisy,' Joseph said, 'how long were you on the island?'

She turned to face him. Did he imagine it, or was there something guilty about her expression?

'Since Thursday.' She stared straight ahead.

'All by yourselves?'

'Yes.'

'Where did you sleep?'

'There's a hut.' Her eyes returned to the water and to the boat that rounded the curve and came into sight. It seemed to him that she was mesmerised by its occupants.

'I suppose', he began doubtfully, trying to shift her mood, 'it might have been fun?'

Daisy regarded him with a penetrating and off-putting stare.

'Pretty stupid remark, eh?' he said.

He saw in her expression a precocious ability to calculate and to take risks on it.

133

'It wasn't fun,' she said calmly. 'We had to do it.'

'Why?'

'Because Mummy asked us to.'

He breathed out slowly. 'So it wasn't your idea – or Will's?'

She ignored him.

She was a daunting child and he was beginning to feel intimidated by her: she was on her guard, or under orders; he did not feel that these rigours were her own. He asked softly, 'Weren't you frightened? At night I mean?' She turned just her head, so that he saw but half of her face and the angle of her cheek. When she spoke, her voice was very remote. 'We know how not to be.'

He imagined then the rituals of these children of Bella's, the forms of comfort, their means of dealing with separation, loss and anxiety. Her back was a testament to her loyalty. Slowly – it seemed to him too slowly – the boat came through the water. At the bank, Will climbed out and helped his mother. He pulled the boat out of the water and made to deflate it.

'It's okay,' Joseph said, 'I'll do it.' The boy looked exhausted; there was a cut on his forehead and his trousers were soaked up to his knees with black water.

It was as if Joseph had not spoken, did not exist. Will continued until the boat was flat and took it up. Joseph watched him carefully, summing him up: Daisy had been aloof, but Will would give him no quarter. He felt his determination quicken: he would find the source of this hostility and overcome it.

Bella's exhaustion was obvious. The quietness of the children bothered Joseph: it wasn't healthy. It had none of the elation one would expect after an adventure, nor were they chastened. Their emotions were too complex for that. He felt that they were bound by obedience to their mother and could not break free from her power. It could be this that made the boy so enraged; it might indeed have nothing to do with Joseph's presence in Bella's life.

They trooped in silence to the car. He walked in front, Bella and the two children behind him. They had closed ranks, these three; a deception tightened the already too-tight bonds between them. One of them was in need of protection from the others and that person must be Bella. Without understanding the meaning of it all, the children would abide by these rites.

He drove the short distance to their home. No one spoke and he did not try to lighten the atmosphere, as he would normally have done. He felt threatened, but he would not allow himself to be chilled out of existence. He could feel the deadly stuff of her detachment; he would watch it carefully for clues.

He followed her into the house. He even let Will struggle with the boat and the oars by himself. When the telephone rang in the hall, Bella walked straight past it. Alison, with the two small children seated before bowls of cereal, looked up quickly. She didn't see Will and Daisy and said, 'The police keep calling.'

Will and Daisy, walking into the room, rushed headlong at Alison. It was the first spontaneous and childish gesture Joseph had seen from either of them. Bella left the room: the noise from the kitchen seemed too much for her. He heard her pick up the telephone.

'Yes, I'm sorry. Yes, that's correct, they are both back home now. Quite safe. No, nothing. I'm certain. Of course I'm certain. I happen to be a doctor. Thank you. On a sort of camp on the common. Yes, I know, but it only occurred to me as a possibility early this morning.' She attempted to laugh, which only revealed the extent of her strain. 'Yes, apparently they did. Yes, both nights. Yes, officer, I too am sorry I didn't think of it before. No. I said, no. He's just not that sort of boy.'

Her voice could be heard in the kitchen. Will's spoon, laden with cereal, was put down in his bowl. His eyes were large and cold as, very deliberately, he turned to look at his sister. Daisy returned the stare. Hearing her mother say coldly into the phone, 'Yes, as you say, messing around,' her eyes held her brother's, demanding his co-operation. There was silence now, in the hall and in the kitchen, and then Bella's clipped voice could be heard again.

'No, I told you: there is *no* trouble at home. This is hardly running away – just a childish adventure.'

Will had got up and moved to the doorway; he stood there, unsure what to do – to go and help her or to keep out of it.

Joseph closed the kitchen door; Bella's voice faded. He turned to Will and said, 'Now, listen to me, Will, you're not responsible here.'

'I don't know what you mean.' Will was surly, but not closed.

135

'I mean that things are going to be all right. This is not something you have to handle alone. Okay?'

He turned to the children in the kitchen and smiled. 'Your mother is under a lot of strain: she's pulled in so many different directions that sometimes she doesn't know what to do. We have to help her.' He was looking at Alison, attempting to encourage her because she too was snared in the web of loyalty, fear and silence.

Will had returned to his cereal, with his eyes down he began to eat as if he had not heard. And yet Joseph was certain there was relief, some slight easing of tension in the room. As he walked into the hallway, he heard Alison say quietly: 'Thank you.' He turned to her and said, 'Alison, I'm going to take care of Bella this weekend. She needs to get right away from everything and everyone. Can you take care of the children?'

'Oh yes, yes.' Her relief was obvious.

He knew that some small measure of trust had been established between Alison and himself, between the two elder children as well. It was slight, but it would do for now.

Walking out into the hallway, Joseph heard Bella say, 'Look, Officer, I'm grateful for your concern, but it's misplaced.' A pause. 'Yes, I realise you have to check everything. I'll come in, but right now I need to see to my children. Yes, of course. Goodbye.' She put down the receiver. The anger had been seeping out of her voice as the conversation approached its conclusion. Seeing her as she stood there a moment to gain breath, he knew that she was a woman who had been pushed way beyond most people's endurance. His curiosity about her had been replaced by compassion. She stood quite still. She did not cry. Voices rose in the kitchen. Alison reprimanded Mary; Harry was yelling. Bella heard all this and it was as if she could not bear it another moment.

She walked quickly to the front door, opened it and stood there, close to the wall where he had written his telephone number among the roses. She leaned against the doorframe and gazed out at the small front garden, raking her fingers through her heavy hair. He sensed some very strong emotion in her and couldn't approach her because of it. But then she turned, feeling a presence behind her, and saw him. Her eyes narrowed in disbelief. In an instant, she slammed the front door and ran like an animal up the stairs, up and up, her body angular and ungainly in its movements, her feet loud on the bare wooden stairs. He found that he was responding without thought or understanding as he ran up the stairs after her.

Chapter Eighteen

By the time she had reached the third floor, he had almost caught up with her. She ran into the study and slammed the door, pressing her body against it. He threw his weight at the door and she was knocked backward, only regaining her balance against a stack of packing cases. They stood there, watching each other.

He thought that this look of hatred and fury stemmed from the time when people cloistered themselves in caves. He moved forward; her hands formed into knots, but she did not retreat from him. She looked at the end of her wits, but she also looked as though she would rather kill him than be confronted by him. He needed to disarm her: he sat down on a packing case, at a safe distance. Breathing a little more easily, they both took up new positions.

'Bella,' he said gently, 'the game's up.' He waited. She watched him. He thought he saw some regret in her features, features he was now studying very carefully, knowing he must read every expression correctly. Then she turned slowly and walked to the small window. With her back facing him, he was shut out.

'Why don't you tell me?'

She gave a low, dark chuckle; it was rather horrible, he thought. Her voice snapped back, all its vitality restored. 'You're not my shrink, you know.' Then she turned to face him. 'And you may as well be certain that I will never play the female patient to your psychiatrist.'

'Ever been to one?'

'No, never,' she said, 'apart from when I was a child.'

He noted the ambiguity.

'You're going to have to tell me,' he said. 'We both know it.'

She turned to look at him with a face full of scorn and disdain.

138

'I have to nothing,' she said. 'You are only here because I allow it.'

'And why do you allow it, if not because you need me?'

She laughed and he felt the lash of her indifference.

'I?' she said coolly. '*I* need you?'

'You?' his voice mocked. 'And who are *you*?'

She winced. 'You know,' she said, 'so you don't need to be told.'

'No, I don't need to be told. But what I need to know is why.'

'So you haven't spoken to her?'

'Her?'

'Rebecca.'

He repeated the name softly, then said, 'I have spoken to her, but I didn't know her name.'

She dismissed it. 'Rebecca's unimportant.'

She crossed her legs and said lightly, 'It isn't so very remarkable. I suffer from amnesia. Lately it has become a great strain – at work and at home.' She looked away. 'I'm tired,' she said vaguely, 'I don't know why.'

'It's probably', he said, 'at least thirty-five years of fatigue. How could you not be tired?'

She said flatly, 'Everything catches up with you in the end.'

'What exactly are we talking about?'

She began to run her hand up and down the spine of a black leather diary.

'The past, I suppose.' She leaned forward so that her face was in shadow.

'Do you both suffer from amnesia?' he asked.

The change in her face was immediate and stunning.

'Oh, clever, clever!' she hissed, like a trapped and spiteful child.

He smiled. 'You are Rebecca, I presume?' As she moved to speak, her mouth clapped shut as if someone else had closed it. Rebecca was gone.

'We don't need you,' Bella said, 'leave us alone.'

'I see,' he said, 'so there is some solidarity between you – if only in times of mutual threat?'

'We don't need you,' she repeated slowly, her tone menacing.

He leaned forward and said earnestly, 'Bella, you have to trust me. And you have to give over a bit, for once in your life.'

139

She was up and furious. 'And why should I trust you?' she spat out. 'Why should I give over to you? So you can put your boot on my neck?'

He was startled. 'Have you never trusted anyone?' he asked.

She laughed. Then, abruptly, her voice lowered and she said: 'Who should I trust but myself?'

'How would you know if you've never tried?'

'And I should trust you?'

'Why not?' He knew why not even as he asked it. How could she be perfectly in control – which she absolutely must be to survive – if she was drawn to a man? Sexuality and love would deprive her of everything she had spent her life creating. She could take a husband in order to have a child, but then he must be disposed of.

'Are you cold?' he asked, seeing that her shoulders were hunched over. Her face buckled with a concentration so intense it appeared to hurt. He was reminded of her behaviour in the nursery and touched her arm. 'Bella,' he asked again. 'are you cold?'

She shuddered but did not reply. Then she lifted her face. It was softer, as if she had just woken from a long sleep. The change was so remarkable that he could not fail to recognise her. 'Rebecca?'

She smiled sweetly. 'Now you know who I am and you won't be confused, like before, in the garden.'

He breathed out with relief. She smiled and tilted her head to one side, as though she was flirting with him.

'And,' he began cautiously, 'where is Bella now?'

She put up her hands with the palms facing him, in a small, theatrical gesture of dismissal, like a conjurer.

'Gone!' she said brightly.

She looked at him and smiled in a way that made him uneasy. 'I can explain, if you'd like. Bella would rather die. That's why I made her go just then. You won't get anything out of her.' Again, that warm look. 'I like you. I'd like to help you.'

'I like you, too,' he said.

'Oh, good.' Her face seemed to be gaining strength, her character coming forward in small but noticeable ways.

'And,' he added quietly, 'I like Bella as well.'

'Oh.' Now she sulked.

'I'm sorry,' he went on quickly, 'I didn't mean to interrupt you. Please – you were going to tell me. I want very much to understand.'

She weighed him up for a while, then she sat on the floor. 'How dirty everything is.' She took a piece of cardboard and sat on that.

She uses her body quite differently, he thought, so much so that it could be a different body. She doesn't have Bella's grace, but she has an earthy, sensual way with her. So altered was this personality that the face shaped itself into new mannerisms; the voice changed quite distinctly, it was as if he was now listening to a recording of Bella. The longer he spent with her, the more she became herself, the less she seemed to be the person he kept thinking she was. It was a peculiar feeling – like a hand wiping away an image, slowly but steadily, until it was gone. He didn't like Bella gone. It was why, seeing her assert herself before, he'd said 'I like Bella as well.' And it had worked: she had retreated for a moment, as if even the name of Bella could reduce her.

'There are two of us, you see,' she said, leaning back just as she had done while sitting on the grass in the garden that day. He said nothing but saw that she watched him stealthily from below her lashes – something, with its overtones of sexual pandering, that Bella could never do. 'There always have been, from before I can remember. Bella was there first, or she says she was, and then I came.'

'Does it make a difference who was there first?'

'Oh yes.' She smiled. 'It's why Bella is stronger. She's the one who has always known everything about both of us.'

He began carefully. 'You have memory lapses?'

'Yes, and she didn't. So she always knew what was going on and I was always confused.'

'Is it still that way?'

Rebecca smiled triumphantly. 'No. Now she's the one who doesn't know what's been going on! I make her go away, then I come and do things, and she doesn't know what I've been doing. Like in the hospital, I can create havoc for her.' She laughed.

'So now, she too gets amnesia?'

'Yes.'

141

'Do you know why that should be?' He sounded calm when in fact he was afraid that she would go and he would be left to try and fathom this out by himself. The mechanics were extremely complicated: how did two people, with very conflicting desires and totally different personalities, manage to live together in one body? He felt ignorant and out of his depth; it was such a rare disorder, one that had only recently begun to get serious medical attention. He knew he could not manage to understand it without Rebecca's help.

'No, I don't know why,' Rebecca said simply. 'Don't you know?'

He laughed, taken aback. 'Me? No, I don't know. Were you hoping I would?'

'I suppose so.'

'Well,' he smiled, liking her better now, 'we'll just have to help each other muddle through, won't we?'

'Do you remember', she asked eagerly, 'asking Bella whether she'd been to a shrink and she said no?'

'Yes.'

'Well, that was because it was me who went, not her. That's the way it works – do you see?'

'A little.'

'Before' – she was anxious to explain – 'I wouldn't have heard her say that – I wouldn't have known about it.'

'Do you hear all the conversations, or just some of them?'

'Just some. It's not so much hearing as remembering them. Some I remember, some I don't.'

The room had acquired the hush of a confessional and he tried to understand why, once again, she had chosen to make him her witness. It had been Rebecca in that odd experience in the nursery with the chimes; now, it was Rebecca who was calling out to him. She had taken charge, she had swept them both – all three, rather – onto new ground. He wondered if it was an act of faith, or mere desperation?

This woman before him now – was she a broken Bella? Or her true self? Who was the primary personality? And on all those different occasions – who was who? Which was which? At the brunch, surrounded by children – was that Bella or Rebecca? How quickly could they intercept each other?

It was odd, but now that he was being offered some explication he wasn't sure that he wanted it. Each side of

142

her character, revealed in fragments over the past weeks, had intrigued him; each view of her was seductive in its own way. Were her moods not so diverse, her character so complicated, her range so large, he might just have lost interest in her. As it was, she had everything, was everything one could want from a woman. The question was: what had brought her to such an extreme? Something or someone had driven her so hard that she had broken in two.

Out of this had come both her predicament and her solution. How simple and brilliant: in one body she could contain and control all the forces in her nature and, at the same time, develop them to their fullest expression. A life deprived of nothing. No wonder she had no feminist rage or resentment: she had risen above everything. His admiration was steeped in pity: she had reached a point where she was exhausted and could no longer proceed with even the vestiges of normality. She was at war with herself.

Rebecca had not said anything for a while. She sat with her hands open and flat on her knees; it was the gesture of a supplicant. He was touched by these hands, these first pointers to her secret, by the roughness of the nails and the delicate, chiselled shape of her fingers.

'Tell me what frightens you,' he said.

She smiled. 'I was always frightened of her strength, now I'm frightened of her weakness. She didn't even know . . .' her voice rose in agitation, 'that I took the children and hid them.'

He frowned. 'Yes, why did you do that?'

She spoke frantically. 'I thought I'd given up and she'd won – she'd take them away. I went round the house with the children, I told them we'd have to go. I'd given up and faced it. And then, suddenly, I couldn't. I knew I'd be locked up in the dark again for years – sometimes getting odd glimpses of them, but never being with them. I thought,' she ended dismally, 'I could break her with the children, make chaos at the hospital – and then maybe I could take over and we wouldn't have to go.'

'Yes, I see. But then of course', he smiled, 'she managed things, she held together and so you had to come back and get them.'

She nodded.

'Are they all yours – the children?'

'Of course not. Just Will and Daisy.'

'And the other two?'

'She had them with Jack – to prove herself as good as me.'

'So who looked after them, when you'd gone?'

She responded with a rush of impatience. 'She did. She had to, she wanted to. She wanted everything that I had. That's why she got rid of me.'

'But still, you see . . .' he touched her hand, 'I still don't see why she would want to do these things to you.'

Her face was fierce with scorn. 'Because she hates me!'

'Can I ask why she hates you?'

'Oh, it's too long and I'm too tired.' Her head dropped for a moment. Then, as he watched, up came the face and down came its shutters, and she said, with a strange mixture of secrecy and coquettishness: 'She didn't want me to go away with you.'

'Who was it on the phone?' he asked. 'Who phoned me?'

'Oh, that was Bella. She wangled the number out of Daisy.'

'So you saw that happen?'

'I don't see it, I just know it.'

He was relieved: he felt sure it had been Bella, but he had to be sure.

'But we will go, won't we?' she said, putting her hand on his arm.

He stared at her. 'But, surely – you won't want to leave the children, will you?'

Her shoulders slumped. He had trapped her: she had tried to forget them, she had wanted to go with him, but now, how could she? He was ashamed of himself; he had done it deliberately because he did not really want her.

She knew it. She turned on him savagely and yelled, 'You want Bella, don't you? Just like William. You think she's more exciting, more clever. Well, you can't have her. I'm here and I'm staying. So get out of here. Go on – get out!'

He did not get out; he waited. In a little while, she lifted her head, slowly she smiled. And what a chilling smile: cool, quiet as a room when the trigger has been pulled.

Watching her, he knew that her calmness was an extreme form of passion: ecstasy beyond excitement, a feeling so

144

powerful that it peaked all sensation. It gave her the ability to act and then escape, without panic, fear or guilt.

It was Bella. Bella looking at him and knowing she had to get rid of him. She'd swatted Rebecca like a fly; now she would turn on him. Still he said nothing. She stood there, waiting for him to leave. But he stayed. He stared her out and then he said, 'Coming with me then, Bella?'

Chapter Nineteen

But although it was Bella who accompanied Joseph to Gloucestershire, she was not his only visitor.

He took her to the house his parents had come to after their marriage, and wondered why he had brought her to a place that was private and particular to him; she wondered why she had come. They stalked one another's thoughts, but for the time being there was a truce. Watching one another warily, they took care not to expose their backs too often. But they both knew that they had linked arms and taken their positions: killers on the dance floor, neither knowing who would strike when the music stopped.

He soon learned to read her face. It was an instrument that she played to perfection. It was the eyes that spoke most eloquently, registering pain and confusion, innocence, childish fear – and then, a monumental ego would emerge: arrogance, wit and ferocious intelligence. At other times, something sweet and damaged came into her eyes, and with it a sense that she was looking for some escape from the web that she had created. Sometimes, if his questions probed too deep, or if he refused to let her duck behind a dishonesty, he would see something click behind her eyes. Then it was that he knew she would stop at nothing to protect the world she had so ingeniously constructed for herself. And which she clearly felt was under threat for the first time. She was right – for he wanted those walls down, those turrets broken to bits and the roof blown off to let the sunshine in.

Bella was exhausted and yet she would not sleep. Finally, Rebecca agreed to take a sleeping pill. But even as she reached to put the pill to her mouth, her other hand knocked them to the floor. And there was Bella, furious to be forced into something against her will. It was only when she agreed to get some rest that the pill was actually swallowed.

When Joseph came back, some hours later, he saw that she slept soundly. He sat beside the bed and watched her, hoping that some truth might surface in her face when she was not fully conscious. But he was touched by the vulnerability and sweetness of the face on the pillow and, not wishing to be trapped further by sentiment, he left the room. Once away from her, though, he felt unsafe and he ended up in the small dressing-room beside the bedroom where she slept. His feelings were as unstable as she was, weaving back and forth, from compassion to coldness, from reluctance to love.

When she woke, she came quietly across to where Joseph sat reading. He saw her come, but didn't look up. She stopped about a couple of yards from him and he could see her naked feet, long and delicate as were her hands.

'Joseph?' Her voice had altered. It was softer and she spoke more slowly. She gave a serious, repentant smile. He closed his book and saw her glance at the title: *The Poems of Robert Frost*.

'I don't want you to think . . . I mean, it isn't always as bad as this.'

'Meaning?' He gave her a hard stare.

'Meaning, all this coming and going – so fast and so often. It is seldom this way with us.'

'That's a relief,' he said coldly. 'Though I can't imagine that either of you could endure it for too long. I felt myself to be going round the bend after a couple of hours.'

'There is a reason for it,' she said with the same anxious need to explain.

'And what's that?'

'It is a struggle for supremacy,' she said simply. 'It happens whenever one of us is going under. She is fighting to stay alive.'

'Isn't that a trifle dramatic?'

'No. Not if you consider that she could be gone for years and years and maybe, one day,' her eyes opened wide with fear, 'one day, one of us might be gone forever.'

'It's not quite correct, is it, to blame Bella for this desire for supremacy? You, if I understand it correctly, are seeking that position at the moment?'

'That is true.' Her hands were held behind her back and she looked the very essence of virtue.

147

'I'm not sure that your motives are any more noble than hers,' he said firmly.

'We both want what we want.' And then she turned her face full on him and said: 'You are no different. You made me lose my footing this morning, in Bella's study, when you made me feel guilty about the children. You were trying to get rid of me.'

'Yes, I was, and it is not something I feel particularly proud of. But I think something else was going on there too.'

She was a little startled. 'What?'

'I think perhaps when this guilt comes, when you're pressed to take care of your children and don't wish to, then, rather conveniently, you cease to be sweet motherly Rebecca and you yourself pull out selfish Bella to get what you want.'

She breathed out quickly, as though he had winded her. 'We both use each other,' she said. She walked away, as if to look at the fabric of the curtains.

When she walked back, she said, 'How long have I been sleeping?' It was a signal that she had had as much of what she called his 'shrinking' as she could take.

'Oh, only an hour or so.'

She pushed her hand through her hair and asked: 'Where is the bathroom?' He was about to say that he had already shown her, had taken her over the entire house when he realized that that had been Bella. He took her to the nearest bathroom and then went to look out of a narrow window at the long gardens he had played in as a child. Later, he went downstairs to make some coffee.

It was here that she joined him, her face shiny and bright, her hair loose about her shoulders.

'It's a beautiful house. How old is it?' she asked, running her hand along the unplastered brick wall.

'Sixteenth century.' He poured the water on the coffee grains.

'Did you live here as a child?'

'My family has always lived here.'

'Always?'

'For as long as the house has been here.'

'Oh, I see.' His curt way of speaking distressed her and she said coldly: 'How nice to have such a long, uninterrupted family line – no disruptions, no – '

148

'Are you Jewish?' he asked quickly.

'My mother was.'

'I see. They are both dead, your parents?'

'Yes.'

'And the rest of your family . . .?'

'Only my mother survived the war.'

'I see. Well, let me tell you a bit about my family then, if you would like to hear it.'

'Oh, yes, I would.' Her face was round with pleasure and she listened very carefully. She was benevolent now and that disturbing ambiguity of her features, which was sometimes so marked as to be repellent, had vanished. She was curled up in her seat like a cat, wearing a different dress from the one she had arrived in. This one was loose and flowing, with a small print on the cotton. He found himself wondering which of them had done the packing.

After the coffee, she announced that she would like to take a walk. Outside, in the open air, she was carefree. Mile after mile they walked, she keeping up with his swift pace with no difficulty, talking to him about Switzerland where she'd gone climbing as a child. The haunted quality had left her; some of his questions seemed to confuse her a little because she did not remember certain times of her life, but he did not probe or push her. She talked about her father who had died of a heart attack when she was eleven. He wondered what bearing this might have had on Bella's choice of profession, but did not ask her about Bella at all. She had regained her composure and, a little to his surprise, Joseph found that he felt quite at home with her.

Joseph accompanied her down to the village shops, and she took great pleasure in buying baskets of food, which she insisted on cooking for him; she cooked easily and well, liking to do it. He noticed that her hands now had the brown, baked look of hands that chopped onions and thyme, stirred stews and kneaded dough. They seemed to have lost any association with the scalpel. She bit the nails of one hand, her left one, and this nervous habit touched him. The sunshine and open air were bringing her face to life and she looked healthy, even strong. It was now much easier for him to treat her in a normal, even affectionate manner.

149

An uncanny instinct in the hidden side of her sensed this affection. Like the flick of a switch, Rebecca was gone. He could very quickly recognise each of them now. Neither had any control of their facial expressions because these were automatic, a result of their emotional state. They both knew this and would sometimes try to dupe him, by turning their backs or moving into a dark corner of the room.

Once, when they'd swapped back and forth too quickly for him to keep track, Joseph was irritated and grabbed Rebecca's arm, swinging her body round so that he could see her. The angry, alert face of Bella looked back at him.

'I know why you did that,' he said unpleasantly. 'You thought I was getting a bit too close to Rebecca, didn't you?' He pushed his face closer to hers. 'You thought she was going to blab, perhaps?'

How smooth and lovely were the lines of her face and how calm her low voice when she said, 'What's the matter with you? Who is Rebecca, really? Some victim of yours from the past?'

He was thrown, but would not take up her implication that he personally was involved in the process of duplication. Instead he took her words at face value and said, 'So, you don't think Rebecca's real – is that it?'

She shrugged lightly. 'Perhaps she's just a fantasy of yours.'

For a second, he actually began to doubt the whole thing; to question his own perceptions, his own involvement in this strange triangle. Until he looked into her eyes and saw that she was laughing silently at him. He made himself laugh; she continued to watch him.

'Bella dear,' he said acidly, 'perhaps we should go back into the kitchen and finish the dinner that you were so dutifully cooking for me?' He hoped that this would flush her out. But she continued to cook the roast lamb as if, indeed, she had been doing it all along. Everything was perfect, even the chocolate soufflé which was only half-concocted when she'd got to it. He was impressed by her composure, even though he felt she used it to spite him. Her dissembling amused him: she had no idea where anything was kept, whereas Rebecca had got to know the layout of his kitchen. He would not help her. He asked, mockingly, how someone with a steel-trap memory like hers couldn't remember where the electric beater was kept. She replied that she had little memory for domestic

150

trivia. 'You mean you only remember the big things? Like a patient suffering from dementia?'

She smiled. 'Precisely.'

He had not unsettled her; in fact, she would put him in his place whenever she could. He was beginning to enjoy her immensely: the antagonism had gone; this was intellectual flirting, but of a very high order. It was hard to score a point off her, even under the circumstances.

'No mercy, eh, Bella? Is that understood? Equals: fifty per cent each way or nothing?'

'No mercy,' she agreed. 'Equals, if you can manage that.'

By now he was too fascinated by the phenomenon to accommodate it. What he really wanted to know was whether the two of them had been doing this nightmare dance always – surely they couldn't coexist for any length of time? They both seemed pretty familiar with it – even quite good at it. Did one dominate for long periods while the other went underground? At least that way some semblance of normality could exist for at least one of them. He came to see that the present see-saw was what neither could bear, whatever their familiarity with it.

They sat down to dinner. He noticed that she'd discarded Rebecca's vegetables and started again, chopping them differently, cooking them very quickly. He did not comment on this, nor on the fact that she'd changed out of the print dress and now wore a sleek blue one that made her seem much slimmer. Her hair was up, every strand in place. She ate less than Rebecca, but talked more.

She got him to converse in a way that was new to him, without rhetoric or striving for effect. Having led rather an academic life, he was, he knew, somewhat pedantic. He couldn't be that way with her because she was too interesting. There was no time to affect a pose or make a pretty speech because the flow was too swift, the currents too deep. They kept up with one another. She analysed the world the way she saw it with ruthless precision. She scrutinised every remark that he made and threw his defences right back into his face. Talking to her was like breathing oxygen.

Then, to his intense annoyance, the supply was shut off. Her voice slowed, her interest faded. In a little while, Rebecca was back. 'Bella was getting tired,' she said.

'I didn't think Bella was getting tired,' he said.

'Nobody thinks Bella gets tired. They think she can just go on and on and on, doing what they want her to do. Nobody sees Bella.'

'Except you, I suppose?'

'Yes, I see her,' she said quietly, 'but I use her too.'

'But just then you didn't, is that it? You cut in to save her from becoming over-tired?'

She smiled. 'I wanted to see you,' she said.

He laughed. 'Could you see us?'

'Only a little.' She seemed a bit downcast. 'I wish . . .' she began.

'What?'

'Oh, nothing.'

'No, tell me.'

'I just wish my education had been better, that I knew more.'

'But, think about it, your brain was educated in exactly the same way as hers, so . . . why not?'

'You don't understand,' she said, forlorn. 'I could never get it back, it's lost – to me, it's lost. I would have to become Bella to have that.'

He was quiet, surveying her. She understood what he was thinking.

'No,' she said, 'I would never do that. I'm not her, you must not want me to do that. It's not possible.' She looked away. 'It would be the end of me.'

'Rebecca,' he said gently, 'you have to believe that your intelligence is just as keen – in fact, it is the *same* intelligence – so if ever you wanted to use it, to learn something, it would be just as good for you.'

'When we were small,' she said, 'and Bella was so tired, when her mind was thin and worn out, I'd come and help her.' She smiled. 'Then Papa would carry me upstairs and make me lie down in the dark. He put some lovely, delicate chimes just outside the window so that when the wind blew they would sound like little bells. He used to say, "Just listen to the chimes, don't think of anything any more, just listen, let your mind sleep until it is better."'

He smiled, understanding her better. She said, 'We've often looked after each other; it's not always like this.'

'No, I suppose it couldn't be. Would you mind talking about it, or would you prefer not to?'

'Why should I not want to?'

'Well, earlier, I felt you didn't want to talk about Bella. Why was that?'

'Because she wouldn't let me.'

'She can stop you?'

'She makes my mind go stiff and dark when I want to tell you something.'

'And now?'

'Now she's tired so it will be all right.'

'What's made her tired? Talking to me?'

'No! Of course not!' Rebecca had a way sometimes of looking at him as if he were rather dense. 'She's tired because of me.'

'Forgive my stupidity, but why?'

'Because she's not used to having me around.'

'Ah ha. So it's new, your being around like this?'

She explained patiently, 'Yes, I've just come back.'

'Well,' he laughed, 'I didn't know that, did I? How long were you away?'

She frowned. 'I don't know, only she knows. But years.'

'*Years?*'

'Yes, she had things to do.'

'And when *you* had things to do?'

'Then she went away – if I made her.'

'So you *can* make her, too?'

'It's what I'm doing now.'

'Yes, of course.' He felt a fool. 'Of course it is.' He got up and paced the room; he was beginning to feel exhausted. 'This won't do, will it?' he said. 'You can't go on like this.'

'No,' she agreed sadly, 'we can't.'

He sat down again, close to her, and said, 'Tell me though, what would happen if you did manage to go on like this?'

'I hate that,' she snarled, 'I hate the way you have of not caring for either of us, just wanting to know – just peering at us, like freaks or something.'

'I do care,' he insisted, 'but how do you think it is for me? I don't know your history. I don't want to behave like a bloody psychiatrist, but there are certain things I have to know, to be of any use to you, to either of you – to all of us, for Christ's sake.' He added, 'I don't understand it.'

'No one does,' she sulked, 'except Bella.'

153

'Well I don't intend to be one of Bella's puppets and I do intend to get her to help,' he said with some determination.

'No,' she said softly, 'you'll have to forget about Bella. She's going away for a long, long time.' But, seeing he didn't like her tone, she quickly reverted to being agreeable. She needed an ally so badly that she was prepared to make a deal. 'If I let Bella out again, will you tell her to go away and leave us alone?'

'I can't do that. She wouldn't do it. She does what she wants.'

'You won't even try?'

'Look, Rebecca, there are times when Bella won't even admit that you exist.'

'She doesn't?'

'No, she doesn't.'

Rebecca looked crushed.

'She doesn't want me to know that there's anything wrong with her, so she keeps shifting her ground.' He wasn't above manipulating Rebecca, so he added, 'It's probably a measure of how threatened she must feel by you at the moment.'

She looked at him with that wide-eyed stare. 'Do you think she's frightened of me?' Instantly, she put her hands up to her temples as if in some pain, said, 'No,' loudly, and left the room.

He thought that that last remark had probably been too much for Bella, and he was right: Bella came back into the room a few minutes later. But she was altered, seeming forlorn in rather the way that Rebecca had been. She barely had the energy to coil her hair up with her fingers, but this she did manage. He let her be and she seemed grateful. A little later, she went to bed.

On Sunday morning, it was Bella who came down to breakfast. She looked much rested, but was still quiet. They read the papers and talked a little. Rebecca made no appearance. He was waiting for a chance to get through to her, but she gave him no opening. He began to think it would be better to be direct, as she so often was, and just ask her to explain how she saw herself. But even in her quietness she had great authority, and to intrude on her was difficult. She seemed so confident of herself and her world that to ask her to explain her place within it seemed ludicrous. She would look up from the paper and catch him

154

weighing these things up, and even her smile seemed to say, don't be absurd.

But she was tender that day. He wondered if she could be thinking of him the way he'd come to think of her. Often their hands touched, in the kitchen, or out on a walk, or he caught her watching him with a look that seemed to be considering him. The quietness between them, the way the day flowed, the landscape outside the stone window, the house which, for him, had always seemed a perfect place – all these things had a sensuality, a sense of waiting, a different, exquisite suspense.

He imagined that Bella might be frightened. Rebecca had suggested it and surely, in some sense, they must speak for one another. Bella was used to being completely in charge; now she was not. It was one of the first indications he'd had that she couldn't be suffering from any schizophrenic disorder. No schizophrenic could manage a life like Bella's; they had the greatest difficulty handling a single existence. The essence of such conditions was disorganisation. Bella lived a life of hyper-organisation; it was an astonishing feat of the human mind.

Sometimes she seemed too composed; sometimes, in what she thought were unobserved moments, she looked sad. In trying to understand her, Joseph found that he was, for the first time, paying serious attention to the dilemma of women in general. All his ranting against the opposite sex, all his disappointment in them, was swept away by her predicament.

She said that she would like to spend one more night there, away from everything. They telephoned Alison: the children were fine, though Joseph suspected that Alison herself was upset and would need a proper explanation before long.

They went to bed early, in their separate rooms. Joseph fell asleep immediately. His dreams were vivid and frequent. Once he woke and thought he saw her standing by his window, looking over the pasture. Once he thought her heard her laugh in her sleep. Much later, close to dawn, he woke again, feeling the most extraordinary sensation of dread. In his dream, he had been choking to death and Bella had been watching him, wearing that homicidal smile she'd worn in her study. So strongly did he feel her presence that he reached out across the sheet and there his hand encountered her silk robe. For

155

a moment, he wondered if she'd tried to smother him with it. Then he fell asleep.

Some hours later, when the sun was shining brightly onto his face, he got out of bed, folded the blue silk robe with a smile and wondered what it could mean. The disturbing quality of the night was dispersed and he went downstairs happily, expecting to find her in the kitchen. It was empty, as was the room she had slept in. Nowhere in the house was there any sign of her presence; it was as if someone had carefully wiped away all trace of her.

Chapter Twenty

Joseph did not go after Bella. The weekend had upset him badly. He needed time to think, and come to terms with the extent of his own involvement with the two women. Most of all, the reason for it. Joseph had never been drawn to a woman of any instability before. And here he was, deeply implicated in the lives of two such women and he had to admit it, almost obsessed by the more treacherous of the two. Bella, for all her outer control, was the more disturbing and the more disturbed. Bella had her own, unique morality and it had nothing to do with society.

Rebecca had loved and needed her husband, William, according to her testimony. Bella seemed to need no one; she had only a biological connection through her children. So how had she dealt with Jack and even with William? How far would she be prepared to go to eradicate any impediment that might hold her back? Bella had made it perfectly plain that she wanted no interference from Joseph – and yet he wasn't convinced. Even in her dealings with him, there was a deep ambivalence. Over the weekend there had been many occasions when she seemed tender, needful even, concerned about him and the direction of his life. And then she'd vanished. And the robe in the bed, preceded by that awful feeling of suffocation in his dream, what had that meant?

By the next day, he could no longer keep away. He returned to London and in the late afternoon he went to her house and knocked on the door, not knowing which of them would appear.

The door opened and a tall woman stood there, a woman with red, curly hair and very pale skin. For a moment, he felt he was losing his mind: was this another personality? He was too startled to speak and took a step backwards, to make sure he was at the right house. But there on the wall, among the roses, were the fading traces of his handwriting. He looked at the woman again.

'Can I help you?' she asked, in a voice with a lovely Highland lilt. She had moved to one side so that he was able to see past her into the house. The Victorian tiles on the floor were now covered with carpeting, a long table stood where a small chair had been; the smell of the house was different. He closed his eyes for a moment.

'Are you all right? Would you like to sit down?'

She had ushered him in and now he was able to see packing boxes stacked in the drawing-room, crumpled newspaper on the floor and the unmistakable disorder of someone moving into a new house.

He shook his head. 'No,' he said, 'my mistake, I'm sorry.' He backed away. Nervously, the woman closed the door. He stood there a moment longer and then walked away. Yes, he did remember her mentioning, vaguely, that the shippers would be coming on Monday to take the last of her things away. And also something about having to stay in a hotel for a day or two – things she had mentioned only in passing. Why had he not paid more attention?

Seeing a stranger in her house had been a shock. Finding Bella gone was worse; it was confirmation of a feeling he'd had about her from the start: she could vanish without a trace, leaving him with this eerie sensation that perhaps she did not exist at all. He returned to Gloucestershire and stayed there until it was time for him to return to America.

Three

AMERICA

Chapter One

Soon after arriving back in America, Joseph endured another of Margy's brunches. Cornering her in the kitchen, where she was making her excellent scrambled eggs, he tried to pump her for information.

'I don't know what you're asking me, Joseph: did you two have something going or something? You didn't? Well, I can't imagine this is professional interest: that woman hasn't a brain cell out of place. Ah ha! I can see by your face: you're bitten. Is that it?'

'Margy, please, can we keep this conversation on track? What can you tell me about her husbands?'

'I need to know why.'

'Why d'you need to know why?'

'Because she's my friend.'

'And I'm not?'

'You're a man.'

'Oh spare me your bile, Margy!'

'Hand me that knife over there, will you?'

'Here. Now, just tell me what you know, don't be such a pain in the arse.'

She sniffed. 'I don't know much. I need to know where you're coming from to be of any use.'

'Margy,' he said, covering his eyes with his hand, 'that really is an absurd expression. Just tell me what you know.'

She threw the eggs in the pan. 'I only knew the second one. Jack: classical pianist, very good, drunk, depressive, committed suicide.'

'I could do better at the police station.'

'Well, what d'ya want me to tell you? The guy stank. He was brilliant but unstable.'

'Why a pianist?'

'Why not?'

'Well, where did she meet him?'

161

'I dunno.'

'Does she like music – opera?'

'Not to my knowledge, wouldn't have time. Would you mind chopping that parsley? Thanks.'

'How did he commit suicide?'

'Fell off a ten-storey building.'

'You don't fall if you're committing suicide. You jump.'

'Sure. Well, maybe he jumped. Who knows? He was plastered, anyway.'

'Was she there?'

'Don't think so. They had separated by then. She'd had it with him.'

'Why would a woman like that marry a drunk?'

'Women marry all sorts of creeps.'

She turned her head to acknowledge the impatient voice outside the kitchen. 'All right, Otto, I'm coming. Can you just get the bagels? Sorry, Joseph, I can't tell you any more. Why not ask her?'

'Is she back?' He felt an exquisite moment of anticipation – and blocked it.

'Sure. I asked her to come today, but she's too busy with the new house. Hey, you helped her get that place, didn't you?' She smiled approvingly. 'That was nice.'

'Thanks.'

A bit later, Bella's friend, James, arrived with his wife. For some reason, Joseph found the sight of him infuriating. What could Bella see in such a specimen? Certainly, his face was handsome and his hair well groomed, but his eyes were vacant. He had that look of a boy so prevalent in the American male: something unformed, even backward in his emotional development, as if it had stopped at high school.

James dominated the proceedings. He was giving a lecture on money: old money with class and political power – and new money with purchasing power in the world of traders and money-changers. It gave a repulsive little glimpse into the workings of a certain kind of mind. Then James and Otto began to discuss a scheme of Bella's, one that Joseph had not heard about. She had, so James said, wanted him to get together the financing for a heart-centre she wanted to create, using new technology and a new wonder-drug that was almost through an eight-year scrutiny by the FDA.

162

Joseph could be silent no longer. He heard his voice roar out across the gentle clatter of cutlery. 'There's too much money in this country being allocated to the wrong thing, drummed up by venture capitalists like yourself, with an eye on their own future health problems. You get corporations to donate vast amounts for cancer and heart research when hundreds of other causes don't get an iota of your interest and certainly none of this superfluous cash.'

'I would have thought', Otto put in mildly, 'both those areas are very worthwhile. Sure, maybe we're all covering research into diseases we're likely to get' – he gestured with his fork – 'eating all this butter and egg, but heart disease kills half the people in this country.'

There was a murmur of relief; Margy passed round a little more smoked salmon. Joseph continued in an even tone.

'Heart disease, and cancer for that matter, are already getting more funding than just about everything else put together. Meanwhile, you have prisons splitting apart at the seams, no money to build new ones, half of the black population below the poverty line and thousands of the mentally ill roaming the streets because there's nowhere else for them to go. Are you saying, Otto, that these aren't worthwhile areas?'

The silence was most uncomfortable, but no one would address the question. Joseph left in disgust. Margy pursued him to the door. 'Look here, Joseph, you don't fool me. I've never seen you like this before. If you think we all stink, then you shouldn't come. What's your problem? James has really got to you, hasn't he? You think he's got something going with Bella? Don't be dumb, she wouldn't give him two cents' worth. Maybe you should tell me what's up with you two?'

'Nothing.'

'So – maybe that's the problem, then?'

'Do you think I'd let a woman like Bella get to me?' he asked.

'Sure. You look and sound like a man who's done for.'

The phrase had a most unsettling effect on him, but he managed to pull himself together sufficiently to kiss her on the cheek and apologise.

'Don't worry about it,' she said lightly. 'You've probably just succeeded in making them put more in the cancer kitty next time!'

'Tell Otto I'll give him a call.'

163

He had to go to California and Texas to visit state prisons and speak to the inmates and officials in each. He was appalled by it all. How could there be any improvement in systems so steeped in frontier justice? He thought of D.H. Lawrence: 'The essential American soul is hard, isolate, stoic, and a killer.' In Texas they told him that, in their lore, there was a defence for homicide that ran like this: he needed killing.

He was impatient with his work, its slowness and what he felt was its intrinsic worthlessness. He would produce yet another report that would be applauded, read and discussed. It would accomplish nothing. He then met a woman at a colleague's house who was so obsessed with gender and women's studies that all his old gripes came back as if they'd never been in remission. He began to quarrel with her, to everyone's delight, particularly the men's, until his temper got out of hand again and he roared at her, 'You have the sense of entitlement of a three-year-old. D'you think all you have to do is moan and bitch and peer at your own organs to have the world fall into your grasp?'

'You are . . .' she gasped, 'the most violent human being I've ever come across.'

Joseph was dismayed by the violence surfacing in him. He was not acquainted with his dark side, it was just that he had never felt it so close. He knew that it was not possible to study evil without living it to some degree, but something maleficent was out. Surely, it must have something to do with Bella, or rather, with his disappointment about her. He didn't like it. What on earth had persuaded him to believe that he'd rehabilitated his bitterness towards women, anyway? The woman at dinner didn't deserve such an attack. What had he done but confirm her opinion of the brutality of his sex?

But after this battle with a puny intellect, he found he was longing for Bella's copious mind and wicked tongue. He had to check himself yet again. He'd decided, at home in Gloucestershire, and again after seeing her empty house, that he must heed her symbols. She had gone. He had been turned away from her house by a stranger. The woman was telling him: it is over, it is done. And yet, hard as he tried, he could not put her out of mind. He decided that until he could, he would not get rid of his rage.

Chapter Two

At one o'clock in the morning, his phone rang.

'Who is this?' he demanded.

'It's Rebecca.'

His disappointment was intense.

'It's me, Rebecca,' she whispered. He felt that she was making the call on the sly and expected to be interrupted at any moment. 'Joseph, I have to see you.'

'What for?'

'Please. I can't tell you on the phone.'

'How did you get this number?'

'I pretended to be Bella and asked Margy.' She added softly, 'She even suggested you might be glad to hear from me.'

'I am not.'

'Oh, I see, oh dear, I . . .'

'Rebecca, just spit it out, what's the problem?'

'It's too complicated. I need to see you.'

He hesitated. 'When?'

'I don't know, do I?' she hissed angrily. 'I don't know when I can get rid of her again.'

'Well,' he said nonchalantly, 'I'll be here for the next two days and then I'm going to Chicago.' There was a long pause. 'Rebecca?' He waited. 'Are you there?'

'No, she's not,' said a low, modulated voice. 'Please ignore all that nonsense; Rebecca's not been feeling very well lately. She gets these silly ideas at night when she imagines I'm asleep.'

'Well, well, well.' He laughed softly. 'How lovely to hear from you, Bella dear. Tell me, why didn't you just slam down the phone? Do you have a reason for wanting to speak to me, after your very rude departure in England?'

'I just wanted to tell you,' she said, 'that it really would be better for everyone, including you, if this thing goes no further.'

'Ah, so you are the one who makes all the decisions, are you? – not just for Rebecca, but for me also. I think that's a little preposterous.'

'You would, because you would prefer to be the one who decides things for us. But that is not the way of it.'

'Well, the thing is, Bella, Rebecca has asked to see me and I intend to do just that.'

'You don't want to see her,' she said. 'You must not use her to get at me.'

'Careful,' he warned, 'the ice is pretty thin on the question of use.'

'Joseph,' she said, 'you must understand, this is not a personal matter. I have nothing against you, I wish you no harm, I just have to do what is best for us. Rebecca is very frail, she could not manage an involvement with you, of any kind. But she will get stronger if she can enlist your interest and help – and you do see that I cannot have that.'

'Oh, I do indeed see that! Very much so. But you can't count on my help there. You're on your own with Rebecca. And so am I.'

'I see.' She could not hide the despondency in her voice.

'Rebecca,' he urged, 'you –'

'Bella,' she corrected him.

'How silly of me. Bella, you really must not try to block me out. I think I can help you – oh, I don't mean shrink you, I know just what you're thinking and how much you loathe all that. I just think we need to be together, to find out . . .'

There was a shriek of pain on the other end of the line and then a plaintive voice said, 'Oh, why must you do that? Why does she stand in front of me so that I'm invisible? Joseph, please let me see you.'

It was no good, he was impossibly entangled.

'Of course, Rebecca, come any time you like. I'll be here.'

Chapter Three

As soon as the line went dead, he changed his mind. He did not want to see Rebecca. He wanted to get out of the whole ghastly mess. No good could come of his involvement. He would have to see her one last time because he'd agreed to it, but then he'd get out. Unasked and unwanted, he'd barged into this delicately constructed paper house. He had looked at these women with scientific curiosity, using the frailer half for his own ends, and now was angry and on the retreat because he couldn't take charge. Well, he had more control of himself than that.

He waited for Rebecca the following evening feeling tense and angry. She did not come. His resolutions peaked, fell and rose again when, on the following night, she still did not come. He was both disappointed and relieved: he had a meeting in Chicago the next day and would be gone for a while. Destiny had for once taken a constructive hand.

At seven o'clock the next morning, as he was dressing, the bell to his apartment rang. He picked up a shirt and went to the door. In the corridor stood Rebecca, very straight and tall, her face calm, her eyes wide and dark. He knew immediately that she was uncomfortable to see him half-dressed and quickly did up the buttons of his shirt. She walked in and sat perched on the end of a chair, her knees close together, her hands in her lap.

'I'll make some coffee,' he said, turning down the music on the stereo.

When he came back, she was smoking a cigarette.

'I thought I'd take it up again,' she said. 'People don't smoke as much as they did last time I was . . .' Her voice trailed away. She turned to him and smiled. 'I like Handel so much,' she said.

'Do you know much about music?'

'Oh yes.'

He sat down beside her. 'The coffee needs five minutes. So why not tell me what the problem is?'

'I'm sorry', she said, 'to bother you like this. I can see you're going to work, but it was important.'

'Important for you,' he corrected her.

'No,' she said softly, 'for you, too.'

'How so?'

'Because you want it.'

He leaned back and spoke with authority.

'Rebecca, we must be straight about all this. The fact is, I've behaved badly. So has Bella, in my opinion. Our relationship has suffered reverses and I think it would be better to call it a day.'

Her face had the most vivid, distressing way of reacting to pain.

'Well, I see . . . I . . . '

'Look, you came here because you needed my help. If I can help, I will, but I want to make it plain that I can't afford to get involved. Professionally is one thing, privately is another. You must see how difficult it would become to separate the two.'

She laughed, a little scornfully. 'Oh, I do see how difficult, yes, I do. But you see, I did think we were involved, were friends.'

'Of course we are.'

'But you are putting me out.'

'Oh Lord! Rebecca, listen, I am simply trying to tell you that I do not trust my own motives in all this and I do not want to make life any more difficult for you – for both of you – because of that.'

She smiled. 'I understand.'

'Don't accommodate me,' he said sternly.

She laughed. 'Oh, you do think you're wicked, don't you?'

'I have not been behaving too well of late.'

'Yes,' she said, as if it did not surprise her. 'The thing is,' she said quietly, 'you're in a bit of a tangle.'

He sat up.

'Yes, you're in a tangle,' she said slowly, 'you want to be involved with Bella, but not with me.'

'I have no desire to be involved with Bella,' he said, rather too loudly.

She leaned back and surveyed him for a long time, making him feel decidedly uncomfortable. He directed his attention to the coffee instead. She continued to smoke, slowly.

'Perhaps you should tell me what's been going on,' he said. 'What made you telephone me?'

'I had no choice,' she said simply. 'Who else could I turn to?'

'Because I'm the only person who knows?'

'Because you're the only one at all. I am in America and I am alone.' She looked at him. 'Bella has brought me here and I know no one, not even a person in a shop who might recognise me.'

Her alienation was so acute that it silenced him. Here she was, in a foreign land, where the only friendships and contacts, presumably, were Bella's; where everything must be shockingly new and strange. She had nothing and no one. He closed his eyes as the implication hit him: she had no one, except him.

They sat for a moment, listening to the music, staring at one another like two strangers in a lift that has got stuck between floors.

'Okay,' he said, 'let's scrap everything I said before. What is it that you want from me?'

'Your help,' she said softly.

'Is Bella forcing you out now that she's here? Has she begun work at the Medical Centre yet?'

'Yes.' Then she said, with a bitter smile, 'She did let me come through for the first week, though.'

'Oh? Why?'

'There was so much to do at the house.' Rebecca sniffed with disdain. 'She's no good at that sort of thing, not the hard work, putting things to rights; she can only do the artistic things.'

He was amused.

Rebecca drank her coffee. 'Then, of course, she went back to work and I've not been able to get out at all. This morning, I knew I could get a long stretch, I felt so strong. There was some sort of scene between Bella and Alison this morning, I don't know what. Alison's been unhappy – about the children disappearing, about her mother who's ill – she was talking of leaving. That's when I came in – Bella can't bear emotion. I tried to comfort Alison.'

169

Joseph was alarmed: without Alison, nothing would be possible. 'Did she agree to stay on?' he asked.

'Yes, you can always appeal to her affection for the children. She feels sorry for them.' Her voice hardened. 'And who wouldn't?'

Joseph refused to respond. 'And so,' he said, 'once you were out, you knew you could stay out?'

'Yes. Bella's supposed to be giving her introductory talk to the students right now,' Rebecca said with some satisfaction.

'But you've cancelled on her behalf?'

'Yes.' She was pleased with herself and then, the next moment, she was clutching at his arm and saying, 'Listen to me, I've got to stay, I have to. Will is unhappy, he feels dreadfully lost and lonely and Daisy is too. They're at some summer camp that Bella's stuck them in, they don't know anyone, they're picked on. They need me at home, don't you see? You've got to help me.'

He took a deep breath: he was in it now; there was no way back. He would have to do what he could.

'Listen, Rebecca, let's look at it unemotionally for a bit. How do you stay out? I mean, how does it work?'

'I can only stay out if she lets me, or I can be stronger and force *her* out.'

'Okay now, how do you do that? Explain it to me.'

'It takes time because her will is so strong. I have to concentrate. I have to disrupt her life and shake her confidence. I do that by preventing her from working.'

'And her confidence now?'

'Is high. She's playing the queen at the hospital and they all love her.'

He had the curious feeling of being sucked into a quagmire. He stood, picking his tie up from the arm of the chair. 'Rebecca, I can't help you with this,' he said bluntly, pulling his tie into a hard knot.

She looked at him a long time and her eyes seemed to say, how can you possibly try to fool yourself this way? She breathed out softly and said, 'Oh, but you can.'

'What do you expect me to do?' he asked irritably.

There was a long pause.

'Help me to kill her,' she said calmly.

170

He spun round and grabbed her by the shoulders. 'You don't mean that, you know you don't!'

She showed her teeth as she grimaced from the pain his fingers were inflicting. 'I do mean that,' she snarled, 'and what's more, you know I do.'

He released her. 'There is only one solution to this,' he said quietly, 'and it's by absorption, by becoming one person.'

'That is what I meant,' she said stiffly. 'Killing her.'

'It's not what *I* mean. I mean becoming one, single, person. Joining.'

'We can't.'

'You have to.'

'You're being simple,' she said, 'you know you are.'

And she smiled up at him so seductively that he moved away from her. She laughed. 'But,' she said, 'there is another way.'

'And what's that?' He was looking at the clock.

'Love,' she said.

'Love?' He laughed. 'Love? Has America got to you that fast?' Her expression silenced him. She was waiting for him to catch up with her.

'Love', she said, 'is the only way to heal us. But –' she looked at him – 'we don't really know how. Do we? None of us. That's why you wanted to get out of this. You know you'll have to learn to love and you don't know how. Bella doesn't know how. It's why you keep skirting one another like wolves.' He was very uncomfortable and said nothing. 'But it's too late, isn't it?' she whispered. 'You are part of us. We have chosen you and, believe it or not, you have chosen us.' She laughed gently. 'So what are you going to do, Joseph?'

Chapter Four

He cancelled his meeting and flight to Chicago. He took off his tie, undid the top buttons of his shirt and sat down opposite her.

'So – we're going on, it seems?'

'Will you?' she asked.

He smiled wrily. 'I never really got out.' He took her hand. 'But we have to start again, from the beginning. First of all, I want you to understand that I have no problem with your – illusionary life . . . false reality . . . whatever we call it. It's the myth you live by, indispensible to you both. What may seem to be a sickness from the outside has been your solution –'

'For *her*,' she interrupted, 'it's a solution. For me, it's a nightmare.'

'I do see that. And you must believe that I've never had any desire to change or "cure" you. When I say that you have to merge, it's because I can't see any other solution. But that doesn't mean the end of you – or of her. There has to be a reconciliation, or you will be stuck this way always. In my bluster earlier – that stuff about the professional and the personal – well, I see now that there's nothing professional here any more, it's entirely personal.'

'That's what I was trying to say when I spoke about love.'

'I understood that. It's why I'm here. Now,' – he moved closer to her so that their knees touched for a moment – 'I need you to tell me everything you can remember. This is not in the nature of what Bella calls "shrinking"; it's simply that I have to understand, in order to go on.'

She shrugged with a small helpless gesture. 'It's difficult. I've not done this before. I try to forget, not remember. I have to start with you,' she said with a frown, 'because that's where it changed. Before,' she said slowly, 'only one of us chose a man. I chose William. She took him from me, but she never chose him. She wanted Jack. I didn't see Jack, much, but I

172

know that she only chose him as a father for the children she planned to have. She never wanted to be a wife, to be under the heel of a man, governed by his life.' She smiled sweetly. 'I liked to be a wife; I liked to be a mother. It was different for me.' Suddenly she held herself straight and proud and said, with touching sincerity: 'My life has had its own melody; it has survived great hardship. To some it may seem a faint echo, but it was the life I chose.'

'So,' he said, gently, 'just like Bella, you would not be imposed upon?'

'No. I would not.' She turned to him. 'And now, you see, it's different. Because we have both chosen you. No, don't protest, I don't know her reasons, but I know yours. Don't look like that. You often think that you're the only one who understands things. Bella makes that mistake too, but sometimes I can see everything. Sometimes, like now, I look straight through glass. I know your reasons. I know about you: you too are broken and hollow; you too have no centre. You too need to be healed.' She waited. 'Shall I go on?'

He nodded.

'You wanted to control us both and make us into one person who would suit you nicely.'

He laughed because it was true.

'Joseph,' she said, 'you have to see me, not just Bella – me. To you, all along, I have been invisible. You used me for information, but it was Bella you wanted. You cannot wrap us both up into one person. Not unless you really see who we both are.'

He nodded.

'I have had to fight', she said, 'for every day of my life.' She looked at him mockingly. 'You think that I am a sweet domestic soul and that she is the rapacious, ambitious one, the brilliant one.' Her voice rose. 'Well, I will tell you: I too have had my dream. When I was a girl I played the piano. I played it – oh, I played it beautifully.' The longing in her voice had spread to her face, and he could not look at her. 'I wanted to be a pianist as much, more than she wanted to be a surgeon. I loved the piano and she hated medicine, she really hated it – the life, the people – and most of all, she hated accommodating mother by doing it. And the thing that I loved, the thing that gave me the greatest happiness – this

173

thing I could not do.' Her voice shook with resentment. 'In our house, her work was given priority. Her brilliance was pampered while mine was smothered.'

He cut in. 'Wait, Rebecca, stop right there: *why* do you think her work was given priority?'

The reason, to her, was obvious. 'Because it was scientific.'

'That's all?'

She smiled. 'You don't understand our house. It was all science.' She added bitterly, 'It was male.'

He was beginning very slowly to understand.

She breathed in and out a few times to compose herself. 'For me to succeed, without breaking, there had to be a deep concentration. I could not do it. I needed quiet, time, freedom – and I could not get them. My concentration was broken and broken until . . .'

'Her brilliance outshone yours?'

She laid her hands on top of one another and surveyed them. 'You are very hard. Yes, it did, it had to. I could not fight all of them.'

'And so you were never the great pianist that you had dreamed to be?'

'No.'

'Why did Bella marry a pianist? And not you?'

She was quiet a long time. 'She married him' – she rested her long fingers against her temples – 'to show me that I could never achieve what he had.'

'To keep you down?'

'For a long, long time.'

'But before that you, too, had given up your dream. You had chosen William, you had married and had children.'

'Yes. I repeated the pattern of my childhood.' She looked fiercely at him. 'But I was happy. Even though I couldn't do it, I was happy.'

He was beginning to sweat. The room was hot. He turned up the air conditioning. He sat opposite her again and waited for her to speak.

Her voice rose proudly. 'Your dream of one woman is folly. You have to take us as we are.'

He was moved. 'But you see,' he offered, 'it's you who can't take it, you're the one who can't take it.'

174

She was steely. 'I've taken it for thirty-eight years . . .' her voice shifted, '. . . but now, now, *she* cannot take it.'

'And why is that?'

She hesitated. 'There have been too many deaths for Bella, starting with Papa's. When he died, she was, she was – as she is now, breaking.'

'How old were you then?'

'Eleven.'

He nodded. 'But surely – forgive me if I'm being dense again – but if there have been too many deaths for Bella, there must have been the same number for you?'

'No, for me there was Papa and there was William. That's all.' She was impatient. 'You didn't listen: only the ones I choose can die for me. Jack was Bella's and he died and now' – she slowed – 'there is one last death.'

For a moment, he was certain that she was referring to his death, but she went on. 'Isaac's death.'

'Isaac?'

'Isaac Roth.'

'The heart surgeon? The famous one who flew around in a helicopter from one operation to the next?'

'Yes. He was Bella's mentor. He allowed her to take sabbaticals while she was working with him; he covered her, monitored her progress, made her stop when her health gave in.' She added scornfully, 'Bella couldn't have achieved what she has without that man, he guarded her all the time. Don't let her convince you that she did it all alone.'

'And I suppose', Joseph said, 'each time he helped her he set you back?'

'Yes. She has always had her allies, people who've supported her – like our parents – but I've not.'

'Well, you have now,' he said.

'Maybe.' She lit a cigarette. 'Anyway, Isaac's death has weakened Bella badly this time. She's frightened without him.'

'She's lost another father.' He frowned and then made a startling connection. He threw up his hands. 'How stupid of me: it's his job that she's taken over in New York. She has literally stepped into his shoes.'

'Let me finish,' Rebecca said.

'No,' he said, 'let *me* finish. There have been too many deaths for Bella because she was responsible for those deaths, wasn't she?' He took a deep breath and repeated, 'Wasn't she?'

'No, not quite.' Rebecca's face was white and her lips trembled, taking on a blue shade as if she was cold. 'No,' she said.

'No?' he persisted, with a determination he had to force from himself.

'No,' she repeated in an empty voice. 'I was responsible. It was me. I was the one who killed him, not her.'

Chapter Five

It was a relief when she asked him if he would mind going out to get something for her migraine.

The sun beat down and his eyes winced with the brilliance of the light on the New York street. There was no vitality in the air and he had little energy left. He walked slowly to the corner and paced the chilled, air-conditioned aisles of the pharmacy, taking his time to find something that might help her. The brands were not familiar to him and he was reluctant to ask for help. The names blurred as he stood there, looking at them. Finally, he grabbed the nearest extra-strength package, some cold seltzer water, paid and left.

Walking back to his apartment, he felt that he needed a little time to digest not only what she had told him, but what had happened to him, too. He was not sure that he wanted to go back inside just yet: it had been exhausting, far more exhausting than any hours he had spent professionally or otherwise. It might be better to go somewhere else. He went into a small deli and sat down at the far end.

The waitress came over. 'You all set?'

He shook himself. 'Yes, I'd like a coffee please, an expresso.'

'Sure. Can I get you something else?'

'No, no thanks.'

A couple were arguing in the booth behind him, Bruce Springsteen was wailing on the juke-box; an Italian beauty made sandwiches behind a counter laden with cakes and pastries. The waitress returned with his coffee.

'Tell me if it's not good, the machine's playing up.' She hung about. 'Sure I can't get you something to eat?'

'Do I look hungry?'

'You look a bit beat, if you don't mind my mentioning it.'

He smiled.

'You from England?'

'Yes.'

'I thought so. Love your accent. You know,' she said, picking up an ashtray from his table, 'you got a voice just like Laurence Olivier, I mean it, just like his. It's great.' She smiled. 'It's the kind of voice you'd just, well, just do anything for.'

'For his voice, or for mine?'

'C'mon.' She put her hands up behind the long, rather straggly blonde hair at her neck and flicked it up. She sighed. 'Is it hot?'

'It certainly is,' he said, tasting his coffee.

'That okay?'

'Very nice.' He smiled again.

'You don't mind me talking to you? Some customers do, some don't.'

'I don't.'

'You on holiday here?'

'No, I'm working here for a while.'

She moved a bit closer. 'What kinda work you do?'

'I'm a psychiatrist.'

'Just my luck,' she laughed, 'just what I'm looking for.'

'I only work with criminals,' he said.

'You're kidding! Is that right? I had a boyfriend once who was, you know, a bit into that.'

'Into what? Working with criminals?'

'Hell no, he just stole stuff.' She went off then to look after some other customers who had just sat down. Joseph drank his coffee slowly. When she came back, he asked for the check. She tore off the scrap of paper and handed it to him. 'Where you staying?'

'Just round the corner.'

'Great.' She smiled encouragingly. 'Come back, now. Maybe I'll even tell you my dreams.'

He got up, put the money and a tip on the table and wondered what her dreams might be. She was still standing by his table, waiting.

'Goodbye,' he said, 'thanks for the coffee.'

'See ya,' she said, folding her arms and watching him go. Her eyes, with their borders of black pencil, were wistful. He smiled at her through the window; she waved and reached to put the money in her pocket.

He walked slowly home. He got into the escalator and rode to the fifth floor. He hesitated outside his door for a moment, then went in, feeling certain that she would no longer be there.

The place where she had sat now mocked him with its emptiness. She had left behind a small lace handkerchief; it was tucked into the side of the chair. He walked over and picked it up, missing her. She had left him a little piece of herself, as if she did not trust him to remember her.

'How laughable,' a low voice said, making him spin round. 'A dropped handkerchief; a courting relic from another age. How like Rebecca.'

'Jesus, Bella! You scared the life out of me,' he said angrily. 'Do you always have to be such a snide bitch?'

She raised an elegant eyebrow. 'Getting to you, is she?' His calm stare outfaced her. She walked to the window and looked out.

'How did you get rid of Rebecca?' He put down the bottle and the box of pills.

'She wanted to go.'

'I'm sure. You don't happen to have a migraine, do you?'

'I never get them.' She turned and smiled at him. 'I hope you weren't gullible enough to believe all that?' she asked coolly.

He knew she might simply be fishing for information. 'All what?'

'That story about killing Jack.' She laughed. 'Rebecca was always so fanciful.'

'Let's see how straight you can be, Bella. How much of that conversation were you privy to?'

'The last bit.'

He sat down and opened the bottle of seltzer; he offered it to her. She shook her head.

'I'm glad to see you're giving up the pretence, at least.'

'The pretence of what?'

'Of there not being a Rebecca, or,' he smiled nastily, 'had you forgotten?'

'Amnesias', she said, with a supple twist of her hips, 'can be removed.' She walked over and sat down opposite him.

'What shall we talk about, Bella?' he asked.

'Don't shrink me,' she said in a light, sing-song voice.

'Not unless I'm paid handsomely for it.'

'What would you like to talk about?'

179

'How about murder?'

'You're the expert. Aren't you the one who spends his life with rapists and murderers? It might be interesting to discuss that.'

'It might have been, before, but I've decided to get out of it.'

'Oh? Really?' She crossed her legs. 'What brought that about?'

'Another conversation. You see, Bella,' he said, leaning forward, 'we poor mortals who are less blessed by the gods do what we can. But there's always some beautiful career inside each of us that never finds its expression.'

'I see. And what is it that lies so beautifully within you?'

'We will see,' he said, with a grin.

'We?'

'Oh yes, we. In case you hadn't noticed, there are three of us now. You, Rebecca and me. And' – he noticed her shift backwards in her chair – 'no one's leaving.'

She rubbed a forefinger across her lip and frowned. Then she caught sight of the ashtray with two cigarette stubs in it.

'Rebecca's smoking again?' she asked.

'Concerned about her health?'

'Yes,' she said quietly, 'Rebecca's never been well.' She pressed her hands together. 'And believe it or not, I came so that her migraine would go.'

'You really don't have a migraine?'

'No. As soon as I come the migraine goes, it always does.'

'That's extraordinary.'

'No,' she said, 'we are biologically quite separate. She gets eczema on her arms which disappears as soon as I come; she has high blood pressure and I do not; our eyesight is different. We are separate, that's all.'

Her manner was so different, so far from the spikiness of moments before that he had to adjust his own mood radically.

He looked at her soberly and said, 'Bella, I think the time has come for us to talk about all this properly.'

'All what?'

'The past: yours.'

She considered it for a moment. 'All right,' she said. 'What do you want to know?'

'The thing that matters,' he said softly.

180

The air had gone still; he didn't feel the heat any more. They stared at one another and he wondered if she was up to it.

'What you're asking . . .' she began, like one playing for time, 'is why this happened, why the ego was broken – what happened to the original consciousness? Is that what you want to know?'

'Yes.'

She looked at him, her face so full of tension that the muscles seemed to be moving, shifting, making waves. He expected Rebecca to appear but then, just as swiftly, her face went still.

'I can't help you,' she said in a reasonable voice, 'because you see, I can't remember.' She stood and tilted her head at him.

'And nor can Rebecca.'

She let herself out.

Chapter Six

It was well after midnight. Joseph sat on the wall outside the Medical Centre until, finally, Bella came out. He watched her walk down the steps and then on towards the corner of the street. Her way of walking had none of the slumbrous quality of Rebecca's movements. He got up and went quickly to her, stopping just behind her.

'Had a nice day at the office, dear?' he said softly in her ear.

She turned slowly, almost as if she'd seen him all along but had pretended not to.

'Yes, I did, thank you.' She looked to the left and right, but all the cabs were taken. 'My,' she said, 'you are persistent.'

'Worse than that,' he said. 'Relentless. I wish I could drive you home, but I don't have a car in New York. Where, may I ask, is yours?'

'I haven't had time to get one.'

'Couldn't Rebecca do that for you?'

The wind blew a strand of hair into her mouth. She removed it delicately; her nails had grown, he saw.

'Rebecca doesn't drive,' she replied and, while he assimilated this, she saw an empty cab, raised her arm and was about to run forward when he pulled her arm down. It was done a little too roughly so that her body spun round to face his. They regarded one another.

He heard himself say, 'Rebecca doesn't drive, eh? Didn't have time to do the test perhaps?'

'She doesn't know how to drive. Besides, she's afraid of speed.'

'I see.' He wondered if he would ever know the truth about anything, or whether it would take the next twenty years to winkle out the facts from both minds. 'You look tired,' he said.

'On the contrary, I feel wonderful.' Simply saying the words seemed to produce the effect: her face lost its fatigued look.

182

'Is it going well?' he asked, with genuine interest.

'Yes,' she said, looking soberly at him, 'it is. I like it. In a way, it's easier for me, less strain. Tonight' – she looked almost radiant, 'I did some very interesting surgery.'

'You've not been doing much surgery?'

'Oh yes, but it is nice to teach again too.'

'No private patients though?'

She shook her head, then looked at him. 'And you,' she said, 'being a civil servant, are you allowed a private practice?'

'Yes,' he said, thinking what a pleasure it was to have such an easy, ordinary conversation with her.

She was becoming impatient.

'It's a bad place to get a cab,' he said. 'Why not come to my place?'

She looked evenly at him. 'We tried that one, didn't we?'

'Yes, and it wasn't that bad, was it?'

'No,' she said slowly.

'Well then?'

'No,' she repeated.

'What about a cup of coffee?'

'I like it here.' And indeed she did seem to. The day's heat had left a balmy warmth in the air, but the wind was cool. The street was busy. A boy skateboarded past them and nearly took her with him. She laughed. She was becoming more relaxed: her work was done; her children were taken care of; she was, for a rare space of time, unhooked. There was actually something rather carefree about her.

'I've been seeing rather a lot of Rebecca,' he said, with a touch of abandon. She stopped looking up and down the street and walked back towards the hospital where, rather unexpectedly, she sat down on the lowest step. She smiled up at him.

'Do you expect me to be jealous?' she asked.

'Well, I had hoped that perhaps you might be.' He grinned.

'Do you want to stir your fingers in my brain too?'

'Is that what I do with her?'

'With her you are mostly soliciting information.'

'I don't care for her?'

'Not much. You do not care for either of us.' There was regret mixed with the anger.

183

'I suppose you probably feel the way many twins feel,' he said, 'that they are not liked for themselves, but only because of their curiosity factor.'

She wouldn't touch the subject.

He sat down beside her.

'Are you good at your job?' she asked.

'It's nice that you should pay a little attention to me,' he said. 'I see you for such short periods of time; we seldom have time for a good conversation these days.'

'Well – are you good at your job?'

'How can any of us know that?'

'Only with results,' came the sharp retort.

'A healed heart?' he asked tartly.

'A successful operation.'

'And what happens,' he asked, 'when there are failures?'

She turned her head to watch the skate-boarding boy, who now did a pirouette in front of her.

'Failures can be kept to a minimum,' she said simply, 'except with the very young, which is why I don't operate on babies any more.'

He wondered how she coped with the inevitable in life: did she deal with the blows of fate or transfer them?

'So you don't take on hopeless cases?' he asked quietly.

'No.'

'Oh, Bella,' he said sadly, 'the world is a hopeless case.'

'I simply meant,' she was rattled, 'surgery cannot achieve the impossible.'

He moved close to her and said, 'Have you never *tried* the impossible?'

'Yes,' she said quietly, 'I have.'

'And?'

'And have failed.' She turned to him, 'But with you, Joseph . . .' For a moment he could have sworn that she considered kissing him. '. . . with you, all your cases must be hopeless. How on earth do you manage it?'

'Because I don't believe in hopeless,' he said quietly – and kissed her.

She passed her fingers very slowly across her mouth as if to erase it, but the act was so sensual that it seemed as if she was touching his kiss.

184

He stood, and reached down to pull her up. He said firmly. 'We're now going to hire a car and I'm going to drive you home.'

'But it's one-thirty in the morning.'

'This is America.' He took her by the arm and marched her off.

The drive through the summer night into the leafy lanes of New York State was very pleasant. A pale moon shone, the crickets were loud and a deer cut across the road, making her gasp. She spoke about her work, about the children, whose adjustment was much on her mind. She was surprised that he knew about Alison's problems. This made him realise that he had always to be on his mettle with her: she had only the vaguest knowledge of his talks with Rebecca – the rest was bluff, or a close assessment of the way she knew Rebecca could behave. Everything she said was smooth, considered, utterly normal; she was in control of herself, nothing seemed to confound her: neither the children's difficulties, nor her own with Rebecca.

When they arrived at her house – newly painted, the roof in process of repair – he stopped the car and sat for a moment, opening his door to let in some fresh air. She did not ask him to come in. Instead, she turned to him and said, 'You know, you ought to be careful.'

'Of you?' he asked mockingly, feeling such an urge to touch her that he could not do it. He laughed softly. 'I know you're quite capable of laying waste a third husband.'

'I wasn't talking about marriage,' she said.

'You'll marry again, you'll come to see that it's unavoidable. You're not the kind of woman a man merely takes up with.'

She turned to face him. 'But you are the kind of man who merely takes up.'

'Touché!' He laughed again. 'Not in your case, however. You know you have me.'

She laid a hand on his arm. 'I think that you have come to feel a kind of love for us, though you may not know which one of us you love. But, you see,' – her hand came back after its small departure – 'I don't want it. I've found a way of living my life precisely as I want to. It may have no great heightened emotions – but it is my creation, my own, unique life. I have no wish to lose it to you.'

He wanted to shake the nonsense out of her. He said patiently: 'Has it never occurred to you that I might not wish to do you any damage or theft? That I might even want to *help* you live your life?'

She said nothing.

'I can see that I'll have to prove it to you. But, remember: your life, yours, yes, and even Rebecca's, does not have to be sacrificed because of me.'

'Sexual love has a way of messing up the best intentions,' she said in a hard voice. Then she opened the door briskly. 'I'm not up to it, I have no capacity for love.'

He pulled her close to him, right across the seat and held her steady. 'Your capacities are all about you – your work, your children, even this house, which already seems in far better health than it was.' He released her and she got out of the car. He followed her round to the front of the car, where she now stood, not moving. 'You have no choice but to trust me' he said quietly, 'you can't go on alone any longer. You and Rebecca have to come to terms, finally; you have to put the past away and begin again.'

'It's possible', she began heavily, 'that you might be right, because I think I can't go on any more.' It was said factually, without self-pity.

'Have you felt that before, that you can't go on?'

'Yes.' She stood very still, looking up at the house. Then she turned to him and, with a slow, calculating smile, said quietly: 'I think, perhaps, you'd better come inside.'

Chapter Seven

Bella flicked on the small light in the drawing-room and he was startled to see the changes she had made there. The walls were a soft peach colour and bookshelves and paintings filled what had once been empty space. Linda's utilitarian furniture had been replaced by elegant European pieces and, on the tables, were cluttered small treasures that the hand reached out to touch: delicate carvings, a pale pink Buddha, small photograph frames, various porcelain and silver thimbles, a little carved owl, an African mask. Everywhere there were bowls of mixed flowers – blooms cut from bushes or the garden – the colours and scents filling the room. Joseph saw a desk he remembered from her London house, a pale rug that looked beautiful against the polished pine floor with its wide boards, and a silver frame with Will's face smiling out of it. 'You've done a marvellous job,' he said, feeling completely at home, remembering the wonderfully eclectic settings of his grandmother's house, where a Jacobean armchair would sit beneath a bamboo-framed mirror and Staffordshire dogs would live happily with lacquered Japanese tables.

It was extraordinary, he thought, how very strong her presence was in the house. These rooms could not belong to anyone but Bella, no one else could have created such an atmosphere. Every piece of furniture, the singular way it was placed, the simple but elegant fall of the silk drapes, the rows of dark leather books (books on anatomy, some very old indeed) – her personality was apparent wherever the eye came to rest. But sitting there, Joseph knew that it was more than that, for the house had a most distinct persona now, it had a life, a sense of order and design – even a purpose. It was as if Linda had never lived here, as if, indeed, Linda had never existed.

He felt sucked into the atmosphere of the room, as if it had been waiting for him to enter it. He was not uncomfortable

187

with the sensation, but he was alert. There was a strangeness here; the room held its breath; Bella's possessions were her witnesses, her accomplices, even as her children were. Other men had sat where he now sat; other hands had lifted the small pink Buddha from its stand and noted its perfection – had they too felt Bella's imposition on all they touched and saw?

She had left him alone in the room and for a while he was not aware that she had come back and was standing looking out of the window. It was an image of her that he remembered from the time in Gloucestershire, when he'd woken to think he saw her standing just so, looking out over the pasture. Looking for something, or someone, it seemed, and yet appearing to be completely self-contained at the same time.

He walked over and stood beside her looking out at the night. The peonies had just begun to break out of their shells and their fragrance drifted through the window. He turned to look at her and saw that she was smiling. She had taken off her shoes and, consequently, she seemed rather small beside him. He took her hand without a word and she did not withdraw it. He knew the potency of silence, but wished he could decipher its meaning as they stood there with the warm air blowing tendrils of hair about her face.

She turned to look at him and he was shocked to see small round tears on her cheeks. She seemed unaware of them and did not brush them away.

'What is it, Bella?' He touched her cheek.

She looked back at the window. She did not answer him for some time.

'They asked me tonight to help with an operation on a small baby, but I couldn't do it.'

She was quiet.

'The failure rate is so very high,' she said. Her voice dropped again. 'Once, when a baby's heart stopped beating, after six hours of surgery, I just couldn't leave the theatre. I asked everyone else to go, but I stayed there all night. It was just after Harry's birth – he was about five months old, the same age as the baby with the ailing heart – and I just couldn't go and tell the parents their child was dead.'

There was a cry from one of the upstairs rooms and she came to a halt, stood very still and listened a moment. When it did not repeat she relaxed.

'I did no more surgery on infants after that night,' she said.

'Yes,' he said, 'I can understand that.' After a little while he asked: 'What did you do, all night, in the theatre with the baby? Did you cry?'

She let her head drop. 'No, I was too sad for that. I just . . . I held the baby.'

'All night?'

'All night.'

And he thought: what do I say to her? That she had a duty – as a surgeon who knows what it is to give birth – to go on with such work, because only she could bring to it a unique compassion? Once he would have said just that. But now he could not.

'You made the right decision,' he said. 'And perhaps you should make more like that – spare yourself a little more of what is unbearable.'

She looked directly at him then, with a kind of recognition, as if to say, you do know a little how it is. He saw how exhausted she now looked, how black and hollow her eyes were.

'I'm sorry,' he said, 'I've kept you up so late and you're very tired.' He touched her cheek. 'I'll let you go to bed. Forgive me – I just couldn't bear to leave.'

'Perhaps,' she said, moving away from the window, 'perhaps you don't have to leave.'

Warmth rose in him, but then slowly it began to evaporate. She had begun to walk across the floor: the moonlight fell on her loosened hair and illuminated her body as it moved with a slow and sensual glide towards the door.

'Bella?' he snapped, shaken and bewildered. And then more slowly, he repeated her name, knowing it was the wrong name.

The woman stopped, she turned her head and let her face reveal itself to him. She smiled imperceptibly.

'Shit!' he snarled, furious with her. 'How can you? I mean, what the hell's the point of it – what's the purpose in duping me that you're her?'

She regarded him in silence and now he could see that her face was sad.

'I wanted,' she began with difficulty, 'I just wanted you to care for me a little. You were being,' she stopped again, 'so tender by the window, it made me cry: I wanted you to be that way with me.'

189

'Even to the point of sleeping with you?' he asked brutally.

'Oh,' she said sadly, 'we are not so much different, we are much more the same than you could ever understand.' She walked slowly back towards him.

'I'm sorry,' he said, 'but that was dishonest. Completely unfair. You deliberately pretended to be her.'

'No,' she said sharply, 'no, you're wrong. I remember that child, too. No, I don't know the name of the rare disorder she had and no, I did not operate on her body for six hours and no, I did not feel her heart stop under my hands. But I did sit there in the dark theatre with her in my arms until the morning, holding her cold little body, and it was *me*, not Bella, who went to tell the parents she was dead because Bella couldn't bear to. Now,' she said furiously, 'do you still think it's unfair? Are you really going to decide what's fair and what's not?'

He sat down heavily in the chair and let his dead drop. He breathed out, putting his hands up to his head. 'No,' he said quietly, 'it's not fair, none of it's fair.' He got up and walked towards the door. Once there, he stopped and turned to her. 'Be patient with me,' he said. 'We have a long way to go.'

Chapter Eight

'Mummy!' Mary called out, racing through the kitchen doors to fling herself at Bella's knees. Bella put down her briefcase with a bang.

'Goodness, Mary, you nearly knocked me over!' She took the child's hand and walked over to the sink where she ran the tap to fill a tumbler with water. 'Want some? You're so hot, you feel just like a sticky bun.' She passed the glass and watched Mary gulp it noisily down. Bella smoothed her hair back from her forehead; she was immaculate after a day's work, dressed in a pale blue dress with a crisp white collar, cut square at the neck. Her legs were bare and she wore soft Italian sandals.

'I like your dress,' the child said with admiration, rubbing a plump hand down Bella's thigh. Mary's hand was dirty and Bella saw the dark streak left on her dress.

'Oh dear,' Mary said with concern and began rubbing at it.

'Don't worry,' Bella said, 'it's only a little mark.'

But Mary had reached the stage when everything domestic and womanly appealed to her and all her mother's attributes made her long to be the same. 'I'll wash it,' she said firmly.

Bella laughed. 'You'll do no such thing. But you can help me put it in the machine later.'

Bella walked to the french windows and looked through them to the garden. The small girl with her helmet of blonde hair came and stood beside her, watching also.

'Where is everyone?' Bella asked.

'At the bottom of the garden. And Alison's asleep – look, over there.' She pointed to a pink body lying on a striped towel.

'You'd better go and wake her up. I'm going to have a shower and change. Do you want to come with me – or go and play?'

The little girl screwed up her face so that her mouth shot out and touched the end of her nose. 'Don't know. Maybe I'll go outside with Daisy again.'

191

She walked off with small thudding steps and Bella watched her go, her head to one side, smiling fondly.

'Don't be long,' Mary cautioned and walked out of the door. Bella could hear her voice calling out, 'Mummy's home,' as she ran down the slope of grass to the trees at the bottom of the garden.

A little later, it was Rebecca who went out into the garden. She stood there for a while, her face torn by the complexity of her emotions as she watched her children in the late afternoon sunshine. Daisy, chased by Mary's laughter, was running up and down the garden paths, in and out of shadow, over the grass strewn with white petals – laughter and more laughter as on and on they raced. The white and blue bells of the delphiniums shook as Daisy leapt over a flower border and entered the long sweep of grass basking in yellow sunshine. 'You can't catch me,' she yelled. But Mary, little trooper that she was, kept on racing, her face red, her thick fringe stuck to her forehead, following her sister.

'Now! Quick!' Will yelled, seeing that Daisy lost her balance and speed as she veered to avoid a bed of pansies. 'Get her now, Mary! Hurry up, you little pudding.' Then he laughed and lay back lazily in the shade, for Daisy had streaked ahead again. 'Too late, Mary, bad luck.'

On ran Daisy with her white dress sharp against the green of the garden. The laughter had ceased in the intensity of the race. The bodies of the little sisters were slowing down and their breath came in tired puffs.

'I've got to the wall,' Daisy shouted in triumph and sank gasping to the ground. 'I'm safe, you can't get me.'

'You're so much bigger,' Will observed, glancing over the top of his SAS Survival Handbook. 'It's not fair.'

'I wasn't running my hardest, not by miles,' Daisy panted.

Mary had rumbled up and she, too, fell to the grass exhausted.

'It was a good race,' she gasped.

Daisy lay with her face pushed into the soft, cool grass. Mary lay on her back with her knees pulled up, squinting at a bee that flew sluggishly into the shaky glare around the honeysuckle.

'Pow!' Will said softly, aiming an imaginary gun at the fat striped body. Then he looked towards the house and saw his mother standing just outside the french doors.

192

'Oh, look, Mummy's back,' Will said, getting up. He began to run across the grass towards her, seeing how she stooped to pull up some weeds from a flower bed. She saw him and waved, her face relaxed and happy. When he reached her, she bent to kiss him. 'You're getting so brown,' she said. In a little while the winded girls had caught their breath and followed their brother. Soon they were all clustered around their mother; she rested her hands on their heads and took a lollipop for each of them out of her pocket. She now wore a red-and-white spotted sundress with a full skirt and no shoes. She wriggled her toes in the grass and said, 'I see Jim's been to cut the grass.'

'Let's throw the frisbee,' Will said to Daisy. 'Where is it?'

'Down in the bushes,' Daisy said.

Their mother watched them run off and sat down in the shade, leaning back on her arms with her legs in front of her. The children had found the frisbee and Will began to flick it at Daisy. 'Let's see how many we can get to,' he said. 'Do try and get it over fifteen this time, Daisy, okay?'

'You drop it as much as me.'

'That's because you're so useless.'

After some minutes, their mother seemed to get restless sitting there on the grass. It was as if she could no longer bear her immobility. She jumped up suddenly and ran across the grass.

'Throw it to me, Will,' she said, 'let me see if I can catch it.'

He stopped with his arm raised and stared at her a moment. She was laughing, holding her arms up, waiting for him to throw the white disc in her direction. With a quick, perplexed grin he shrugged. 'Okay,' he said, 'here it comes.'

Up she rose in a slow, graceful leap, her hand straining, the long fingers flexed, her eyes fixed on the frisbee as it began to descend and she caught it in its flight.

'Brilliant!' Will exclaimed. 'I didn't know you could catch like that. Now throw it to Daisy.'

'I'm not quite sure how to throw it.'

'Hang on, I'll show you.' Will ran up eagerly. 'Here, curl your fingers round the lip of it, no, like this, that's it, now flick it sideways.' It spun lightly away from her with the grace of a paper boat caught by the wind. 'Yes, that's right. Only, next time, do it quicker,' Will said, marvelling, for he had never once in his life taught his mother how to do anything, nor could he remember her playing with them this way. Perhaps when they had been very small, but even then he couldn't be sure.

He ran back to his place and soon the frisbee was flying back and forth between the three of them with soft flipping sounds – back and forth and up and across, curving like a bird into the sunshine, hitting the leaves of the trees, alighting on the rhododendrons, landing in their hands or rising above their heads.

'We've done seventeen,' Will said, 'let's get to twenty.' He threw the frisbee towards his mother, hard and high. Daisy, with a spasm of anxiety, called, 'Run, Mummy! Don't let it fall!' She clenched her hands and shook them, jumping up and down as she saw her mother run and jump, her hand straining, the frisbee spinning as, with her head upturned, her hair running down her back, she reached – and missed. The disc came plummeting down to earth.

'That's enough for me,' she gasped, 'I'm going in to make supper.'

Will picked up the fallen frisbee and stood there a moment. He looked up at the blue sky and saw the leaves falling in straight lines under the trees; he heard a dove call and felt a sleepiness descend on the day. It reminded him of other days in another country and he was reassured. He saw how his mother strode across the lawn; he thought how nice her hair looked when it streamed down her back that way. He saw that Daisy, too, was watching her go.

'Will you play again, Mummy?' he called after her.

She turned. 'Of course,' she said lightly, 'we'll play every day and soon we'll get to fifty.'

Chapter Nine

In the kitchen, Alison, with a very burnt face, was watching Harry as he spooned tapioca into his mouth with rapid and dedicated attention, not spilling a drop. She looked up. 'I didn't hear you come home, Bella. You're early.'

'A little.'

Alison gestured towards Harry. 'He woke up grumpy, so I decided to feed him before the others.'

'That's fine. I'll do dinner anyway. You really got burnt, Alison.' Bella looked at the inflamed skin as she walked to the sink.

'I know,' Alison said, touching her face and wincing. 'I fell asleep.'

Now that Harry had polished off his tapioca, he had time to notice his mother's arrival. He acknowledged it by tossing down his spoon and beginning to climb down from his chair.

'Just wait a moment, Harry,' Mary ordered, requisitioning a dishcloth and applying it to Harry's mouth. 'You're a real mess.'

'We're going to have to watch Mary,' Alison said with a laugh. 'She's over-domesticated and she's barely four!'

Harry was now settling into his mother's arms with his thumb jammed into his mouth; his fingers were pulling at her loose hair with curiosity; with a snap of her white teeth, she bit his cheek gently and put him down.

Bella walked to the pantry and went in. The walls were thick, with flaking plaster, and the windows had wide screens, which gave it a wonderfully ventilated feeling. The survey had revealed that there had once been a stream running under this part of the house. The air in the small room was fresh and Bella kept her butter, fruit and vegetables in here. There were rows of empty preserving jars, waiting for the summer fruit, and a large jug of homemade lemonade. She reached for the butter, put it on top of a bowl of eggs and walked back into the kitchen.

Mary had left the room. Alison, looking shy and hesitant now, said, 'Bella, can I talk to you about something?'

'Of course.' She put down the bowl.

'Well,' Alison began, 'it's my mother . . .'

'Yes, I was going to ask you – have you heard from her since the operation?'

The voice was concerned and Alison relaxed: Bella was going to be all right. That tension and stiffness that Alison expected whenever she was about to ask an indulgence, or had a difficulty, was absent today.

'Well, she only went home yesterday.'

'Heavens, Alison, I told you to telephone home!'

'I didn't like to – you're so generous as it is . . .'

'Don't be silly! I've told you before, you *must* call home whenever you like. I know how hard it is for you to be so far away at a time like this.'

Alison felt tearful but bit her lip: she knew the one thing Bella could not take was tears. 'I'll ring tomorrow,' she said, glancing at the clock and seeing it was too late to call London. 'But what I really wanted to know, Bella, was . . . ' Now her voice had retreated again. '. . . I know it's awkward right now, but I really would like to go home – just for a week, I mean. I just . . .' Her voice cracked, but in a moment she went on, 'Do you remember, you said I could when I was upset last time? I don't like to ask.'

Bella turned away; her face darkened and her features began to undergo a strange erosion. Anxiety and disturbance hovered around her mouth, drawing it into a hard line. Then instantly, as if by some alchemic process, all this was gone. She had donned a new face and turned back to Alison with a smile.

'You absolutely must go,' the soft voice insisted. 'I was going to suggest it myself, but I've been so busy and it made me thoughtless.'

'Oh no,' Alison cut in, 'not at all. I just feel badly because I don't know how to cover my absence. In England, when I took time off, I could always ask Sally to stand in for me, but here, well, I don't know anyone and I hate to leave you stranded . . .'

196

'Don't give it another thought.' With a lovely sweeping gesture, Rebecca whirled Harry high into the air, and looked up at him, her face shining with happiness.

'Do you think I can't manage my own children? Goodness, it's a wonderful idea: I'll take a week off, that's all.' She turned back to Alison. 'I'll book you a ticket right now.'

'But won't it be . . .? I mean, I can wait until you see about your schedule at the hospital?'

'Nonsense! They can manage. Here, pass me that phone, and find me the travel agent's number. Come on, Harry, you can help me.'

_____ Chapter Ten _____

Joseph had gone to ground after his confrontation with
Rebecca. He'd written the first draft of his report and
barely left his apartment. He was edgy and restless and,
when the phone rang, he snatched it up before it could ring
a second time.

'Hello?' he snapped.

'Joseph, it's me, Rebecca.' The voice was hesitant. He didn't
reply and she went on quickly, 'I didn't telephone you before
because I was confused and I didn't know what to do.' Still
he said nothing. 'Well, I just wanted to tell you,' Rebecca said
softly, 'that I'm sorry about what happened the other night. I
really am – I shouldn't have done it, it was unfair, as you said,
and I feel badly . . .'

He said slowly, 'I'm the one who should apologise. Everything you said was right. It's taken me some days to distil the
meaning, but it was quite fair.'

'Oh,' she said.

'Rebecca.' His voice was gruff. 'It's a time of change,
of reversals. For me as well as you, even Bella. Things
are coming to a head.'

'Oh, don't say that,' she whispered.

'Why not? It's the only way out of this, and there _is_
a way out of it, Rebecca.'

'I don't know, I don't know any more.' Rebecca's voice had
lost all its confidence. 'When things reach a crisis, I . . . it's
always me who cracks.'

He didn't know what to say to comfort her. But, in
an instant, she was furious with him.

'Look, I'm doing _all right_; I'm doing very well. She's been
gone for days now and I look after the children, all of them,
and it's fine. I can live without her.' Her voice turned low and
hard. 'Nobody knows. Nobody has ever known anything was
wrong: people would see me or see Bella, as the children and

198

Alison do, and that would be it. There isn't a problem, we can go on like this. As long, as long as I – don't go under. As long as you don't take her side.'

'I'm not taking sides, Rebecca, I just want to understand. I'm concerned equally about you both.'

Her voice was tight. 'Oh, well, I don't know what to do about that.'

'Can you accept it?'

She was silent a long time. 'Only if I felt you really cared for me,' she said.

'Rebecca,' he said patiently, 'I do care for you.'

'Well then I'll try,' she said valiantly.

'Good,' he said. 'Now, when can I see you?'

Her voice changed utterly; it became ripe and sweet. 'Any time,' she said. 'I'm always here. And Alison's gone.'

'Alison's *what*?'

'No, she's just gone home to London to be with her mother. She's had an operation and Alison's gone for a week.'

'But what about the hospital?'

'I took the liberty of taking a week off from the hospital. Just wait!' she demanded, 'don't take me to task about that. I had to do it because there was no other way.'

'I see. What does Bella think?'

She was petulant. 'I don't know. She's not been here – I told you.'

'Okay, we'll leave it at that – but these are the things that we're going to have to sort out, once and for all, you can't –'

She cut in swiftly. 'Why don't you come and have lunch with us tomorrow? It's Saturday, so I don't suppose you're working?'

'My work is becoming the least of my concerns,' he said, with the old sharp ring in his voice.

'Oh good, come as soon as you can. No time is too early. I'm up at six. See you tomorrow!'

Joseph sat at his desk a long time, thinking. And then he went over to stand by the window where, once, Bella had stood, waiting for him to return with the pills he had gone to get for Rebecca. It chilled him to remember how she had turned and he'd see that one woman had become another. It was this duality that had eaten into him for days: the essence of it, and what it meant for him. He had come to the conclusion that he

199

must live with it. It was too late to pick and choose, to say, I will take this and discard that; I like this aspect of the woman but not that; I would like her to be this way and I will not put up with that side of her life. It was too late. He was dealing with the finished woman, the final version. The mould had set and it could not be broken and remade to his specifications. The woman was. She simply was. And, as it happened, she was extraordinary. She deserved unconditional love. Rebecca was quite right: love was the one thing that could cure them. Bella was entitled to the highest admiration, for she had built out of the misery of her early inheritance a life of exemplary self-government. Her life was her creation: she had duplicated herself in order to combat the world. Her mind had the startling brilliance to behold itself.

The only question was: could he do it? Was he worthy of such a task? A man went out into the world – so he believed, so all mythology told him – on a quest to conquer his demons, to bring them to heel. In this way, he achieved real manhood. Was he capable of such self-knowledge, could he look directly into the eye of the mirror and not through the projections of the prison? Could he love the woman as she was? Because he knew that if he could not he too would remain maimed and incomplete. He would be the broken half of a man, unable to engage fully with either a woman or the world.

If he did not do it now, he never would. He was no longer a man at the starting gate. He was thirty-four years old. If he was not careful, the race would finish and leave him where he was.

Chapter Eleven

Joseph woke the next morning believing he had turned a bend in the river. He got up early, left his apartment, rented a car and was driving down to see Rebecca by nine o'clock.

When he got to the house, he walked round to the back, from whence came a great deal of noise. Daisy saw him first and came up to him.

'What's all the noise about?' he asked her.

Daisy looked out across the lawn. 'The rabbit's got out of its hutch and the cake for tea has just burnt. Mummy spent the whole morning making it. Mary fell in the poison ivy again.'

'I see. Not a lot's been going on then?' He smiled at her.

'I haven't seen you since England,' she said.

'Ah,' he said, 'but I have been here.'

'Mummy says you found this house for us,' she said with an appraising stare.

'Hm. Sort of. How'd you like it?'

'It's nice,' she said, 'I like the garden specially. But I miss our old house.'

'Yes,' he said, 'I do, too.'

She stared at him with the same sober interest. 'I lived there,' she said, 'from before I was born.'

He laughed. 'Oh yes, your claim is much deeper than mine, but I'm fond of the house because I got to know your mother there.'

She looked sideways at him, precisely the way Rebecca often did. He was disconcerted.

Looking down the length of the garden, he could see Rebecca; she was laughing her head off. First decent bit of laughter he'd heard from either of them, he thought. This was the real thing, from the belly, not the brain. Will was walking slowly towards him, trying hard to look nonchalant. He was just a jump away from those painful years when his self-consciousness would really begin to plague him.

201

'Mummy', he announced formally, 'is having a little trouble catching the rabbit.'

'Well, why the hell don't you catch it for her?' he asked, precisely as his father would have done. It rather shocked him, this reversion to type.

Will said, 'I think she's enjoying it.' Which, Joseph now saw, she certainly was – leaping in and out of the bushes with a recalcitrant rabbit dodging her with the skill of a breed well used to avoiding the cooking pot.

He had a fierce desire to see her and walked down to the bottom of the garden, Daisy just behind him, treading on his shadow each time it moved.

'Got him!' Rebecca whooped, snatching up the rabbit and running to stuff it back in its hutch. Then she came up to him, breathless and laughing. He took a good look at her and whistled.

'Don't you look beautiful,' he said approvingly.

She smiled and pushed back her hair with both hands. Her face was different, very noticeably so. It was vivid, but not in the way he was familiar with. This face had come to life; Rebecca was radiant and she did not mind his scrutiny. She took his hand and walked him up the lawn to the terrace circling the back of the house. She pointed out the sweet-peas she had planted and the rows of foxgloves along the white walls. Her voice was bright as a sparrow's.

On the terrace, she stopped at a table and poured lemonade into blue-rimmed Mexican glasses. Then she flopped down into a chair. One of the children (the one he remembered her calling 'Bella's brat') settled down on her lap and began playing with the material of her skirt.

Joseph looked at the poison ivy rash on the girl's arm. 'Pretty nasty,' he said.

'I've got some good stuff. This is the second time she's had it.' Rebecca frowned at the child. 'You just have to keep out of that long grass, Mary.' Mary ran off to where the other children played among the trees.

Joseph watched her hurl down the grass towards a clipped hedge where Daisy's crouched form could be seen digging in the earth. Pools of orange fell where the shade did not reach. Birds – he did not know their names or recognise their calls – swirled up into the sky. The scent of the roses drifted in the

202

warm wind and made him feel the most profound peace. He looked across at the woman sitting in her chair; she was smiling in a mysterious way. Her skin was a warm russet shade and her nose wore a little saddle of freckles which suited her. She was barefoot and brown, wearing a white dress with red dots.

'I think you'd like to know, wouldn't you, how I'm here?' she teased.

'Well, you did say that Bella had been gone, so . . .'

'She came back yesterday.'

'Oh?'

'But not for long.'

'Did something happen?'

'No.' She pulled her chair closer to the wicker table and rested her round arms on its surface. Her breasts looked fuller. 'She was only here for a little while, but I left her a note. I wrote it some days ago,' she said, drumming her fingers on the table. 'I told her I wanted to have the weekends from now on.'

'That was rather enterprising of you.' He drank from his glass, watching her over the rim.

'And why not? She doesn't usually go to work at the weekends, not unless there's an emergency, and there hasn't been one yet. This job's better,' she beamed, 'easier. Not so many patients to visit and all that. More of a nine-to-five job.'

He laughed, enjoying her matter-of-factness, her ease with herself and with him.

'Do you always write notes to one another?'

'Oh stop it!' She laughed. 'We used to write notes, we rather had to. But,' she looked at him, closing her eyes, 'now we don't really need to; we can talk through you.'

'I'm not sure that's such a good idea,' he said doubtfully.

'Anyway, did you say anything to Bella, to help me, to get her to let me out more often? Did you say anything about what we discussed, about trying to work with rather than against each other?'

'No, I haven't seen her.' He frowned. 'Why d'you ask?'

'Well, it's just that normally she ignores my notes, or scratches them out. This time she said yes.'

'Just yes?'

'That's all she wrote. I can't understand why she would let me take over,' she said with a quick, bewildered shake of her head. 'It's not like her.'

203

'Maybe she agrees.'

'I think,' Rebecca said softly, 'she may be letting me take over now because she wants to go away.'

'Why?'

'I don't know,' she tilted her head to one side, 'but of course, she would always rather I took over than that any man should take her over.'

'That,' he said, 'may well be true.'

'Anyway,' she continued quickly, perturbed by his tone, 'I don't want to talk about Bella. I want to talk about what's happening to me here.' She leaned forward. 'It's an astonishing country, isn't it?'

'America?' he asked vaguely. 'Yes, I suppose it is.'

'I've never been anywhere like it.' He had to remind himself that it was indeed a new world for her, quite different from the Europe of her childhood.

'A woman came here the other day,' she said, 'called Linda. She used to live here. She asked me if I'd like to join her Women's Group.'

He laughed loudly. 'You didn't go?'

'Yes I did. I didn't know what a Women's Group was. I thought perhaps they might swap recipes, or something like that.'

'Fat chance!' He laughed again: she was like a castaway returning home after years on a desert island.

'Did you learn to the contrary?' he asked drily.

'Yes. They sat about saying how horrible men were. Well, of course women have always loathed men and men have always disregarded women, but this was something quite other.' Her eyebrows shot up. 'Quite violent.'

'Has the women's question passed you by, Rebecca? Can I be that lucky?'

'Don't be facetious. If you're a woman it never passes you by.'

He regarded her with amusement. 'You're certainly a quick learner.'

She ran on. 'You'll have to explain something to me.' She frowned and stuck out her lip. 'You know, they were so un-private. They expected me to tell them my emotions.'

He gave a snort. Spilling their guts is an American pre-occupation. The men', he added, 'are very good at it too.'

'It's all clichés, though,' she said, puzzled. 'They never say anything profound.'

He said, in a different way, 'I do think though, that maybe you rather liked it, Rebecca.' She had found some relief in talking and thinking about a subject other than herself. It was heady to her. Her curiosity was a relief to him, too. It would be interesting to see the world through the eyes of someone who had been absent from it for years.

'I liked being called by my name,' she said happily. 'They use names a lot.'

He frowned. 'She must have called you Bella?'

'No,' she laughed. 'I said she'd got it wrong, that my name was Becky.'

'That could be risky.'

'Why?'

'Well, what if she comes round here, asking for a Becky? Alison, and the kids, you know . . .'

She lifted her head with determination. 'I don't think you understand, Joseph. Things are going to be different; I'm going to be here a lot, maybe all the time.'

They surveyed one another in silence. Then she got up quickly and reached over for his hand. 'Come into the kitchen,' she said. 'You'll get burnt sitting there. And I have things to cook.' He followed her, watching her body; she moved slowly, voluptuously. Turning her head, she said sweetly, 'I can tell you things. You know, as we agreed, for me to tell you things.'

'Be careful,' he warned. 'It sounds to me as if the notion of living without Bella has become very appealing to you.'

They had entered the kitchen. It was a homely room, very different from the parts of the house he had seen. The style was so out of keeping with the drawing-room that he realised Rebecca had put her stamp on it, expelling Bella from the kitchen.

'What's the matter?' she asked sharply. 'Don't you like it? I just took out that pale sofa. It's a silly thing to put in a kitchen. I want it my way,' she said plaintively. 'I want to live here in my way. I could even,' she hesitated '. . . well, I could make a life here, I could give piano lessons.'

'You've been doing a lot of thinking.'

'Of course.' She was gathering up bowls, spoons and ingredients with easy familiarity.

'If you make a life here, does it mean Bella loses hers?'

'I don't know. Perhaps.' She looked unhappily at him. 'That would hurt you, wouldn't it?'

'I can't imagine Bella not working, and that's what it would mean.'

She went to the other end of a long pine table and took a book out of the drawer. 'I found this cookery book the other day. It was my mother's. I can't imagine why Bella kept it.' She put on her glasses and began to look for a recipe.

'Does Bella wear glasses?' he asked.

'No, her eyes are perfect.' Her voice had speeded up. He saw that she was frightened and unsure of herself again, so he changed the subject.

'Your mother was German, you said, last time?'

'German Jew.'

'Tell me about her.'

It was as if she must make up for lost time, must cram in as much living as she could in the time allotted her.

'Mother made me write out all the names of her family who had been killed by the Germans. The names went on and on. She said, "We will remember them, each and every one, but we will have no grievance, we will not live like martyrs. Instead, we will make a triumph of our lives to erase what was done to us." '

'Did you lead an orthodox life?'

'No. Not in any way.'

Her childhood was real to her. She told him stories and small things that had happened to her, or to Bella. She spoke of a time when their relationship had been almost close: when each had kept a journal so that the other would know what had been going on. He wanted to know if these journals had survived, but let it pass. She was at pains to let him know Bella's vulnerability as a child: her fear of the dark, her asthma. She told him that Bella was punished by being locked in a cupboard for hours on end. When her asthma got very bad she would go into a trance and let Rebecca come. The asthma would disappear and she could bear the darkness. Sometimes they would swap many times, so that the work could be done before their mother came back to unlock the door.

As she spoke, a picture began to emerge, vague in detail, but clear enough in terms of sequence. He was sad to see how few landmarks there were in her later life, particularly after the birth of William and Daisy. If she'd surfaced then at all, she had little memory of it. There was a brief appearance around the time of Mary's birth and there were more frequent memories leading up to the birth of the small boy. After Harry's birth she could remember nothing for a long while; her place had been taken by Alison. These were clearly the years of exceptional accomplishment for Bella. She had reached a perfect balance as a consultant, doing exquisitely delicate open-heart surgery and achieving a world-wide reputation.

According to Rebecca, the marriage to Jack had been very difficult: 'He couldn't keep up with her and took more to drink.'

'How do you know this?'

'Bella kept a diary. She recorded his behaviour, his visits to clinics and finally, his fall from the top of a hotel in a state of paralytic inebriation.' Rebecca used these last words as if they had quotation marks around them, which made him feel that she had indeed read them.

Then, cautiously, Joseph asked, 'Do you remember how you told me before that she made you kill? Do you remember that?'

She nodded. 'I didn't mean it quite the way it seemed.' Her manner was sneaky and she moved away from him.

'What precisely did you mean?'

Anger seemed to make her regress. She laid her hands helplessly on the kitchen table and leaned forward.

'I just meant that she made me come when Jack was in trouble.'

'You said before you never saw Jack.'

'I meant, only a little: when he was sick, when he was unhappy with her, when he couldn't do his concerts – she made me look after him.'

'Rebecca, I wish you wouldn't lie to me, it's difficult enough to follow as it is.'

She twisted her hands. 'I'm sorry.'

'That's all right,' he said more gently. 'But tell me: why were you so obliging?' Her face was so desolate that he was moved to pity. 'I'm sorry,' he said, 'I didn't mean to be harsh. But why *were* you so obliging to Bella?'

'Because' – she breathed in slowly – 'I could live again. I could see my children. Don't you see, don't you see *anything*?' Her hands were incapable of working now; they had a useless look about them. She was wringing them in a way Bella sometimes did.

He got up and put his arms about her. 'Rebecca, I'm sorry. I didn't say it would be easy. But it will help. That much I do promise you.' He took a knife from the table and began to slice the tomatoes. 'Don't take any notice of me,' he said, 'I'm just impatient when you contradict yourself.'

'My life contradicts itself,' she said, pulling at the round leaves of some basil.

He held her wrist a moment. 'I'm just trying to get the facts straight.'

'I know. I'll try not to confuse you.' She was quiet and then she said softly, 'You shouldn't think she was cruel to Jack. I think she even loved him once, in her way. But she was terribly disappointed in him. That's what he could never bear.'

'Disappointment is a most efficient killer,' he said. 'It could probably chalk up as many deaths as heart disease.' He looked directly at her. 'Being kind to Jack, Rebecca – it can't really be put down to helping him die, can it?'

'Don't you see,' she asked in a wondering tone, 'what it did to him to think that Bella, the woman he adored, was the one who took him out of bars, collected him in taxis from strangers' homes, cleaned up his vomit? He didn't know it was me, not her.'

'So he killed himself?' He was matter-of-fact.

'No,' she said sadly. 'He wanted to, he wanted so much to end it. But you see, he couldn't. He was too weak.' Her voice had become dreamy and remote. He abruptly stopped chopping and looked at her.

'What are you saying, Rebecca?'

'He was standing up there, the wind was blowing, I remember the lights' – her voice was thinning and falling – 'and then he turned around and saw me standing there.'

'And?'

'And he said, 'I'm sorry, Bella, I can't even do this for myself.'

She turned her face until it was close to his.

208

'And did you?' he breathed.

'Oh yes,' she said softly, 'I did.'

'You pushed him?'

'Yes. Very gently. It was what he wanted.' She smiled forlornly. 'It was the only thing to do,' she said.

Chapter Twelve

Daisy came bursting through the door, tripped and crashed to the floor. Instantly, Rebecca came to and rushed to her daughter, who was now crying. She rocked her gently to and fro.

'I'm sorry, Daisy,' Will said sheepishly from behind, where he stood watching. 'I shouldn't have been so rough.'

'Is she all right?' Joseph asked, walking over to where Rebecca was rubbing Daisy's leg with slow movements.

'Yes, she hit her leg quite badly, but it's okay.' Rebecca looked up at him. 'I just can't bear pain,' she said. And with that, she put the balcony, and its consequences, completely away from her. Joseph felt that, for now, he must do the same.

'Come and help me take the lunch out, Daisy,' Rebecca said, pulling the girl up.

'Will and I will help too,' Joseph said, watching Rebecca as she stuck large spoons in salad bowls and sliced bread. The children, he noticed, had lost their slightly spooked quality and seemed really quite normal. Rebecca was asking him questions about American politics. Will was putting glasses on a tray. Daisy had recovered. They went outside to lunch. 'Put the things on the table under the big tree,' Rebecca called out to Joseph, 'not the one with all those horrible little beetles. Daisy will show you where.'

Lunch was a delicious affair. They sat around a large table with a blue-and-white tablecloth and feasted on chicken and tarragon, tomatoes still warm from the vine, homemade bread, Pouilly Fumé, apple-cake and brie. It was very hot, but Rebecca pulled her chair into the sun and sat there, baking.

'What's the summer camp like, Will?' Joseph asked.

Will was quite friendly. 'It's not bad. The other boys are okay. We do lots of sport but they don't know anything about cricket. There's one guy I quite like.' Already, his English accent was losing its purity and Joseph felt he could even discern a slight thaw in the chill of his character. With his sisters, Will was a protective and guiding influence, as he was with his mother. But today he began to give over a little to Joseph – and there was some relief in it. He had learned too well the burdens of being the man of the house. It was as if he could accept that his mother's happiness was in some way due to the man who had entered their magic circle. Will would tolerate him on those terms.

Rebecca was lying back in the sunshine and Will was cautioning her about the ozone layer.

'But of course,' he said, eating grapes one by one, 'it doesn't matter so much with you because you never stay in the sun.' She looked at him over the white rim of her sunglasses. 'I've never seen you brown in my life,' he said, still eating the grapes, still watching her.

'Oh, I've been tanned before,' she said; then added, with just a touch of steel, 'There was life before you, Will, you know.'

'Was there?' he said with a mischievous grin.

Observing this little exchange, Joseph was aware of how right she had been when she'd said that the children were oblivious of her predicament: they would accept what they saw and heard. He, however, found it much harder. He was watching Rebecca carefully. So often with her, he felt the sense of a fugitive identity, even an imposter's. She didn't possess Bella's sense of entitlement in the world. Joseph could not forget the man on the balcony; the way he must have turned and sought some grace and mercy from the woman watching him. Whether Rebecca had actually pushed him, or led him, or merely watched him fall, who could say? If she felt Bella had forced her to certain actions, she quite often embellished them. It gave her some freedom from guilt. This made Joseph consider something else: who had the moral imperative to exist? Which of them had killed? He had always been drawn not so much to physical as to moral danger, and now he felt it all about him. He could not reconcile any of it; there were no boundaries here. How could any judge in a case like this decide who was guilty? And he did not just mean of the two of them, he included Jack.

211

Rebecca looked up at him in a haze of heat and smiled. 'A penny for your thoughts?'

He laughed uneasily.

She began to involve him in a problem she had with the house and went on to tell him about amusing incidents that had arisen from Alison's absence. She was very engaging. He knew that her intention was to distract him from darker things. She put a straw hat on her head and the limp silk roses fell over the brim. The wine was going to his head as he lay under the young green leaves of the tree; a cloud passed over, dimming the sun. The children had gone indoors. it was very quiet.

She came and sat close beside him and lying there, very still, he seemed to feel a burning come off her body, as if she was flaming, or something was flaming, inside her. He opened his eyes and looked up at her and then beyond her into the tree. Her face had taken on a perfect immobility, her mouth was soft and set and her eyes very dark. He waited – for he had decided long ago that she would have to be the one to make the move. In these moments, his head cleared and he looked again at her face, to read it, but it was illegible. The sun had ducked in again; the wind had risen and it shook the leaves above their heads and sprinkled shadows over her cheeks.

She whispered something he could not catch and then, very tenderly, kissed him on the mouth. His hand rose and grasped the back of her neck, where the heavy hair felt damp. He held her there, hard, mouth to mouth, mind to mind, seeking knowledge. And then he forgot what he was seeking and kissed the woman, again and again, seeking forgetfulness.

Then the first drop fell. The wind in the trees made the leaves tremble and shake. Rebecca lifted her head and let the raindrops peck at her warm skin. There was a sudden gale in the trees. Lightning flickered in the distance, followed by a clap of thunder. Rebecca laughed and jumped to her feet, then bent to pull Joseph up.

'My cake!' she said and ran to scoop it up like a mother rescuing a baby.

He stayed there a little longer, letting the rain drench him.

Later, in the kitchen, he helped her paint the cupboards.

212

'With Bella, everything has to be white, or something delicate or refined,' she said with a little sneer, opening up a large tin of paint. 'Look at this lovely colour.' She stirred it with a wooden chopstick. It was a deep pumpkin shade, very warm and earthy, and immediately she began to apply it to the woodwork. He had to admit that it looked very good, though it completely altered the look of the kitchen.

He took up a brush and said, 'Won't this get on her nerves?'

'No,' Rebecca said brightly, 'the kitchen's mine. When we shared a house, the one you liked, we had an unspoken agreement. Certain rooms were hers and others mine. Do you see that pine dresser?' she pointed with her wet brush to a glass-fronted dressser with drawers beneath it. 'Bella would never have bought that. I found it the other day in an antique shop. It's Swedish and the lines are too clean for Bella. She likes French and English furniture, very old, but our tastes have always looked all right together, a bit wayward – a French armoire in one room and a modern chair in another – but it's okay, it works.'

'Yes, rather well,' he said, realising that this paint, now that it was making an effect, looked fine.

'I shall fill that corner with plants,' she said, 'and you really must look in the pantry – I bought a lovely old rolling pin.'

He stopped painting for a moment and watched her lavishly flinging colour at a door.

'Rebecca,' he said, 'this may be indelicate, but we're here to find things out – how do you manage about money? Is there an arrangement about that, too?'

She laughed. 'Oh, you mean, do we both use what one of us earns?'

He raised an eyebrow and smiled.

'No,' she said gleefully. 'I have my own money. It was left to me, not to her, you understand, to me, by our mother. Bella wanted none of it. And,' she laughed, 'I invested it, some years ago of course, and it did rather nicely. I took it all out when we came here. The exchange rate was very good, so I think my timing has been excellent.'

He sat down and laughed, really laughed, at the sheer wonder of it. 'You're quite something,' he said, beginning to feel the kind of respect he had always reserved for Bella.

When the room was finished – she wouldn't stop until it was – Joseph went upstairs. He was in the bathroom, washing the paint off his hands, when the door slammed to behind him. He spun round, startled.

'What the hell do you think you're up to?' a low voice snarled.

'Bella!' he laughed, 'how delightful! But, I didn't think you were supposed to be here.'

'What's going on?' she asked.

He picked up a towel and began to dry his hands. 'What's going on is that Rebecca is very much in charge of things, astonishingly so.'

'I know,' Bella said. 'I can't get rid of her.' She stood there stiffly, regarding him.

'Rebecca's view', he said, perching on the end of the bath, 'is that you're afraid, that you're giving over to her because you can't bear to give over to me.'

'Rebecca is strong only because of you,' she said, ignoring his remarks. 'She's strong when she loves someone.'

'And you feel weakened by that emotion, don't you?' He rose and walked over to where she stood with her back pressed against the door.

'I don't trust you,' she snapped. 'And I certainly don't trust her. What is she trying to do?'

'Give her a break, can't you? She's like someone out of jail – she's just glad to be out.'

'She should be in jail.'

'What d'you mean?' he snapped.

'Nothing.'

'You're referring to Jack's death?'

A smile of appreciation barely touched her lips. 'That was brave of you,' she said, 'not to dodge the issue. I'm surprised she told you.'

'Well, she did.'

'She must . . .' she gave him a long look, '. . . feel rather safe with you.'

Did he imagine it, or was there something wistful in her eyes? If there was, it was instantly banished. She walked over to the window and touched the end of a fern.

'She didn't tell you the truth,' she said with quiet devastation.

214

'No? What is the truth then?'

She turned slowly. 'Oh, she did push him, if that's what you're asking, but not for the reasons she gave. Not because I made her, not because I couldn't live with his behaviour.' She spoke in a circumspect manner, keeping her eyes fixed on his face. 'I had already left Jack by then, our marriage was over. No – what Rebecca couldn't bear was his music, his brilliance. She was driven by envy. She often is.'

Joseph slumped. 'This is impossible,' he said. 'It gets more and more convoluted. I suppose I just have to accept that there is no "truth". Only your truth or hers.'

'Isn't that the way it is with everyone?' She smiled, 'You will see, as you go deeper, that we are all much the same, dear Joseph, we are not so extraordinary that you will not be able to recognise yourself in us.'

It was chilling, the quiet wisdom of it. 'How much more agreeable', she said softly, 'to concentrate on what's amiss with us.'

'You're quite right,' he said, 'as always.'

'It's nearly over now,' she said in a tired voice that took him back to past conversations.

'What is?'

'Everything. You will see.'

'You're not trying to tell me that the mighty Bella is going under?'

'I don't know,' she said, with unsettling detachment. 'I'm tired. And I want my children to be happy . . .' she hesitated, '. . . more happy than they have been with me.'

She turned back to the window and looked out at the garden. In the silence, the sound of children's laughter reached them. 'They are different now, aren't they?' she said sadly.

'Bella,' he said, walking over. 'You must not think that way. You've been a good mother.'

She stood close to him and did not mind that he saw the tears in her eyes. 'But it is not all I wanted,' she said.

'Why should it be?' He took her face in his hands. 'Bella, there is no one on this earth I admire more than you. Don't lose heart. We'll get through this and find a way to live, all of us. I promise you.'

For a moment she let her head fall forward onto his chest. Then she lifted her face and smiled a little. 'No,' she said, 'I

215

have tried, we have both tried, but it is not possible. One of us will have to go.' She very softly touched his cheek. 'I don't know who it will be,' she said, 'but I do know now that it depends on you.'

She left him there.

Chapter Thirteen

He stayed upstairs a while longer. Bella was right, the whole matter was approaching a crisis and he had been the catalyst. Once he had hoped that the two of them could resolve it between them; now it was far more complicated. Rebecca seemed to have no inkling of the dangers. Her attention – how could it not be? – was taken up with staying alive. And she was succeeding. Bella was not fighting back. Yet having seen her, having felt her despair and ambivalence, he could understand why.

He went slowly downstairs, sensing that it would be Rebecca he would find. She was not in the kitchen. Coming across Will in the hall, he asked, 'Where's your mother?'

'In the outside shower.'

'Oh, I didn't know there was one.'

'It's the best one, the pressure's really strong.'

'What have you got there?'

'Swiss Army knife. Want to look at it?'

Joseph took a look and said, 'It's much more sophisticated than mine.' He looked at the file, screwdriver and can-opener.

'Look,' Will said, 'it's even got a toothpick. My grandfather gave it to me,' he said proudly.

Joseph looked at Will. 'I believe you're going to be an explorer?'

Will shrugged. 'Well, most of the world's gone, but yes, something like that. Or maybe I'll just find an island somewhere, or a forest where no one has been, and just live there.'

'By yourself?'

'Yes.'

'And you'd start from scratch and tame the environment?'

'No, I'd leave it as it was, but I'd learn how to survive in it.'

'Interesting. Always wanted to do that?'

Will nodded. Then with a grin he said, 'When you have time, will you tell me why you work with evil people?'

'Oh,' Joseph said, 'they're not really evil, most of them, they're just sick. Bad things were done to them when they were small and they couldn't recover.'

'Maybe,' Will said doubtfully. 'I'd like to see your knife, is it a very old one?'

'Nearly as old as I am.'

Will smiled. He strolled off, stuffing the knife back in his pocket.

Outside, on the terrace, it was as if no rain had fallen. The heat was thudding down and the heavenly blue of the morning glory spiralled into the shade among the eaves of the roof. Joseph could hear water falling hard against wood, and followed the sound. The outside shower was just that – outside: there was nothing around it, just a spray coming straight out of the wall. She was standing under the streaming water, her hands up to her hair. He watched her a moment, interested to see if he could tell which of them it was. He couldn't. Then the water was turned off and a hand groped for a towel hanging from a hook. He took it off and passed it to her. She took it, smiling at him, unperturbed by her own nakedness. It reminded him of how shy she had been in his apartment, the day he had met her at the door half dressed. She dried herself and put on a blue silk robe very similar to the one that had been left at his house in Gloucestershire.

'Ah,' he said. 'Good, I've been meaning to ask you something for ages.'

'Yes?' It was Rebecca. In spite of himself, he was disappointed. Whatever the sweetness of Rebecca, something was missing when Bella was not there.

He sat down on one of the steps leading to the lawn and motioned to her to sit beside him, which she did, shaking her wet hair.

'When we were in Gloucestershire – you remember that?'

'Of course.' She threaded her arm through his. 'It was nice, I liked that house.'

He was pleased.

She was brisk. 'What did you want to know?'

'It's a small thing,' Joseph said, 'but it bothered me.' She gave him a smile and he went on. 'Well, at the end, when

218

Bella left the house, very early on Monday morning, when I woke up I noticed that a silk robe rather like the one you're wearing now was lying across my bed. Do you happen to know how it got there?'

'You're asking *me*? Or you're wondering if you slept with her?'

'No,' he said drily, 'I'm not wondering if I slept with her. I didn't.'

'Well, if you did, you wouldn't forget,' she said cryptically.

He raised an eyebrow.

She went on, 'She's very sexual, you know.'

He let it pass. He was suddenly very aware of Bella, just below the surface, like someone swimming under water, who might at any moment break through.

Rebecca took a packet of cigarettes out of her pocket and lit one.

'So,' Joseph said, 'you don't know about the robe?'

'Yes, I do.'

'Well?'

'It's mine. I put it there.'

'When?'

'During the night, very late. I woke up and I thought maybe she might have tried something with you, so I went into your room.'

'And what did you do?' His dream returned to him, with its strong sense of suffocation.

She blew out a long lazy stream of smoke. 'I took off the robe and threw it across your bed; it landed on your face but you pushed it off.'

'And that's all you did?'

'I wasn't thinking of killing you,' she said evenly, 'if that's what you're getting at.'

'Not at all. But what did you do it for?'

The old sneaky look was back in her face, but he found it less offensive now; it was the childish side of Rebecca.

'I thought', she began, 'that if I left it there, she might think . . .'

'That she'd slept with me,' he finished for her.

'Yes. I know it wasn't very nice.' She looked down. 'But she was forgetting things then, and there was a time' – her face took on a defiant mask – 'when she used to do things

219

like that to me. She used to upset me, making me think I'd done dreadful things that I couldn't remember doing.'

He was quiet a long time, imagining the implications of it all. Rebecca kept on smoking, nervously now, as if she was in a hurry.

'And then,' Joseph said, 'you went back to bed, thinking that at some point she'd go looking for the robe?'

Rebecca took a brush out of her pocket and began to draw it slowly through her hair. She was more settled again; the agitation had gone. 'I'll explain properly. That night, I didn't want her to come back. I liked it there, you see, and she'd pushed me out a lot all day. So I stayed awake once I'd got rid of her. That's the best way to keep her away: if I sleep, she takes over. She doesn't sleep much, she never has. So I stayed awake.'

'Did you wander round the house?'

'How did you know that?'

'I saw you looking out of my window, once, but I wasn't sure – I thought I might have dreamt it.'

'Yes.' She smiled tenderly. 'That was me. I sat by your bed and watched you while you were sleeping.' She looked away, her face flushed. 'I wanted to sleep with you,' she said softly, 'I still do. But it's . . . difficult, for you, I think.' She pressed her lips together hard. 'I think maybe you can't make love to either of us because, well, because it would seem like an infidelity. Do you mind my asking you about this?'

'No. The time has come to discuss it, but I admit I'm not sure what's to be done.' He looked directly at her. 'I don't think there's a way round this one, Rebecca. I think that, for me, this is where it really doesn't work.'

'Does that mean you don't want to sleep with me?' she asked painfully.

'No. It means that I can't sleep with either of you, and that way – well, how can we exist? Properly, I mean?'

Bella's words echoed in his mind: 'We have both tried, but it is not possible. One of us will have to go.' He felt once again the sensation of Bella's presence, so close that she seemed to be looking over his shoulder, watching them. It was creepy. He had felt it under the tree, in the rain, when he had kissed Rebecca. It was here now, only stronger.

Neither of them noticed for a moment that Will had come out. He stood behind them for a moment quietly, until Rebecca turned and looked at him.

'What is it, Will?' She quickly shook the distress from her features and smiled at him. 'Is something the matter?'

'It's the hospital, Mummy,' he said. 'They want you to go in. There's been an accident, I think.'

Chapter Fourteen

Rebecca went reluctantly into the kitchen. She picked up the red telephone book with all Bella's hospital numbers in it, and called the cardiac unit. She told them she could not come in – that she'd already explained that she would be unavailable. Then she listened in silence for a moment, her face becoming frantic.

Joseph had followed her and now watched her hang up. 'Should you have done that?' he asked quietly, coming to stand next to her. 'She's on call, isn't she?'

'She's not supposed to be, it's not my fault there's no one available.' She turned away from him angrily. 'It's *my* business,' she snapped.

'Well, not entirely.'

'Well, then, it's my weekend.'

'I thought you were going to try and help one another?'

'Don't interfere,' she said desperately. 'Bella's right, it's no good when someone else is involved. You start trying to interfere and it's hopeless. Just leave us alone.'

He went and stood in front of her. 'Please don't act as if I'm making it worse. Why can't you get it into your head, finally, that I'm trying to help?' He was angry and exasperated. 'Why do you both feel such a strong sense of threat – as if everyone's trying to get at you?'

'You're just trying to get Bella back.'

'I'd say the same to her if the situation was reversed. You should know that by now. You should know that I am trying, in my own bungling way, to help you, to protect you.'

'Keep out of it, you're not the referee.'

'Okay,' he said, flinging his hands out in a gesture of surrender. 'Do what you like.'

Daisy appeared with a dismembered video game. She opened a kitchen drawer and pulled out a screwdriver. Joseph looked at the bits and pieces in her hand. 'Will you be able to put it together again?' he asked.

'Unless something gets lost. Mary's always taking bits and that's a problem.' Her head was down, her brow furrowed with concentration as she turned a tiny screw. He pretended to watch her, whereas, in fact, he was watching Rebecca as she paced up and down – angry, torn and impatient.

'Oh, it's no good!' Rebecca burst out furiously. 'It's all spoiled anyway, because I'll just feel guilty.'

'Daisy,' Joseph whispered, 'can you go and do that somewhere else, would you mind? I just need to talk to your mother about the hospital.'

'Okay,' Daisy said, scooping the things into her hand.

Joseph walked over to Rebecca, put an arm around her shoulder and led her to a chair. 'Look,' he said calmly, 'it might not take long. Did you find out what the problem was?'

'No. I don't understand what he said.' She was wringing her hands. 'Some complication and there's no one else who can deal with it. Oh, I don't know. I didn't really listen, these doctors with their big words.' Her hand went up to her forehead.

'Now listen,' he said, crouching in front of her and taking her hands in his own. 'It's not that difficult. We've had a wonderful day. It's six o'clock. The rabbit is back in his hutch. The sun will go on shining. I'm here to look after the kids. You can afford to do this.'

'No!' She shook her head violently. 'I won't do it, I *won't*. I don't want to go.' She turned and began tearing at the pink petals of some geraniums in a blue basket on the table. She was as rebellious as a child.

'Look,' he said, 'let's try and do this differently for once, shall we?'

'You just want to get rid of me.'

'Rebecca!' he chided. 'Now listen, for Christ's sake. I'm quite happy with you, it's time you knew that. I can't spend my life trying to prove it to you. You've got to take it on trust now, or we can't get on. Today has been wonderful, I've been very happy here with you.'

She looked sharply at him. 'You mean that?'

'Yes, I do. Now, all I'm suggesting is that when something isn't working, you have to try something else. You only have two choices: to keep Bella out of the hospital, which will look very bad for her, or to let her go in.'

'*You* never have these choices to make,' she said dully.

'I know that. All I am trying to do is to help you make the right choice.' He felt useless suddenly – but the real assistance he could give her was with the children, so he repeated: 'I'll look after the kids. It doesn't matter when you get back.'

Slowly she began to gnaw at the nails of her left hand. 'You don't understand,' she said sadly. 'I've never had a chance like this before.'

'Come on, woman! You sound as if you'll never have it again!' He grabbed her hand from her mouth. 'You'll have days and days more like today!'

She looked at him, her eyes wide with knowledge.

'No,' she said quietly.

Suddenly, her vigour returned and she clenched her hands. 'Look at me,' she said, 'I'm here, I'm actually *here*! Before, she'd have wiped me out the minute the phone rang. But I've managed to stay.' She became excited. 'Don't you *see*? I'm stronger than her now.'

'That's precisely it,' he said quietly. 'It's why you have to exercise some mercy. And not just for her. Someone may be dying at the hospital.'

'Oh, that's a dirty trick!'

'Yes, it is.'

'You love all this, don't you?' she snarled, 'pulling the strings, watching us suffer, getting close to our horrible wishes. Of yes, I'd like to kill Bella right now, of course I would, and you know it. And now I'm wondering if she's trying to come back to injure me. Maybe she's planning some way for me to do myself in through all this – through you.' Her voice was high and hysterical. 'Yes, it was William who killed me last time, loving him did it to me. And now there's you. She knows it, she knows just how to get rid of me.' Her head fell towards her chest and she began to sob. Lifting a face glassy with tears she whispered, 'I should have known it from the start, that she would use you to do it.'

'Love', he said firmly, 'has never killed anyone. You have the power to be reduced or strengthened by whatever you feel. Why are you falling to pieces now?'

'Because I have no choice,' she said, rising. Her face cleared of all its woe; she walked to the window where she saw her children playing in the soft light; the doves were calling in the trees and the morning glory had closed its petals for the night. He walked over and took her in his arms and held her close. He was awed by the difficulty of her choice and the courage it would take for her to make the right one.

She looked up at him and said, 'I'll go. How could I not?'

'I'll be here, when you come back,' he said quietly.

He went with her as she walked through the kitchen and began to make her way dejectedly towards the stairs. Even as she began to ascend them, he saw how her movements began to change.

'Will you ring the hospital for me?' she said, her voice low and calm, her back straight and steady. 'Tell them I'm on my way.'

Chapter Fifteen

After Bella had gone, Joseph walked into the kitchen, where Will and Daisy were playing Scrabble. He pulled out a chair at the pine table and said, 'Okay, this is what's happening.' They both looked at him expectantly. 'Your mother has gone to the hospital and before she went she gave me my orders. I'm staying with you lot,' he grinned, 'until she gets back. Anyone with objections, speak now.'

'I'm hungry,' Mary said, drifting in from the garden. 'Where's Mummy?'

'She had to go to the hospital,' Joseph said, 'someone was very ill. She said she'd be back as soon as she can.'

The child was crestfallen.

'Come over here, Mary,' Will said, 'come and help me make a word. Mummy will be back soon.' Joseph saw that the boy spoke as much to comfort himself as his sister. Will looked down at the board; Mary stood beside him with her head to one side.

'Has axe got an "e" in it?' Will asked.

Joseph looked around the kitchen, at the freshly painted cupboards, at a salad that Rebecca had begun to make, and felt suddenly lost without her. Upstairs, Harry began to bellow.

'I'll get him,' Daisy said. 'He'll be grumpy, he always is when he's slept too long.'

Will pushed the Scrabble board to one side. Mary got up on his knee. They both looked at Joseph.

'Well,' he said, 'this is going to be an adventure.' He looked rather sheepishly at Will. 'Your mother said that Mary and Harry should have a bath. I think I'm going to need your assistance.' He saw, with pleasure, that the boy would co-operate. He toppled his sister from his knee and assumed an easy-going manner. 'I'll show you,' he said. 'They go in the bath together, that's what Alison usually does, anyway.'

He led the way upstairs. On the second floor, where the bedrooms were, the house had a wonderfully comforting quality. Each room was painted a different colour – Will's was a bold blue with lots of white woodwork. It reminded Joseph of Greece. Will took him into Harry's room, which had hundreds of small paper birds hanging from the ceiling, sharp scraps of colour blown about by the wind. Will took a cotton shirt out of the chest of drawers. 'This'll do, now we just need to get something for Mary to put on.'

To reach Mary's room, they had to walk past Rebecca's bedroom. Joseph had last seen it when he had looked around the house with Bella. Unable to help himself, he walked in and stood there, looking at a brass bed, polished like a new penny, with a brilliantly white sheet tucked neatly round it and a pile of pillows heavily crusted with lace. Hanging from one of the brass knobs of the bed was the red-and-white spotted sundress. It hurt him to see it. Curtains billowed at the long windows and, on a French armoire, stood a pure white orchid in a blue bowl. Beside the bed, on a low table, were a pile of medical journals, a dish of mixed roses, and Virginia Woolf's *The Waves*. Whose room was it? He didn't know, he couldn't tell, he didn't care.

He wanted to lie on the bed, to push his face into the pillow where her head rested. He wished she had not gone; the house felt so forsaken without her; how much more so it must feel to her children.

'Joseph?' With reluctance, he walked down the corridor to Mary's room which, he found to his amazement, was a carbon copy of her mother's. Except for the dolls. For here, in beds and cradles, shelves and chairs, in little sprawled heaps sitting on cushions, were dolls of every kind. Some with staring blue eyes and china faces, others soft and ragged, in well-worn clothes; some that looked just like babies, one with a bottle in its mouth and another dressed in a doctor's outfit.

Will was pulling a long nightdress out of the cupboard. 'Mary loves dolls,' Will explained, seeing Joseph's startled face. 'She collects them.' Joseph nodded and followed him out. 'And, at the moment,' Will added with a grin, 'Mary wants to be mummy. Before, she wanted to be a boy.'

They turned into the bathroom, where Daisy was filling a great old tub with water while Mary added vast quantities of bubble bath. It was the bathroom where Bella had appeared slamming the door behind her. He walked to the window and stood looking at the fern she had touched, remembering how she had nipped off a broken stem and how her finger had dug into the soil to make sure it was damp. Even as she had been discussing her fate, the possible fading out of her now tenuous existence, still her hands had been busy. He smiled, loving her. Loving them both.

'They like all this rubbish in the bath,' Will said, chucking in ducks and buckets and empty shampoo bottles. 'You can leave them in here for hours. Harry doesn't fall under the water any more – though you can't leave him alone, not without Mary.'

'I see,' Joseph said. 'I'm certainly glad you're here, Will. I could have made a real mess of this.'

'You'll get used to it,' Will said, phlegmatically.

When the two little ones were in the bath, Joseph sat down in the wicker chair and stretched out his long legs. Will was sitting with his back to the wall and his knees drawn up; there was no particular reason for him to stay. Daisy had gone and it had been made clear to Joseph that he was the sentinel. Joseph waited a while to see if he had anything to say, before remarking casually, 'You are a good son, Will, to your mother. I thought you were something of a prat when I first knew you, but I've come to see what a good man you are.'

Will's face lit up with sudden pleasure.

'It's not easy, you know, to be a good man. It takes many years. You've made a good start.'

'Thanks,' Will said. 'You don't have any children, do you?' he asked, making the same kind of direct connection as Bella, reaching the heart of the matter.

'No.'

Will got up, with the pretext of throwing a duck back into the bath, and said sharply, 'Are you going to marry my mother?'

'Yes,' Joseph said immediately. Then he laughed. 'Though I would prefer you not to tell her just yet, since' – he shrugged lightly – 'I haven't asked her.'

Will smiled, but it was a lonely smile. And it was more than that: it was an orphaned smile. Joseph found it hard to take; it was like a replica of his own face when his mother had left him at boarding school and gone to join his father in China – not returning for three years.

'Will,' he said, getting up and whisking Mary and Harry out of the bath, 'what shall we have for dinner?'

'What can you cook?' Will asked doubtfully.

'Oh, most things, but since we had such a huge lunch I thought we might have some pancakes. Okay with you?'

'Yes,' Will said.

Downstairs, in the kitchen, Daisy was still working on her computer game. 'Just keep away from me, Mary,' she warned. 'Touch anything and I'll kill you.'

'That's one of my fishing hooks,' Will said, retrieving it from the table and putting it in his pocket.

Daisy clucked furiously, scooped up her pieces and left the room.

A little later, Joseph heard the sound of a piano in a room far away. He lifted his head and listened, feeling slightly spooked, wondering if Rebecca had returned.

'What's that?' he asked.

'Daisy. Mummy bought a piano last week. She hasn't played for years, too busy I suppose, but she taught Daisy that tune.'

They both listened to the sad sweet notes of '*Für Elise*'.

'She plays well,' Joseph said. 'Did she learn that in such a short time?'

Will was pouring apple juice into a glass. 'She had lessons once,' he said, taking a gulp of his juice. 'Then Mummy stopped them.'

Joseph said nothing.

Mary came and stood directly in front of him. 'When are we having the pancakes?'

'Right now,' Joseph said, rallying. 'Who's going to show me where the things are? I need a bowl, a wooden spoon, eggs, milk, whole-wheat flour, butter and milk. This is a recipe that a friend from California taught me.'

Will laid the table. Mary put on an apron. Joseph flicked the pancakes. The piano in the other room had ceased. The phone did not ring. Finally, Joseph asked Will, 'Does your mother usually ring you from the hospital?'

Will shook his head. 'Not when she's operating, she can't. She will when she's finished.' He looked at Joseph. 'It could take all night.'

229

'She must get very tired,' Joseph said, lamely. And, with a painful flash of recognition, he saw how he had never given her any help. How he had never given any woman any help. Occasionally, he had cooked and cleaned, heroically going through the motions of assistance; but he had never given any real help. He had never looked to see exactly what help was needed. He realised, with sadness, that he had never even given real consideration.

The faces round the table looked up at him eagerly as he handed round the pancakes, pouring maple syrup onto Harry's and cutting it up for him. He found that his own appetite was gone. He was exhausted.

'Can I have some more milk, please?' Mary said, distracting him. He got the milk, poured it and gave some more to Harry, who knocked it all over the floor. Mary hit him. 'Don't make a mess, you silly baby.' Harry bawled. Everyone stopped eating. Will told Mary not to hit Harry. Mary hit Will who almost hit her back and then did hit her back. She screamed. The phone rang. But it was not Bella. It was Linda.

'It's you, Joseph,' she purred. 'Well, fancy that. Oh, *you're* looking after the kids while she's at the hospital? How nice.'

'What do you want?' he snapped, rattled.

'I just wanted to ask Becky to a dinner party – she's real nice.'

'She can't come.'

'You don't even know when it is,' Linda said furiously.

'Well?'

'Next week. Friday.'

'I'll tell her you called, Linda, but I think she'll be away.'

'Yeah?'

'Yeah, now I have to go.' He put down the phone in time to see Mary wallop Will on the arm and rush out of the room.

Now the room was empty, apart from Harry, who sat, surrounded by the debris, calmly eating every scrap of food off the plate next to him.

'Well, Harry,' Joseph said wearily, 'so this is family life?'

Chapter Sixteen

By nine o'clock that night, Joseph felt the relief of a mother whose children are all in bed. He wandered around the house, waiting for the telephone to ring, but Bella did not call. He was concerned about when she would get back – about who would get back.

He had left the kitchen spotless, knowing that was one way to help her. Then he sat in the drawing-room – Bella's room – for a long time. This was the room he liked best. He fell asleep on the sofa there; when he woke up, it was two o'clock in the morning. He couldn't get to sleep again and paced around the house. No child stirred or cried and without their bustle he understood the intense loneliness of a childless house.

He seemed to hear birds in the trees outside and couldn't imagine why they would sing at that time. But one cry persisted, sharp and high, and he wondered if it was a mother up with her chicks. He felt peaceful and rested and longed to have her with him; to spend these cool, quiet hours, shorn of interruption, with her.

Later, around four o'clock, when the first light had leaked into the dark sky, he arrived at the piano room and found that he could not leave it. It was a small, white room on the top floor, which may once have been a maid's room. No attention had been paid to it: there were no curtains at the windows, the floor was bare. The only object in it, apart from the piano, was a large jug of pink lilies that filled the room with a sweet and cloying scent. It reminded him of tuberoses in the rooms of the dead. Clearly, Rebecca had appropriated this room in Bella's absence. She had bought a piano and a stool and had set up life here. There was a pile of music scores, some well used, others brand new. He noticed there was a lot of Chopin. He wondered how well she played. He sat down and ran his hand over the keyboard lightly, feeling pleased by Rebecca's assertiveness, this insistence on a room of her own. He felt it was due.

He sat on, watching the sky lighten through the smudged window panes. The room, for all its starkness, had a strong atmosphere. He didn't know if it was the scent that gave it its sad quality, or if he was bringing this to it. He glanced at the floor and saw something he had missed: a piece of paper that must have fallen out from among the sheets of music. It was the rough copy of an advertisement, offering the services of a music teacher. The handwriting was round and large, very clearly formed. He was touched by this. He was watching the slow unfolding of a woman who had, for so long, been prey to her own hesitations. He put it in a prominent position on top of the piano, so that she would find it and proceed with her plan. It seemed to him, then, that if he and Bella could nurture Rebecca, they all might flourish. And if Rebecca could only find the confidence to put away her rage and envy, she might come fully to life.

Hearing a sound behind him, he thought he must have woken one of the children. But when he looked round, it was a woman, not a child, standing just beyond the doorway, standing very still, in the darkness of the corridor, her eyes on the piano. He looked hard at her; she said nothing. She remained camouflaged by the dark, but now her eyes were trained on him: huge, dark eyes, seeming to take up the whole of her face. He wanted to go to her, to hold her, but he stayed where he was.

Her silence was disturbing, but he detected in it the deadly calm that Bella possessed – or, was possessed by.

'You must be absolutely exhausted,' he said quietly. 'Let me get you something – would you like a drink?'

She shook her head, turned and began to walk away. He got up and followed her down the stairs. It was Bella, he was sure of it, excited by it; even though her body was slowed by fatigue, still it was her walk, not Rebecca's.

She had gone into the drawing-room and stood there, in the centre. The grey dawn filled the room with neither light nor darkness but a pale, tender glow; it was that moment before the first warmth touches the morning sky. Her face, in its exhaustion, looked ravished and ravishing. He had an unholy sense of how she would look after they had made love.

232

As they stood there regarding one another, he could think of nothing but their bodies commingling. Then she said abruptly, 'Thank you for staying with my children. I really appreciate it.' It was as if she was dismissing him.

He smiled and shook his head. 'I'm not going anywhere. I think, perhaps, you don't even want me to.'

She put both hands up to her temples and smoothed the hair back from her face.

'I'll get you something to eat,' he said firmly. 'You won't have eaten anything since lunch.'

'I'm not hungry.'

He walked over to her and led her to a chair. 'At least sit down. What was the problem at the hospital?'

'It was', she began with a hollow voice, 'a baby, with a hole in its heart.' She looked directly at him. 'The one I told you I couldn't operate on last time. She had deteriorated since her operation and was brought in having difficulty breathing.' She bit her lip, then snapped: 'There was nothing I could do. She needed a transplant, but there wasn't an infant donor – we tried everywhere. There was nothing I could do,' she repeated angrily. She turned and spoke directly to him for the first time. 'For a little while we thought we might have found one: there was a crib death and the heart had been resuscitated. The parents gave permission for transplantation, but it didn't work.'

'The baby died?' he asked gently, taking her hand. She nodded. 'Oh Bella, I'm so sorry. But at least you did it.'

'I had no choice,' she said dully. 'I was the only person there who could do it – we had a miserable surgical team as it was. It was just a terrible night, things went wrong, people were slow . . .'

'But even in the best circumstances, the chances were almost nil?'

'Yes. Of course, I know.'

'No one could have done any more, Bella,' he said, rubbing the fingers of her hand. He hesitated and then asked, 'Did you speak to the parents?'

She looked sharply at him. 'Yes,' she said, 'it was me.' But now there was something resigned, almost vanquished about her. Her courage daunted him; he felt he had nothing to offer her in the way of sympathy or support.

233

She got up and walked away. She sat down in another chair, further away from him. She wrung her hands, just once, but hard, so that he felt it must hurt her fingers. In a while, she looked down and began to speak in a dreamlike way, rubbing her hands up and down the cream silk upholstery of the chair. It was strange for him to watch her; it was as if she was deliberately trying to distance herself from some recollection, yet, by the distress on her face, she was failing.

'I took the baby to them – the parents – afterwards,' she said slowly. 'They had a room in the hospital. When I went in I put the baby in the mother's arms. It was terrible,' she said, her voice wavering, 'it was so small, only four months, and so very white –' She stopped, her face aghast. 'Like one of Rebecca's dolls,' she whispered. 'I couldn't speak, but the woman – she came and she put her arms around me, so that the child was between us for a moment. The father came and he stood there, watching us, and he seemed – oh, so lonely . . . . I couldn't bear it. And . . .' She began to sob and through the sobbing came a wild flow of words: 'I *told* them I would not operate on babies, I told them, I can't do it. And when this one died – it was as if the baby had become Rebecca. It *was* Rebecca, I know it was.' Tears were pouring down her cheeks, bloating her eyelids – her whole face was awash. It was unrecognisable.

He wanted desperately to comfort her, but did not know how. He wanted to understand the full nature of the grief that was, finally, breaking her down. Believing she was afraid of her power to destroy Rebecca, he said urgently: 'Bella, Rebecca has not died.' He crouched at her feet and took her hands. 'She's really quite strong now – strong enough to let you go to the hospital tonight – even though she didn't want to, she did it.'

Then Bella did a remarkable thing. She reached out and placed her hand tenderly around Joseph's head and bent down, kissing him on the mouth. It took him back to the first day he had seen her – her, not Rebecca, in Margy's house, when she had touched James's arm with a gesture equally provocative. The memory was sweet to him now, as was the kiss, and he wanted to take her entire body into his custody, to save her from every damn thing that stood between her and this soft sensuality.

She touched his hair lightly. 'Poor Joseph, it is so hard for you to understand.' She sat up again.

'Well, I hope that this time you'll at least try to help me,' he said.

Her voice was weary. 'What we have been seeing this past week is a form of remission.' Her voice was quite flat now. 'It happens before she goes, when she still has a little life left. She knows it and I know it, but at times, of course, she chooses to forget it and believes she can have a full life.'

'Like with William?'

'Yes.' She rubbed her hand across her face. 'It's so hard to explain. She's never had a chance. Just like that baby' – her voice broke – 'just like that.' Again she looked directly at him, as if now she did want him to understand. 'She's struggled so hard for a life, but it has to be through me. She's a little like a ghost,' she whispered.

He considered this and then asked, 'So, you pull back – she doesn't force you out?'

She nodded. 'I let her come.'

'As you did for those years with William?' He frowned. 'Why? And why for so long then?'

'For the children. I wanted them to have a childhood.'

'As you did not?'

'Only Rebecca could give them that childhood. I couldn't do it . . .'

He took her hand. 'Are you sure that she'll go?'

'Yes.'

'For good?'

'I think she has gone,' she whispered. 'I felt it with the baby, that she had gone. That's why I feel so weak.'

'Bella,' he pleaded. 'You must let me help you and be with you. Please understand that I am not a threat. I understand you. I love you. I know what you are and how you got to be that way. We are all that way. Has that ever occurred to you?'

With a swift movement she got up, walked across the room and went to stand with her back to the window. 'Joseph, this is no good. It won't do. I don't want any involvement with you, I never did. You have become entangled because of Rebecca. You must go.'

He too was standing now and he strode over to her and said angrily, 'Bella, for God's sake, what *is* it that frightens you? You act as if I'm trying to annihilate you. Can't you see – I love you. I'm in this for me – I need you, and I want to make you see that you need me and that it won't injure you to be loved by me.'

Her voice was quite remote. 'You are quite right when you say that we are all the same. It is why you spend your life in prisons. You hide behind those malfunctions just as you hide behind mine.' There was no malice in her voice; it was just cold.

'And now, for a change, let's look at *you*, Joseph. Let's look at your private life, shall we? Because you're right: we are all broken, all unwhole and yes, all criminal. How many lives have you broken into and pillaged? How many times have you crept out of the back window when it looked as if you were going to have to connect with someone? How many corpses have you left in your wake? Apart from one wife? You're always trying to break me on two dead husbands. All right, let's have a reckoning. What's your quota?'

'That,' he breathed out, 'was probably one of your more brilliant pieces of surgery. Congratulations. I can't fault you on a single incision. You've opened the spinal column and exposed the nervous system. If I'm not twisting and jerking too badly, it's only because I've been aware of the malignancy for some time. But' – and here he smiled like one who would always return from the dead to haunt her – 'I'm alive, Bella, I've survived. You've not led me to the balcony of a ten-storey building, nor administered me a lethal dose to help me out of my pain. Here I am, Bella. No – don't be alarmed, I won't touch you, have no fear.' He stood solidly in front of her. 'I'll bleed, but' – he smiled – 'I'll keep on coming. So, what will you do? How are we going to go on? Because go on we must and we will. Together.'

She turned and ran across the room. Her body had lost all its grace; it looked heavy and awkward. At the door, she stopped. She turned to look at him. 'What do you want?' she asked.

He stayed where he was. 'You,' he said calmly. 'You, for all the reasons you have given and for a thousand more. I will do you no damage because now we both know I can't – the same goes for you. We have seen one another. We know what we both are. The knives are on the table. It is time for mercy.'

236

She began to walk very slowly back to him. An extraordinary energy possessed her face; there was in it such power and desperation – such terror – that he was bewildered. She stood looking at him, her face black with hatred. He recognised her.

'You're trying to kill me,' Rebecca hissed, 'you and Bella, you're trying to kill me.'

In an instant, she had grabbed the marble lamp from the table, lifted it high and brought it down. His arms flew up to protect his head and the lamp was knocked back towards her. It struck her temple and then crashed to the floor, gouging the wood. Rebecca fell; with one slow movement she lay still.

Chapter Seventeen

When the ambulance came she still had not regained consciousness. Joseph woke Will and asked him to look after the children till he got back. She was taken, at Joseph's insistence, to her own hospital, in New York, and there she was dealt with immediately. He left the hospital after initial examinations had shown that the concussion was not severe, and returned to her house.

Later, when he called the hospital, he was told that she was being examined by a neurologist and undergoing tests. There was nothing he could do but wait. Though he had wanted to be with her when she regained consciousness, the children could not be left again. He found it hard to be separated from her; as the hours passed, he grew more edgy and upset. He could not pull himself out of it; the things that he had managed with such ease on the previous day now drove him to distraction: Harry's crying for his mother; Daisy's scream as she fell on the path; even the sky on this long, slow Sunday was too lambent, too blue. He kept to the dark, longing for silence and solitude.

The children, reassured that their mother would soon return, reverted to their old ways in a manner that he found callous and incomprehensible. Only Will was quiet, even solicitous but, sensing Joseph's tension, he had become more distant again. Joseph began to see that his suffering was due to the fact that he could not do as he chose to: he needed to escape into his own head, but no such self-indulgence was available to him here. It threw into sharp relief the disparity between their lives: he never had to answer to anyone, while every moment of Bella's life, in a hospital or at home – was accountable to someone. At the end of her day, somehow, the books had to balance. Her self-discipline was so severe that he could have no comprehension of it. No wonder she gave him no quarter. He had always admired her dedication and discipline, but had never, until now, begun to understand what drove her.

But now, in her house, children had to be fed and watered; Harry had to be comforted; Mary had turned belligerent and kept asking for Alison, who would not return until the following day. Joseph's nerves were frazzled; he was at the end of his tether by three o'clock. He could not think in peace for more than a few moments. Rebecca's lament, in their first real conversation, that her concentration had been broken and broken, now struck him forcibly.

He knew he had to right himself or he would be of no use to her, nor to her children. The first thing he had to face was the drawing-room. He had avoided it all day. Now he entered it again. Sunlight fell in golden pools across the gleaming furniture and made a halo around the small, circular table where Bella's little treasures were laid out. He walked over and picked up the pink Buddha. He was just a glance away from the place where she had fallen, but his eyes refused to look at the floor.

The room had lost all its tranquillity; it had become the scene of the crime. The beauty of Bella's things, the care and attention lavished on them, all this had been broken into and defiled. Lying on its side, a small distance from where it had violated the wood, was the lamp. The deep gash in the pine reminded him how the blood had poured across her face and into her closed eyes. More terrible even than her last words had been the expression on her face after she fell. Staunching the blood with the pressure of his hand, he had seen in her face what she had become. What, he now felt, he had made her become.

He saw it still: her face, masked by unconsciousness, had seemed almost blind in its vulnerability. But there was something transcendent about her, beyond any physical personality. Lying there, she seemed to have become universal, reminding him of Goethe's 'eternal female leading us upwards'. Her flight had brought him lower than he had ever been: he had become inculpated in her sorrow, there was no line to cross and escape it.

Now, picking up the lamp, he found that his hands were shaking. He was sure of it now – Rebecca was dead. And he, in so many ways over and above the physical and violent one, had killed her. He broke down and sobbed.

'Is she going to die?' a small voice asked, from just behind him. Joseph felt so frail that it seemed the voice came

239

from within his own brain. He lifted his head from his hands and saw how Will's eyes were trained on the floor, where the blood had spilled and dried. Instantly, Joseph righted himself; he reached out and took the boy's arm, drawing him close.

'No Will, she's not going to die . . . I just felt . . . you know,' his voice splintered, 'so sorry for her, for all she has had to endure.' The boy did not understand.

Joseph began again. 'Will, your mother won't die. She's conscious and the doctor at the hospital says she's going to be fine. She has a bad cut on her head, but there's no internal damage.'

'Can I see her then?'

'Not today, she has to be very quiet. Perhaps tomorrow, or the day after. I'm going to see her tomorrow and after that I'll be able to tell you exactly how she is. But there's nothing to worry about. It's a big cut, but it didn't penetrate.'

'I still don't understand,' the boy insisted, 'how it happened. Why she was carrying – whatever it was – when she fell?'

'She was very tired, Will, very, very tired. She'd been operating all night. She should have gone straight to bed. It was my fault, I wasn't looking after her properly. It won't happen again. I promise.' He got up and put his hand on the boy's shoulder. 'It's four o'clock, Will, and time for tea. Let's go and see how the little ones are doing. Harry should be up soon.'

The words, the way they led him away from his anxiety into a haven of normality – all this Will recognised from his life with his mother. He took the comfort offered and was grateful.

Chapter Eighteen

The following day, as soon as Alison got in from the airport, Joseph went to the hospital. He waited for a moment or two outside Bella's room, to try and compose himself. When he went inside, he saw that she was sleeping. Her face was quite blank. Her head was swathed in bandages and her face was pale; it was a little wasted so that her eyes seemed deeply set in the bruised sockets. He watched her a long time.

When she woke after an hour, she looked at him and he was horrified to see that she did not seem to recognise him. He moved over to the chair beside her bed.

'How are you feeling?'

She said nothing; she barely looked at him and closed her eyes again. Pain welled up inside him and, trying to locate its origin, he realised that something had altered. Something was wrong: all about him he felt a great sense of emptiness. His sadness was so acute that he moved over and gathered her into his arms. But holding her he only felt the emptiness more. He returned her to the pillows; she smiled then, a smile quite impossible to decipher.

When she next looked at him, her face had a wistful quality: childlike, lost and quiet.

'Rebecca?' he said, doubtfully.

'Why do you call me that?' She seemed afraid.

He felt his hands begin to sweat. He looked at her again, but she had turned her face away. He could barely breathe.

'It's odd that you should mention that name,' she said gravely.

'Why?'

She smiled. 'I remembered her again, for the first time, here, in this hospital, the night that the baby died. When I took it to its parents it was as if I was carrying Rebecca.'

'I'm not sure that I understand,' he said.

241

The wistful, lost quality was back in her face. 'It's just so sad,' she said.

'What is?'

'Rebecca.'

He looked hard at her face for any sign of dissembling and found none. Her face was calm, the eyes clear, her hands still on the white sheet. He hesitated, unsure of her; she was vulnerable, but it was not Rebecca's vulnerability.

'Can you tell me?' he asked.

'You mean, can I tell you who Rebecca was?'

The past tense was deeply painful to him.

'Yes,' he said, 'if you're not too tired.'

'No, I'm not tired.' She looked at him with her old sharpness. 'And I think, perhaps, you will understand now.'

He knew that she had been right not to tell him before, on all the occasions he had tried to prise it from her.

She thought for a little while, with her eyes closed, and then she said: 'Rebecca was my sister.'

'Your sister?'

She nodded. 'My twin sister.' She wrung her hands, just once.

He leaned forward. 'Are you sure you want to tell me this? You don't have to.'

'Oh yes,' she said, 'I do, I must.' She looked directly at him. 'When I was little, I heard my parents arguing one night. My father was very angry and he said my mother was unnatural – inhuman – something like that, I don't remember precisely. He accused her of killing his child. It took me many years to work it all out. But it seems that when my mother got pregnant it was an accident; she didn't want children. She made that very clear to me all my life,' she said bitterly. 'But my father managed to persuade her to go on with the pregnancy for a few months. It seems they had been told they were going to have twins. They even chose names for us.' She smiled wryly. 'Bella and Rebecca. But then she changed her mind and had an abortion. The abortion didn't work, but by then it was too late to do anything about it.'

Bella turned her face away and stared bleakly out of the window.

242

'When my mother came to give birth, there was only one of us. The other baby, my sister, had been scraped away.'

When he was at last able to speak, his voice was no more than a whisper. 'The dead baby,' he said, 'was Rebecca.' He hesitated. 'And the remaining baby – was you?'

'The remaining baby,' she said, 'was called Bella.'

Chapter Nineteen

When Joseph next saw Bella, her face had lost its empty quality and her voice had the low melodic tone that he associated with her. She apologised to him, 'I'm sorry I was so tired, last time you came. They told me I slept all day and night without waking up.' She looked into his eyes. 'I hope it didn't upset you, what I told you?'

'It upset me,' he said quietly, 'but it's helped me to understand.' He took her hand. 'And I'm not surprised you're tired. You've been living too much, for far too long.'

She nodded, quickly, fiercely, as if she did not want to pursue it.

'Don't worry,' he said, 'I won't ever try to shrink you.' It was said softly, lovingly.

But she was quick to raise her standard. 'I wouldn't let you,' she said.

He smiled. 'You seem', he said, 'much more yourself.'

'I can go home in a few days.'

'The kids will be pleased. They miss you a lot.'

She looked at him with gratitude. 'They told me you've been looking after them more than Alison. Taking them round New York, even to Long Island. It's very kind of you.'

'It's the least I could do.'

'What about your seminar? I've been taking up so much of your time, I feel guilty.'

'The seminar's over,' he said. 'I just have to finish writing up the findings. Then I'll stop doing the prison circuit.'

She looked at him shrewdly. 'Won't you miss your lost souls?'

There was no doubt in his mind: it was Bella and no one else. She seemed softer, a little chastened, but he never, for a moment, had the sense that she would disappear and be replaced by someone else. She seemed fixed; she seemed not to remember being any other way. He was the only one who

244

remembered now, and he was determined to shield her from the burden of the past.

'Joseph,' she said, 'why are you doing all this for me? Why do you keep on coming?'

'I warned you,' he said, 'that you wouldn't get shot of me.'

'You act, sometimes,' – she looked away – 'as if we were lovers.'

He saw that she was afraid that there was something she could not remember, something that compromised her.

'No,' he said, with regret, 'we were never quite that.'

'What were we?'

'We were enemies,' he said.

'Enemies?'

'Yes. The oldest kind: man against woman, woman against man.'

'So there was no love?' She was confused, her voice quiet. But in all of this, he saw with relief, she was not trying to pretend, to cover her lapses; she was asking him direct questions about things she was unable to recall. There was something about her that seemed dependable now.

'Yes,' he said quietly, 'there was love, on my side at least, great love. It's just that I didn't know *how* to love you.'

'You seem sad,' she said.

'I am. I feel we have been widowed – all of us.'

She looked closely at him. 'Why do you say, all of us, when there are only two of us?'

His face twisted. 'You were like two people to me.'

'Was I?' She moved her head with the most economical of movements. 'I never wanted to love anyone,' she said.

'Have you never?'

'No, not really. I don't know how to, either, and I was never sure that I wanted that – it seemed, you know, rather dangerous.'

'It is. That much I have learned.'

'All I ever wanted', she said, 'was to be a surgeon.'

He took both of her hands in his. 'But you are. You're the best there is.'

She moved away from him and the old penetrating stare was back. 'I think,' she said carefully, 'that I was not that to you.'

'Not what to me?'

245

'A surgeon. I was not a surgeon to you.'

He watched as a tiny chink of light entered her eyes. 'What were you to me?'

She looked him straight in the eye. 'A woman surgeon.'

He was silenced.

She looked at him steadily now, her eyes glittering. 'I never wanted to be a woman anything – not a woman surgeon, not a woman doctor – not a woman anything,' she said with cold precision.

'It's understood,' he said. 'It's taken me a long time, but it is understood.'

'And', she said, as if to warn him, 'I never wanted to be a wife either. I wanted just to be myself – to do things not as a man does, not even particularly as a woman does.' She shrugged her shoulders in joyful triumph. 'I am,' she said, 'that's all.'

'I understand,' he repeated. 'You move with greater speed across the water, but I'm catching on.' He bent forward. 'But there are a few things you have to understand, too. You are a woman. A fine and exceptional woman. Not a scientist with no heart like your mother, but a real woman. You've shown me how far short of a man I've always been; I can help you in the same way.'

She smiled; she seemed to be considering him, and herself, in the most cool and objective manner.

'Come on,' he urged, with a wry grin, 'this is the best offer you'll ever get.'

She laughed, then she narrowed her dark eyes and said: 'Maybe.'

'Oh no, that won't do! That was not said with the confidence of a woman who believes she can be and do whatever she chooses.'

'You will have my reply in a week,' she said firmly.

Chapter Twenty

Before Joseph brought Bella home from the hospital, he went up to her bedroom and there, hanging from the brass bedpost, just as she had left it, was Rebecca's lovely red-dotted sundress. Seeing it, he knew, finally, the loss of her. He picked up the dress and held it against his face. It still smelt faintly of her: a pungent, spicy smell, quite unlike Bella's. He held it a long time, feeling acute pain. He began to search the room, desperate for some other traces of her. There were so few: the ribbon she had worn in her hair, the brush she had used after her shower, a pair of pink espadrilles that Bella would never set foot in. The roses she had picked that day were long dead; they were still there; the room was exactly as it had been.

It was so hard to believe that she had really gone, that he would never see her again. Her death was as real to him as her life and unique character had been. And now it was gone: just as she had begun to create a life for herself, it had fled from her.

He knew that once he had taken her things away there would be no trace left. It had always been her deepest dread. But now his old dream of a merging between the two of them was as dead as she was. Rebecca was gone; no turn of her head with that flirtatious smile, no sway of her body as she walked with a child on her hip. The image of water cascading down her naked body under the shower came back to him; he saw her brown legs and the freckles across her nose; the way of her laugh; the intemperance of her anger; the bitten nails on the fine narrow fingers; the way she would smother a vase with flowers and fill a kitchen with the full blown scent of her cooking. No more, Rebecca.

He sat down and wept.

When he looked up at last, he saw, hanging from the back of the door, her blue silk robe. It seemed to rebuke him; he could not touch it. He was filled with his own treachery and betrayal and he knew that it was something he would have to live with always. The loss of Rebecca, his part in her downfall – it was something that would never leave him. For him, there would always be three of them. He vowed then to spend his life shielding Bella from this new ghost of Rebecca. She must not remember, and that meant that he could never forget. Bella must have no part in his guilt. He would take the profound responsibility that Bella had once taken; he would absorb Rebecca within himself, so deeply and so sincerely that Bella would find no trace of her.

He began to search the room methodically. He came across the black diary in Bella's desk and began to read it, seeing the frightening messages that had gone between them. He put the book in his pocket, to destroy it. On the bureau was a stack of music-scores: Chopin, Debussy and Brahms. He took these too. Would the piano have to go – or could he convince her that she had bought it for Daisy, as Will believed? He felt that he could. He went through the clothes in the cupboard and took out every dress he had seen Rebecca wear. He removed the Virginia Woolf from the table beside the bed and replaced it in the bookshelf. He put her glasses in his pocket. He then went from room to room in the house, banishing Rebecca for all time – from Bella's rooms and from those Rebecca had considered her own. He did all this with the utmost pain. But he did it for love, for love of Bella.

Much later, when he went downstairs, Alison was filling all the vases with flowers from the garden.

He smiled painfully.

The children were excited, painting a welcome banner on the kitchen table. He found that he was walking over to the drawer in the pine table; he took out the recipe book which had belonged to her mother. He found the page – splattered with egg and milk stains – with the recipe for the apple cake she had made that day. He began to make it, doing all the things he had seen her do that day, the last day in her life. He chilled a bottle of the same wine, laid the table under the trees with the same blue and white tablecloth and Mexican glasses. He prepared the chicken as he had seen her do. And then he went to fetch Bella.

When she walked through the front door, she stopped and looked around with happiness. The children threw themselves at her and, a little nervously, she held her arms out to them. Joseph saw her head bend over their heads. Her hair was pulled back at the nape of her neck, but it had lost some of its severity, for little strands tumbled across her forehead. He wondered if she had done it in a gesture of vanity, to cover the bandage on her temple. She picked up Harry, lifting him onto her hip with a sure, practised movement; she bit his cheek and he caught a glimpse of her white teeth. Mary clung to her blue dress, crumpling the cloth. Will stood beside her like a sentry.

He felt suddenly that she was complete and had no need of him now. He turned and began to walk away.

But she called after him. He stopped and looked at her.

'You're not trying to chicken out, by any chance?' her low, throaty voice mocked.

'Certainly not,' he said, restored by the flickering, combative quality of her face.

Mary was tugging at her mother's skirt.

'The rabbit got out again, this time for ever.'

Bella raised an eyebrow.

'A rabbit? Do we have a rabbit?'

'We most certainly do,' Joseph said quickly, 'or rather we did, until a few days ago.'

In an instant, the strain left him, the sense of awful anticipation. It would be all right. He could protect her: he knew how to do it. Where the two of them had done their nightmare dance, cutting in on each other whenever the music changed, he could make a different harmony. What they had never been able to achieve, so deep were their rivalries, he could now do.

'We are going to get another rabbit,' he said firmly. 'Kids like animals around.'

She frowned, but he insisted. 'Don't worry, I'll take responsibility for it – you have quite enough of those. Mary will help me.'

Mary raced out into the garden, calling Daisy to follow. The two little sisters ran down the path, jumping in and out of the beds of foxgloves, chasing one another across the grass pooled in yellow sunlight, down, down to the end of the garden where, Joseph now thought, it might be rather nice to have a vegetable garden.

Bella smiled. 'I'll just go upstairs for a moment. I won't be long.' She handed Harry to Alison.

'I'll help you with your things,' Joseph said.

Once upstairs and in her bedroom, she looked about her.

'It's good to be home,' she said. 'Everything is so beautiful.'

He said nothing.

Sunshine flooded in through the windows, making the pine floors shimmer. Diaphanous white curtains swelled out as the fan whirled in the ceiling. On her pillow was a bunch of pink and lilac sweet peas, tied with a ribbon. She picked them up and smelt them, untying the ribbon. She wound it through her hair. He closed his eyes; with her arms lifted in that gesture she seemed to be Rebecca. But then, with an impatient tug, she pulled the ribbon out and dropped it into her pocket.

She walked to the cupboard and opened it, looking for something cooler to wear. Suddenly, she turned her head and saw the red-dotted dress still hanging from the bedpost, where he had left it. He moved forward with a quick, protective gesture, but she didn't notice. She held the dress up and the full skirt billowed out in a gust of wind from the fan.

'Is this mine?' she asked, looking at him.

'Yes,' he said, turning his face away, 'it's yours.'

'Oh, how lovely,' she said. 'I think I'll wear it.'